RAFT BABY

# RAFT BABY

## BONNIE DUNLOP

*thistledown press*

Thistledown Press Ltd.
410 2nd Avenue North
Saskatoon, Saskatchewan, S7K 2C3
www.thistledownpress.com

Library and Archives Canada Cataloguing in Publication
Title: Raft baby / Bonnie Dunlop.
Names: Dunlop, Bonnie, 1950- author.
Identifiers: Canadiana (print) 20200279823 | Canadiana (ebook) 20200279831 | ISBN 9781771872027 (softcover) | ISBN 9781771872034 (HTML) | ISBN 9781771872041 (PDF)
Classification: LCC PS8607.U544 R34 2020 | DDC C813/.6—dc23

Cover painting, *Moberley Lake*, by Alison Newth
Cover and book design by Jackie Forrie
Printed and bound in Canada

 Canada Council    Conseil des Arts
for the Arts       du Canada                        Canadä

Thistledown Press gratefully acknowledges the financial assistance of the Canada Council for the Arts, SK Arts, and the Government of Canada for its publishing program.

# RAFT BABY

*In memory of E. Jean Lines, mother and teacher,*
*whose words I have used in the quilt description*
*that appears in* Raft Baby
*Thank you Mom, for everything*


*For Shayne — who requires bedtime stories*

# ONE

## 1.

Condie Meadows Nursing Home
Manning, Alberta
June 10, 1994

The walls in Lily's room are painted cream — real cream that has risen to the top of the crock. Not exactly yellow, but nowhere near white. The winter-white trim, newly installed and four inches wide, is a pleasing note.

Dean, our cheery handyman is always adding little touches like that to make this place feel less like an institution and more like a home.

Harlan Miller, who just turned eighty-eight and was finally forced to give up living alone on his ranch and riding herd on his Red Angus cows without help, dubbed this place "the finishing barn" on the day that his children moved him in, nearly two months ago. How they convinced him to give nursing-home life a try, I have no idea. I do know that they have no intention of letting him return home no matter if he settles or not.

The three other male residents — men are few and far between in homes for the aged — have really taken a liking to the name and often joke about it. But it's no joke to Harlan.

The director is not amused either so the term hasn't quite made it into the vernacular.

The east sun is streaming in and Lily's tough little money tree plant is, as usual, not growing, but not dying either.

The lacy curtains her daughters have hung across the bay window on a silver rod create pleasing patterns on the opposite wall, shapes shifting in a desultory manner as the breeze tickles the curtains with lazy fingers.

The poor old girl is sleeping soundly this morning, her papery eyelids flicking.

Her chest is rising and falling so gently that I stand beside her bed and listen, just to make sure.

I don't want to wake her, so I put her breakfast tray on her little metal table. Thankfully, she doesn't hear the rattle, for Lily is really quite deaf. She thinks we all mumble and that her daughters don't enunciate clearly, not anymore. She's taught them better, is what she says. She absolutely refuses to try a hearing aid.

Nothing wrong with my hearing, she says. I hear all I need to hear.

I know I am supposed to wake the residents, make sure they eat. But today, for Lily, I can't. She looks so small, and so very tired.

When they come to retrieve the trays, perhaps some steely woman, much less attuned than I, will wake her, cajole her to take a bit of congealed porridge and drink her cooling tea.

But I know Lily. She will sweetly ask for brown sugar, not white, to top her porridge and to have her cream warmed a bit. She will not take one sip of her tea unless it's served piping hot and in a bone china teacup. Today the kitchen has sent a green ceramic mug. Obviously someone new has started and not checked the copious notes concerning the residents, what they like and what they don't. I know that for Lily, this definitely will not do, and maybe that's why I decide to let her sleep.

And maybe I let her sleep because the last three nights I worked she was wide-awake and restive. Struggling out of her bed, straightening her sheets again and again, climbing back into bed but not settling, flicking through the channels on her TV. Up again, straightening the sheets, fluffing the comforter. Checking the money tree to see if it needs water. Taking up a pen and a notebook but writing not a single word.

Her daughters tell me she used to be a great one for making lists at the end of a day. A blueprint for tomorrow's tasks. Lily, it seems, was never without a plan. Until now.

There are four books stacked on the bay window ledge, two poetry books, one a thick blue volume of Robert W. Service and another slim grey one by Mary Oliver, a poet I have never heard of. Mary Oliver's book is well read, dog-eared and underlined here and there, so I read those passages when I get a chance. They mostly centre on nature and wild animals and birds. Also love. I am curious to know what it was in those poems that really spoke to Lily.

What she was thinking? Before.

There is also one paperback murder mystery, and a tattered black Bible, its bindings loose and the gilt on the edge of the pages thumbed away. Although she has given up reading entirely now, the books remain. Sometimes, she chooses one, holds it, but she never turns the page.

Getting old, Lily once told me, is all about managing small losses. But eventually, those small losses amount to something big. Like having to leave your home. The physical sorting and packing was beyond me by then, she said, her eyes round and earnest behind her smudged glasses. Thank God for the girls. They handled that for me, and very efficiently too. But it was up to me to prepare myself — mentally, I mean.

How did you do that, I wanted to ask. When you had no choice but to leave your home and all of the jumbled pieces of your life?

I am at a place in my own life where I am trying to imagine a leaving, but I have no idea where to start. I wish I had asked her, when she spoke of it, but I was not courageous enough, so I let the opportunity slip away.

I pick up Lily's Bible, stroke the black leather, softened by years of use and maybe by the dependable caress of the sun. When this room came open — we all know how vacancies occur in nursing homes — her daughters requested the move. Mama likes the sun, is what they said. And to the director, that seemed reason enough. Lily, with her undemanding nature and sharp wit, has become a favourite around here.

A refracted ray from a crystal knick-knack, two tiny teddy bears on a mirrored teeter-totter, makes little rainbows, on the ceiling, on the walls, rainbows everywhere.

Lily doesn't stir, so peacefully asleep.

It has been only two days since I worked three straight twelve's, which are a real killer, health-wise and home-wise too. So tonight, I am already tired, partly because of my schedule and partly because Donovan has been out of sorts lately, and I have no idea why. He spends all his

11

spare time out in the shop, as far as I can tell, although I'm often not around. Maybe it would be different if we'd had a family. Some kids to bind us together at the end of a long shift. That would have been nice.

I used to take him a beer, usually an ice-cold Pilsner, perch on his welding stool and watch him work, admire the muscles delineated beneath his blue tee-shirt, the round rise of his amazing butt.

I don't do that anymore.

He's gotten bored with welding and moved on to woodworking, although I have no clue what he eventually does with his long oaken shelves, grooved to hold plates, his mahogany gun racks, his sturdy little stools. They are not in our house, and once they are finished, they are not out in the shop either.

Maybe he gives them away? But to whom?

Most nights, when he is finally done hammering and sanding and oiling and comes inside, he quickly eats his supper, sometimes even standing over the sink with his plate. I'm certain he does this even when I'm not home, when I've dished up and left his meal in the fridge for him.

Our lovely little dining room has become a lonely place.

Once done shovelling the food in, he buries himself in the Blue Jays or Monday night football, or God help me, poker on TV.

He hasn't forgotten his manners entirely, because he does remember to thank me for the meal. But only with words, no quick hug or a kiss.

The tension in our house is thick, thicker than the wide slices of whole wheat bread I use to make his sandwiches for work. I can eat in the kitchen at work for a pittance. I thank God for that choice. At least there's company there.

Tonight, I really am tired, bone tired, so that if I get all of my residents sponged and fed a late-night snack and tucked in for the night, I will likely find an empty room and crawl into bed for a few blissful moments myself.

Just a small nap when all of my people are doing the same. What, really, could be wrong with that?

When I came on shift last Friday night, which also happened to be the full moon, we did reports. I was told Lily had been restless, unable to settle.

I would be restless too if I had to live in this place, so I went to see if there was anything I could do.

I heard the water running as I approached her door.

Dear God, not again.

I found Lily by the sink. She had stoppered it and turned on the water full blast. It cascaded over the counter's edge and fell to the floor like a miniature waterfall.

She was smiling, such a wide smile. She turned to me, light in her eyes. "Do you hear it? Do you hear the rapids?"

I reached for an armload of cardboard-stiff towels stacked on the open shelves on the opposite wall. "Yes," I answered. "I'm afraid I do."

"When I was a baby," she said, "I was set adrift on a raft on a great shining river. They say babies have no recall, but I, for one, know that's not true. Sometimes I still feel the rise and fall of the water beneath my craft, the brightest of stars lighting my way. The great yellow moon hanging so low I want to touch it. But I cannot, for I am

13

bundled tightly and all I can really move is my eyes. I can hear the rapids. Coming closer. Rapids I can feel but not see."

I reached around her and quickly turned off the gushing tap. "You've had so many big adventures in your life, haven't you, dear?"

Then I clapped my hand to my mouth. When I started working here, I vowed that I would never be rude or condescending, never call a resident "dear" and I had just done both. These lonely old people are not my dears, but they are someone's, and they deserve, at the very least, my respect.

I threw down a couple of towels to stem the spreading tide. Water in the bathroom I could take care of. Water in the whole room would be something else.

My arms around Lily, I guided her across the treacherous tiles, slippery now with a thin film of cooling water.

I marvelled at the remarkable smoothness of her skin, the silver sheen of her long thick hair, a dark wing swooping from her temple to her chin. The streak is a natural lowlight, nothing to do with the hairdresser who comes here weekly to butcher the residents' hair. The men are virtually scalped with a clipper, number one I think, which leaves the hair almost invisible, and the poor women inevitably end up with either a tight frizzy perm or a no-maintenance almost-brush-cut. But not Lily. She is adamant that her hair is not to be cut even one smidgen shorter, only trimmed with extreme caution. A quarter of an inch at most. A sign of vanity I admire.

She is shrunken, but not quite a shadow. Four years ago when she came here, there was a lot more to her.

"Round and firm and fully packed," she would comment, when I was helping her with the bath. "That's what my husband always said and it's still the truth after all these years."

It's nowhere near the truth right now.

"How about you rest for a bit now?" I pulled out the sturdy stool she needed to step up and into her bed. I eased her down and tucked the covers around her thin shoulders.

"I made this quilt, you know," she said. "With my own two hands."

This was not new information; she'd told me many times before.

She held out her hands, her knuckles knotted with the arthritis. It was hard to imagine those gnarled hands holding a fine needle, sewing such tiny even stitches in intricate patterns.

"The blend of colours in this quilt means to depict the way in which the northern landscape and the northern people are attuned to . . . " Her voice trailed off.

Above her bed, on the cluttered bulletin board, there is a square of stiff paper — white once, but yellowed now and curled at the corners. It is one of her most treasured mementos, the detailed description card that goes along with a public art exhibit, explaining the inspiration behind the creation.

Her daughters have talked of her quilting prowess, as if trying to make us see past this aged woman before us into the vital person she used to be.

She was an award winner, her quilts taking first prize at all the area county fairs and once two of her creations were chosen to tour the province in a folk-art exhibit.

There is a picture on the board of a much younger Lily standing next to a woman with a halo of frizzy red hair, round, wire-rimmed glasses perched on her turned-up nose.

The woman is brandishing an impressive red ribbon, holding Lily's hand.

The quilt tucked around her was the lone remainder of her craftsmanship, the others now treasured keepsakes for her girls and her three granddaughters, who fill these silent halls with giggles and blaring music when they come to visit. The crack of bubble gum, the waft of a lemony, light perfume.

One of her quilts, the one that won the province and went on to be in a Canada-wide art exhibit, was purchased, at a ridiculous price, Lily has told me, by a folk-art collector from Toronto. Part of exhibiting your art is being willing to put one piece up for sale, Lily said. She had been sure her price was too high, that her quilt would be safe. She was wrong. She could have sold them, every one, she said, but she didn't quilt for money, only for love.

And the amount of cash she was paid for the award-winning quilt made her shake her head when she told me, as if she really couldn't believe it, even now. But the sum didn't make her eyes shine with happiness, like they did when she talked about the special quilts her grand-daughters now possessed.

Her hands brushed the chocolate-brown edging, back and forth, a soothing movement, it seemed, and she started again, at the beginning. "The blend of colours in this quilt means to depict the way in which the northern landscape and the northern people are attuned to the changing seasons. A centre yellow block represents the sun, lending brightness to the . . . the . . . "

I leaned closer to the card, picked up the dropped thread of her thoughts.

" . . . lending brightness to the white, grey, and blue squares of the sky. Then a hint of springtime green, deepening to the verdant hues of summer. Blossom time brings flowers of yellow, peach, and coral. All too soon these colours will fade to the vibrant gold and deep rusts of autumn. The yellow blocks in each of the corners re-affirm that the sun will shine on all four seasons."

Lily was smiling, a beatific smile, so I continued.

"The black feather stitching is reminiscent of waterfowl in fall migration. The way they stitch the filmy grey fabric of the sky. Then comes the first skiff of winter snow. The pure white squares, which ring the entire piece just inside the binding, like whipped-cream snowdrifts, are indicative of the endless winter and all the hardships that winter in the north entails.

"A random touch of green stitching on the white squares, features a floral motif, lending assurance that Mother Earth will always bloom again . . . There's a little more," I said. "A bit like a postscript, I think." I took another deep breath. Reading aloud has never been my forte. Perhaps it's a good thing I never had a child. Or maybe that would have been Donovan's duty, settling the children into bed with a story.

"Scraps from my own ragbag were sewn by hand in the pioneer tradition. Plain colours signify the 'plain folk', proud to have settled in the Peace River country. So very far from their homes."

17

"Thank you," Lily said and she pulled the quilt closer. "How in the world did you know to come and help me? Sometimes I ring my buzzer for what seems like hours and nobody comes."

"Instinct," I said.

And the fact that I could hear the cascading water.

The water was icy cold and so were her hands.

"Rest for a bit, okay Lily? I've got to mop up the bathroom. Don't want anyone slipping and breaking a hip, now do we?"

"I love it that you always call me Lily," she said. "No matter how many times I tell them, the others insist on calling me Lillian. It even says Lillian on the sign beside my door. And the picture of me posted there is quite poor too. I have never liked being a Lillian. A Lily, however, is something quite different." She took my hand in hers. "You do know," she said, "that I rode down the mighty Peace River in a very small raft. I hardly think a little water on a bathroom floor will do me in."

She's an interesting woman and she makes me smile. And I wonder what her story truly is.

## 2.

The Peace River
September 24, 1897

Trapper Jackson John had been paddling against the current since the first pink blush of dawn. His muscles were screaming with every pull. Waves smacked his bow and he was he was fighting hard to face the onslaught. The roiling water rushed past his canoe, grasping at its birchbark skin with frantic fingers, as if to slow him down.

The Peace is not called the mighty Peace for nothing, he thought. And I'm so damn tired you'd swear I was drunk. Six whole days of scouting and nothing. Nothing at all.

He hadn't spotted any beaver sign; of his sister-in-law Isabelle and her greenhorn husband he'd been unable to find a single whisper. No one had seen them, not the Dene, not the travelling missionaries. Not the lone trapper he'd come across. And he'd found no blackened campfires, no sign of human passage, nor messages scratched on massive rocks. His only lead had been the letter that had found its way to Annie via a willing courier and blind luck.

Isabelle had written that Edward was finally discouraged, almost ready to give up his dreams of gold. Was considering how to take her home. She told Annie that she hoped they would meet somewhere along the shores of the Lesser Slave Lake when the autumn leaves had coloured the shores a riot of oranges and yellows and browns.

*Until then,* she'd written, *say a prayer for me, for I have not yet quite convinced Edward we must leave this place. And I fear we are not well equipped to travel, not even the two of us, and especially not when the baby comes.*

*I hope you've already received my letter telling you that news and how frightened I am of the whole idea.*

*I have quit talking to Edward of my fears, although at night, they keep me awake. He would only assure me that things will work out fine. Which so far, they have not. Not by a long shot. By being wakeful in the blackness, can I avert the peril I feel gathering about us like towering storm clouds?*

*Most likely not. However, let us hope.*

*Your loving sister, Isabelle.*
*PS — I need you Annie. More than ever now*

He pulled again on the paddles, but his heart wasn't in it and he knew it was time to take a rest. The worst thing a man can do while travelling alone is to keep going past the point of exhaustion. Bad things happen then, most times, and Trapper meant to get back to Annie as soon as humanly possible, no stumbles along the way. He'd already been gone too long. The thought of Annie keeping camp and waiting patiently to see her sister again was almost more than he could bear.

His powerful arms were aching, his back sore from the long day of sitting. He groaned aloud. Then in an open spot on the south bank, he spotted a circle of charred rocks and a neat pile of wood. He blessed the unwritten law of the trail: use what you need and leave a leg-up for the fellow coming behind.

He angled the canoe, muscles flooded with adrenaline, and aimed for the shore. The opening was small and if he missed it, he had a jagged outcropping of rock downstream and a solid wall of forest to contend with. He didn't really feel up to any such challenge just now.

With one mighty surge, he escaped the pull of the current and then paddled easily to shore. He beached his canoe, tying it to a sturdy aspen, its fluttering leaves laced with the first tinges of fall finery, golden yellow, ochre, and flaming orange under the fading forest of green. He tugged on the rope, satisfied his canoe was soundly anchored.

He raised his curled hands to the endless sky, flexed his stiffened fingers. He rotated his back, heard the crack of his cramped knees as he straightened. The growl of his stomach told him it had been ages since he'd finished his last pinch of achees. How many hours might it take to pound dried caribou to a powder? How much perseverance? Whenever he received the gift of achees, he was always grateful. Sometimes at the end of a hard day, he just boiled up a little water and added achees, scavenged for some edible greens and maybe a few mushrooms and tossed them into the pot for his evening meal. Or while paddling, he would reach into his soft leather pouch and put a pinch of the powder into his lower lip, like chewing snuff, only better.

With steady purpose, he gathered dried grasses, inhaling their sweet scent. He snapped small brittle sticks for kindling and laid a perfect fire. Soon, he had a battered potful of the Peace boiling above the blackened stones.

He was hungry and he was tired, but he forced himself to the edge of the clearing and chopped a fragrant pile of balsam boughs. When he was satisfied with their arrangement, he was tempted to collapse onto his newly made bed.

Not just yet, he thought, stretching his cramped arms wide. Not just yet. In the bush, preparation could save your life. When all my chores are done, there will be plenty of time for rest.


"Tea time." He poured one cup of the boiling water into a thick green mug and set it aside.

He'd shot and dressed a mallard duck at the end of yesterday, when it was too late to start a meal. Now he unwrapped the carcass, and squatting beside the coals, he slid it into the blackened pot and poked it down with a stick.

He fumbled in the bottom of his knapsack for his bag of loose tea. But then he stilled. For upstream he'd spotted something.

A tangle of logs? Something aflutter? A flash of red? All borne with frightening speed down the mighty Peace.

"You've been alone too long, my friend," he muttered. The sun had eased his aching back, and the promise of a good strong cup of tea and a biscuit or two was uppermost in his thoughts. But his eyes were drawn again to the river. A craft of some kind? Hurrying down the Peace? He stood and shaded his eyes, staring hard at the water. He shook his head, checked again. "I am not hallucinating."

Grabbing his canoe, Trapper scraped its bottom on the rocky shore in his haste. "It can't possibly be, but I know what I am seeing."

Finally afloat, he paddled toward the middle of the river, his muscles flooded with sudden strength. As he neared, he saw it was a raft, solidly built. He was glad when he saw a small red flag snapping at the top of an upright stick, for it was a bad sign to begin imagining things while travelling alone on the Peace.

Trapper John began to swear — a string of inventive curses, some even he had never heard before. For on a cradleboard, wedged between two short lengths of birch and secured by rope, he could see what appeared to be a baby, wrapped in a blanket.

He rode the river, his eyes darting between the bone-chilling water rushing by and the bucking raft. He positioned himself alongside, and leaning low, nearly caught its edge. So close. He turned his canoe, paddled hard, and pulled alongside the raft once again. This time he managed to grab the crosspiece and hold on, his fingers clutching hard.

Silver glinted on the burnished blade of his skinning knife as he slashed the ropes securing the cradleboard. He grabbed it and hauled it into his canoe, cursing still.

Holding the cradleboard close, he loosened his grip on the raft. Like a too-small fish thrown back, it hurried down the Peace.

"Excuse my language," he said, when he looked down at the baby. "It just that I never dreamt . . . "

A baby? He hadn't partaken in any pipe ceremonies lately or chewed on any unidentified plants, but could this be a dream? Or was it a vision? The Dene sometimes talked of visions, crazy talk.

When it gave a small mewling cry, he knew for sure the baby was real. He feared who it might be and wondered why in God's name any child was alone on the Peace.

The baby's features were fine and a fringe of curls peeked out from beneath a bonnet. A girl, he thought, a flotsam baby girl for sure. As he paddled shoreward with the child, he was calculating her chances.

At the very least, and against great odds, she'd found her way to him.

Once ashore, and his canoe again secured, he undid the tidy knots securing her, one by one, until she was free.

Who? Why?

Her lips were cracked and tinged with blue and as he'd loosened the bindings, one arm had fallen free, as if she were a rag doll who had lost too much stuffing. But her eyes were bright and focused on his face.

"Tough luck," he told her. "Trail smarts I got, but when it comes to babies . . . well . . . "

He held her as if she were made of spun glass. "You're safe and sound," he told her, "but definitely soggy on the bottom."

He spread his groundsheet over the fragrant balsam, laid her down with infinite care. How to change a diaper? He could track and hunt and fish, barter with the best, and find his way across this goddamned country entirely alone, but changing a loaded diaper was something entirely new.

He drew a deep breath, steadied his trembling hands.

Eventually, he fashioned a crude diaper from two of his regulation dotted red bandanas, lining them with soft sphagnum moss. Moss more efficient than a sponge, he knew. Probably a lot better for a baby's bottom than soggy doubled flannel.

She tolerated his fumbling efforts with surprising patience. When he'd finally finished, Trapper lifted her languid body and tucked her head beneath his chin. With a rusty voice, he began to sing an off-key lullaby.

The baby drifted off to sleep.

When the flesh of the duck began to drop from its bones and became a thick gruel, he laid her again on his bed of balsam. The baby stirred, stretched and opened her violet eyes. Her gaze was solemn and she seemed to be taking his measure. Strangely enough, she did not cry. But surely she would be hungry. And all he had to offer was the thick juice of the stewed duck. He could add some water and a little sugar from his tea supplies, but that would be it. Would it be enough? God knows how long it had been since she last was fed.

But how would he manage to feed such a bit of a thing? He'd never fed a baby before.

Or had he? When he was a boy, he'd sometimes helped his father with newborn calves too weak to suck. His father would dip a rag into milk and put its end into the sickly calf's mouth while John held its head and murmured prayers.

"Suck, please suck. For if you don't, my father will whack you a good one right on the head and then you're a goner for sure. Come on! At least try!"

Remembering, Trapper John untied his bandana. Easing himself down, he pulled the pot closer. "Okay," he told the baby, as he picked her up once again. "We might as well give this a try. And I'm hoping it suits you, as it's all we have for tonight. Not one thing more. Except for tea, of course, and I don't think that's quite all a baby requires."

He soaked the bandana's knotted end in the mush. He let it cool a bit before he held the dripping knot to the baby's bowtie lips.

For a moment, she lay unresponsive and then she began. The sound of her greedy smacking made him laugh aloud.

It was slow going, and messy too, but the baby was amazingly intent, watching him with ancient eyes. She sucked hard on the knot, indicating with a tiny whimper when she'd sucked it dry and it was time for him to reload.

"What in bloody blue blazes will I do with a scrap of humanity like you?"

The rising colour in the aspen leaves had confirmed his hunch that this year winter would be closing fast. He couldn't travel far hampered by a baby. Perhaps he could keep her alive for a while, but he knew he didn't have the time or the resources to trek very far. Women's work, he thought, and longed for Annie, in their main camp, seven days of hard paddling ahead.

The Dene? They had invited him close to their fires. Shared their caribou stew, and often sent him on his way with a pouch full of achees and two pair of soft moccasins. Maybe the Dene?

He held the baby to his chest, the heft of her as light as the down of a duck. His rough hands tried to be gentle on her back.

Pat, pat, pat. Pat, pat, pat.

His efforts had exhausted him and the sun was still warm. And although he'd been sure he would never, in his lifetime, fall asleep with a baby cradled in his arms, he slumped, his eyes became heavy, his breathing measured and slow.

The baby felt it, and matched her breath to his.

Snuggling deeper into the wiry nest of grey that fronted his massive chest, the Raft Baby slept.

Trapper broke camp just after dawn, the baby snug in her cradleboard and his arms ready to battle the river. A little breeze had come up and it was at his back. He was thankful for the help, and if he'd have believed in God, he might have said a prayer of thanks.

They made good time all morning, Trapper paddling hard and the baby watching his every move. Thankfully, she did not cry. Eventually, the rocking of the river lulled her to sleep, her thick black lashes spikey shadows on her chapped cheeks.

Just before the sun reached its zenith, he saw smoke rising along the north shore and was thankful that the Dene had not yet broken camp.

"Wake up, Raft Baby. We have important people to meet."

The baby's lips puckered as he touched them with a blackened forefinger. She yawned wide and began to wiggle.

His arms tightened around the cradleboard. Her violet eyes found his and he suddenly had an urge to turn his canoe and paddle hard, back to Annie, to home.

The old woman watched from the shore, shading her eyes with the edge of a leathered hand. She waved him in, wading into the icy water to steady his canoe.

"You are back, my friend," she said. "And bearing a gift. I have been waiting, for I dreamed of it last night. This one has been sent to us for a reason." She reached for the child, carefully unwrapping her, balancing the baby on the wide plane of her hip. She pointed to a silver scar on her right middle toe. The scar was tiny but perfectly shaped.

An arrowhead, sure as she was born.

"This scar," she said, "is much older than the baby. This child will survive the trials of life and live to a wise old age."

The trapper reached out, ran his coarse finger across the small scar.

"She will know things," the old woman said. "Things that cannot be known."

## 3.

Edward Armson
September 30, 1896

Edward stared, unblinking, at the riverbank. Idly, with a willow stick, he traced a map of their trek north. His banker's hands had become tough and calloused, his blue-white arms now brown, sinewed. He stretched, felt the unfamiliar bulk of muscles along the length of his back, heard the pop of his middle-aged knees.

Scruffy brown bushes hung low over the water, their leaves curled from an unusually dry stretch of blistering heat. The little river now flowed sluggish and slow, nothing at all like the mighty Peace, into which it fed.

Lowbush blueberries were hard to spot, the small clusters hanging close to the ground, almost hidden. Their season was nearly over, but Edward's mouth watered thinking of holding a handful of their luscious midnight blue. He searched and eventually managed to find a sparse few. All the bending and twisting made his back complain and his arms were scratched and bleeding. The berries were small, tart from lack of rain. His mouth puckered, his lips purpled from the scanty juice. Not really worth all the effort, he decided. Kind of like searching for gold.

He scuffled the shore with his boot. Toffee-coloured sand and, beneath that, brownish sand, fine-grained and mixed with mud.

He eyed up the riverbank, looking for a tell-tale patch of grainy black. Now that was the sand most likely to be shot with gold, sand that he had been hard pressed to find. And even when he found a promising vein of black sand, he'd come up skunked when it came to gold. It was as if the gold were a living thing, allergic to light. Seeking safety deeper and deeper in the earth.

A raven swooped and landed on a low-hanging branch. Edward's red plaid shirt hung on the same tree but the raven seemed totally unconcerned.

Cerr-aw, cerr-aw, cerr-aw.

He tossed his stick but the raven ignored it, staring at him for a moment before taking wing and riding an updraft into the puff-quilted sky.

He cleared his clogged throat, spat in the dust at his feet.

"Maybe old Raven's got the right idea."

He reached for his shirt and tied its arms around his slimming waist. The flannel had been a foolish choice, for it was too hot to wear once summer arrived, and it didn't do much to keep out the cold in winter either, although he liked the feel of its softness against his skin. His shirt was red and black, one of the few things he'd purchased back in Ottawa, before their trek began. Somehow he had gotten the idea that a gold miner would need a plaid shirt. So much for bringing a little luck from home. Didn't work. Not one bit. Either time.

He'd dreamed going back to Isabelle at the end of day, of dropping a few small nuggets negligently on the table beside her supper plate. The larger ones saved until later, when they'd sit together listening to the snap of the fire, the lonesome call of the loons. Then he would slip the biggest one into her open palm.

"A penny for your thoughts," he'd say. "Or maybe a little more."

He heard a rustling, a small sound, so at least he could rule out a bear. And although his head knew this, his heart did not. He scanned the area. There was not one speck of garbage at the claim, each lunch carefully buried after he'd eaten his fill.

Sometimes, he dreamed about black bears, and he woke up sweating and shaky. The literature about the Peace River country had all been positive and full of possibility. No mention whatsoever of bears.

Now he knew a bear was dangerous, and not just to humans. A bear would trash another's den, kill their cubs, steal their food. There was no worse place in the world to be than between a bear and her cub. Ferocious mothers. And quick.

He struggled to get a clear breath.

Maybe this was how Isabelle felt, this threatened feeling that no amount of common sense would dispel.

He had come to think that the Hudson's Bay Company was correct, bears should be shot, skinned and tanned and their lovely shining fur used as a rug to warm that first icy step out of bed on a freezing winter morning. Those mornings where the smoke, if you were lucky enough to have embers left and get a decent fire going, went straight up into the frosty air. Thinly, as if exhausted from the burn.

Perhaps he could make a little money doing just that. But when he thought of getting close enough to actually shoot a bear, his hands trembled, as if a strangle of palsy had set in.

He stood, shaded his eyes with the edge of his hand and peered into the thickest part of the bush. He picked up his axe, tested its sharpness with his thumb. At first push, nothing. He steadily increased the pressure. Finally, a small bubble of red appeared, confirmation that his axe was dull, and maybe confirmation that he would never be proficient in the basic skills so necessary in the north.

He rummages through his camp gear, not really surprised to find that that's he's left his whetting stone at home. There's the troubling rustle again, only this time much closer. He hefts his axe.

A striped squirrel runs from beneath the low-hanging blueberry bushes and he laughs aloud. Only a squirrel, searching for his stash.

At least the animals are doing what nature intended, following ingrained behaviour, trying to stay alive.

Only a man would be stupid enough to leave his natural habitat, to be out in the countryside alone, searching for gold.

He is starting to think a monthly wage, even a paltry one, wouldn't be so bad. You didn't ever read anything about gold mining being a thankless job, how panning for gold day after endless day was hard and back-breaking work. Boring too. No one told him how gold would work its way down as far into the earth as it could, how its very heaviness helped it to hide. Gold had a mind of it's own, it was tricky and shrewd and showed itself to only the chosen few.

It had seemed so easy, back in Ottawa. He'd heard talk of gold everywhere, easily found, and he dreamed the solid feel of a nugget in the palm of his hand.

So maybe in the end, no one ever really told the truth. About anything. He took comfort in the thought, if only a little.

4.

The Bank
Ottawa, 1894

Edward unwrapped his cheese sandwich, the bread limp and white, dried at the edges despite its doubled wrap. He thought longingly of the overstuffed buns his wife used to make, layers of roast beef cut thin enough to see through, old cheese, grainy mustard thickly spread. A few crisp pickles in a little lidded jar, buttery shortbread she would wrap and tuck in for his dessert.

His eyes dropped to his left hand as he realized how long it had been since he'd even thought of Bethany. The indent that had once branded his flesh was now entirely gone.

Getting a job at the bank had never been a big deal. Pretty hard for Mr. Witherspoon to check his glowing references, considering the slowness of the mail and that England was a very long voyage away.

And he had been a clerk on the docks, so his references weren't a total lie.

Luckily, the Bank of Montreal had gotten itself into a bit of a mess, from the top down, and his boss was in a hurry to hire.

The bank building was elegant, with rich limestone corbels on the corners, portals carved and fine. The tall walnut doors darkened by years of polish and the

34

push of sweaty palms. Edward noticed that it was hard for the frailer customers to open those massive doors. Sometimes, when he saw a bone-thin old lady struggling, he'd leave his desk to help. It was pathetic how grateful the elderly were.

"It's nothing," he'd assure them. "Glad of an excuse to leave my desk for a minute."

He thought of the banks in England, with their proper doormen. Perhaps Mr. Witherspoon should consider it too, as most of his customers, if not feeble already, were edging up there fast. But he didn't offer this idea, even at staff meetings where new ideas were encouraged. Be damned if he'd take a chance on becoming a laughing stock.

He hated Mondays. Longed for freedom. It turned out the job was only a little bit better than the one he'd left behind. He had expected to become a financial expert, approving massive loans for important men, but he was only a glorified clerk, checking ledgers and processing unimportant papers. With very little chance to impress anyone, certainly not his boss who he hardly ever saw.

A red ant crawled across his finger and he quickly picked it off, pinched its body between his forefinger and thumb. He was about to squeeze when he saw a breadcrumb, almost as big as the ant, held in its tiny pincers.

"Scavenging my leavings, were you? Well, you're determined, I've gotta' give you that." He flicked the ant sideways onto the grass. "Go on home with your precious booty," he said. "Take care of the wife and kids."

The ant stayed put, stubbornly clinging to the crumb. Edward watched for a moment, then reached out, squished it between his thumb and forefinger. If you don't have enough sense to grab a chance to escape when you get one, he thought, then you might as well be dead.

The sky was bluebell blue, wisps of high clouds floating in and out of his view. He watched a lone Canada goose gliding down for a landing. The soft grey of its underbelly, the black neck elongated, a slash of white on its underside like a bank robber's kerchief.

The goose was lower now, low enough that he could hear its excited cry, see the creamy grey-brown underside of the wings shading to the larger darker feathers. Wings no longer generating power, but gliding, gliding, gliding majestically down, a renegade leaving the flock. But no, as the bird got closer, he saw it was not one, but two, in tandem, down and down and down.

He scrambled up, watched them for one more minute until they were in front of him, bobbing on the water. Geese mate for life, so if the gander leaves the flock, his mate must follow.

He considered the geese, how they migrated when the urge was strong but then returned to their birthplace every year, as if they had no say in the matter. Funny, he'd never once felt an urge to return.

At the edge of the granite walkway, he bent for a moment to polish a splatter of goose shit from his shiny shoes.

Two pair of shoes clicked into his field of vision. One in very high heels — black patent, shiny, and the other in shoes of chocolate brown, low sheen and of a sensible height. Shapely ankles, muscular lower legs.

He straightened quickly, a rush of blood pulsing to his head.

The women wavered in his sight. One was smiling broadly and she grabbed the other's hand. "Only one more week. I can hardly believe it. And I can hardly wait. But first, our business at the bank."

"Edward Armson," he said, blinking to clear his dizziness. "If you ladies are doing some banking on this beautiful day, perhaps I can help." And he scrambled ahead of them to open the ornate door and ushered them inside. It was shadowed, cool, and he blinked, blinked again.

Annie, he soon found out, was the sister who'd flashed him the luminous smile. "We do have some business we'd like to get tidied up."

"Then I'm your man." His heart thumped and his palms were damp. "Edward Armson," he repeated.

"Annie Olson," the dark-haired woman said. "And my sister Isabelle."

Isabelle put a hand on Annie's arm. "Can you give us a minute?"

Edward could hear their conversation, no effort required.

"But Annie, what about Alfred? Didn't you set up a time with him? I don't think we can just. . . . he always handled things for Papa, and for us too."

Annie tossed her hair, blue-black in the muted light. "I'm so sorry Isabelle, but in all the excitement, I clean forgot about setting an appointment. Maybe it's fate, with me starting a new life and all. Alfred was a perfect fit for Papa, but sometimes a change is as good as a rest." She opened her handbag and withdrew a sheaf of papers. "Isabelle, let's see what this fellow has to say."

Edward reached for the papers.

"I'm relatively new here," he said. "But I have loads of experience and I'd be honoured to help you. Whatever you might need."

Annie offered her hand. "Annie," she said. "And my sister Isabelle. Now we're officially acquainted."

And that was how he'd met the beautiful Annie Olson, and her sister Isabelle.

He led them into his cubicle, because calling it an office would be too much of a stretch. Annie strode ahead, her shiny black hair swinging as she walked.

"We need to set up an account with joint signing authority," she told him. "For I am heading north as soon as I marry. Which is going to be Wednesday next, so we don't have much time." Her brown eyes sparkled. "I'll be Mrs. Jackson John. Otherwise known as Mrs. Trapper John. Maybe I'll just sign everything that way right now and be done with it.'"

Edward grabbed a pencil, pushed its lead hard against a small white pad. He was dazzled by Annie's beauty, and he was somehow angry too. Angry because of his growing feeling that his 'new start' was no better than his old life, maybe worse as he'd left his buddies behind. A crappy job and just his lousy luck, the beautiful sister was already taken.

He heard Isabelle suck in her breath and saw her face pale. "No Annie. Don't even think of it. We'll come back next week, after the wedding. When you really are Mrs. John. You don't want to jinx yourself."

Annie returned alone the following week, and she signed the papers quickly, the letters large and looping and bold, slanting forward as if she were heading somewhere in a hurry. She popped the pen back into the inkwell, rubbed her palms together.

"Mrs." she said. "Me! Married. I can hardly believe it."

As she turned to leave, her giggle tinkled like crystals caught in a breeze and Edward felt a moment of pure envy for Trapper John.

"But I am worried about Isabelle. She thinks my marrying and heading north with Trapper is just plain crazy. Dangerous too. I'm afraid she'll sit around and mope when I'm gone."

His hand strayed to his right trouser pocket, and he caressed his lucky marbles. He could really use a little luck right now. When he heard the tell-tale clicking, he pulled his hand from his pocket as if it had been scalded and straightened a pile of papers on his desk. "I do have quite a bit on the go just now. But if you like I can check on Isabelle for you."

That wasn't exactly true, but who would trust a banker who admitted he hadn't much to do. "Maybe I could come up with some excuse to call her down here for a consultation once in a while."

Annie was quiet for a moment, running her fingers through her gleaming hair. His own fingers curved as he watched her charcoal locks lift and fall.

"Isabelle's a private kind of person," she said. "She's never been one for collecting friends so I couldn't think of anyone. At least, with you, there's a plausible excuse." She smiled and his heart beat faster. "But let's keep this between us.

I know Isabelle would hate the thought of me arranging anything for her. Even if it's just popping in to see you at the bank."

"I understand completely," Edward replied, happy to share a small secret with Annie, happy to share anything at all. "You can count on me."

When he offered his hand, Annie took it in both of hers, gave it firm squeeze. "Thank you. Thank you so much."

Blushing wildly, he led her back to the belly of the bank where a tall man commanded the counter, his black hair askew, eyes sapphire ice. Every woman in the place was sneaking glances but he seemed totally unaware. A smile flooded his face when he saw Annie.

"Why hello, my darling wife," he said, pulling her to his side. Then he turned to Edward. "You must be the new advisor the girls have been telling me about," he said, extending his hand. "I'm Annie's husband, Jackson John."

Edward quickly straightened his tie and put his hand out.

"They tell me you're the man who'll make their money grow."

"I certainly intend to." Edward's hand seemed so much smaller now, enveloped in the man's massive mitt.

"Call me Trapper." He released Edward's hand. "Doesn't make a lick of difference to me. For I've got Annie. Riches enough for any man."

"Congratulations on your marriage," Edward said. "And take good care of this girl. Her sister tells me she's stayed close to home up until now and sometimes adventure is not all it's cracked up to be."

Trapper grinned. "Adventure and Annie," he said, "go together like peaches and cream. No need to worry. We'll be just fine."

The man loomed large, taking up all of the available room. And the oxygen too. The female tellers were watching him, barely drawing a breath.

Trapper's massive hand rested on Annie's delicate elbow.

Ready for action, Edward thought. They'll be gone in a shot.

"Bye for now," Annie said, turning to him for a moment. "And thanks."

Edward watched them walk away, heads close, arms swinging. And when they stepped outside, a sudden clearing of the clouds, sun shining brightly on their shoulders.

The balance in Annie and Isabelle's account had made Edward's heart race. Thank God for spring, he thought, and the Canada geese and that he'd stayed too long at lunch. It was pure chance that he'd gotten his hands on such a healthy sum, but perhaps now his boss would take note. Give him more responsibility, and along with that, the promised raise in pay.

Although maybe not, because Mr. Witherspoon had asked him pointed questions as to why Annie and Isabelle had decided to hand their business over to him.

"Just blind luck," he'd replied. "Right place at the right time? But believe me, I'm more than grateful."

"Humpph," Mr. Witherspoon had replied and Edward wondered just who had been handling the account previously. Mr. Witherspoon himself? Had he been Papa's old friend?

Well, too bad if he had. The years roll by and one generation gives way to the next and that's just the way things go. Or should go. Be damned if he'd feel guilty for his good luck with Annie and Isabelle Olson. About time something good happened.

The land of opportunity, it seemed, for everyone but him.

Edward considered shifting some of their money from the safety of savings into shares. He dreamed of a letter to Annie, advising her that she and Isabelle were now not just comfortable, but independently wealthy.

Of course, he would add, I took no chances with your initial investment. Just played with the interest and made it grow. A talent of mine.

Stocks in the Bay were probably the safest, but he was a bit ticked off with the Bay just now. He'd been down at their ostentatious office more times than he could count, hat in hand. Wrought iron railing above a low wall of stone. The façade ornate, with gargoyles glaring from every corner and huge blocks of black granite outlining the carved oaken door. A doorman in grey and maroon suit. If the building was meant to intimidate, it most certainly did.

The farthest he'd ever penetrated was to chat with the dazzling Darlene, a receptionist with a nameplate, a bronze and black plaque that looked quite official. How did a woman end up working for the Bay in the first place? Someone's precious daughter, someone's niece?

Last Wednesday, on his half day off, he'd tried again. Nothing wrong with making yourself memorable.

He'd slid two sheets of vellum paper onto Darlene's desk, remained standing there until she finally looked up.

"Oh hi," she said. "Sorry I don't recall your name, but weren't you in just last week?"

He nodded, pleased that she'd remembered.

"This," he said, "is a full list of my skills and accomplishments. At least those that I can put in writing." He raked his fingers through his lanky brown hair. "Accounting is my specialty, but I am also a bit of an outdoorsman. I feel I'd be a perfect fit for one of your outpost jobs." As he pushed the papers toward her, his fingertips had brushed hers. "We all know who really runs places like this." He flashed his most charming smile, and he hoped his dimples were deep today and that she had a fondness for the boyish look. "Who can influence things a bit one way or another, if they so choose."

She straightened his papers, folded her hands. "I'll keep you in mind, but we're flooded with applicants just now. And there are only so many positions. Even at the outposts. And of course, there's experience required there."

He'd seen the ads. the Bay had jobs open everywhere.

"If you hear of something, something my particular skills might fit, could you at least make sure the brass sees what I've got to offer?"

She took a paper from the right side of her desk, marked it with a red pen before putting it into a pile on her left.

"I can try," she said, and pulled another paper from the untidy pile.

Edward's colour rose. If there was one thing in the world he really hated, it was being ignored. Loudly, he cleared his throat.

43

"Sorry," she said, when she finally looked up. "The boss insists the filing be finished every day by five. And it is about the only thing I'm in charge of here."

He grinned. "No doubt you're underestimating yourself. You probably run the place. Sometimes all it takes to get yourself noticed is one good word from a sweetheart like you."

As the door closed behind Edward, Darlene ran her fingertips across the silky scarf looped under her collar and then slid his neatly written papers into the trash can beside her desk. She was nobody's sweetheart and she could spot a snow job from miles away.

Maybe he had hurried his decision. All that lovely money, sitting there, doing nothing all. the Bay was a good solid stock, their assets spread both near and far. But if the Bay didn't have enough foresight to hire him, why should he advise anyone to buy their stock, now that he was in the position to do so?

After endless study, he settled on gold.

*Dear Isabelle,*

*I am hoping you can come by the bank on Tuesday next at 10:30 AM to discuss some ideas I have for increasing your portfolio. With Annie gone, I wish to consult with you. And of course, I require your approval before I make any changes to your accounts. I look forward to seeing you again and I am sure we can come to some consensus regarding future plans.*

*Yours truly,*
*Edward Armson*

He dropped his note into the outgoing mail and marked Isabelle's name on his calendar for ten o'clock

Tuesday next, as if it were preordained he would see her again.

But that night, in his twisted bed, it was Annie he dreamt of, Annie who called out his name.

He was leaning against the oak railing that separated customers from staff. He checked his watch against the time on the big bronze clock hanging on the north wall of the bank. Ten past ten. He wiped his slick palms on the crease of his pants.

For it was he who needed Isabelle, and not the other way around, as Annie had thought. He'd been too impatient, not willing to leave such a large sum in a low interest account and he'd begun investing without the required consent. Just a bit at first, but as his trading made them some real money, he became much more bold. He felt sure Isabelle would understand, once he'd explained.

Or maybe he wouldn't actually explain. Just get her to sign a few papers. Most people failed to read anything thoroughly before they signed. Some didn't read at all.

He desperately needed her written consent, for without it, his job, as puny as it was, would be on the line.

Not that it should be, he thought, for he'd already realized a tidy bit of profit for the Olson sisters. And for the bank as well. And wasn't profit what banks were all about?

"Thank you for coming," he murmured, grateful when she finally showed.

"So sorry I'm late. A crisis next door," Isabelle explained. "My neighbour let her little dog out and he didn't return. Mildred is eighty-two and has hip trouble, so when she knocked on my door in obvious distress, I

45

told her I would search for Frisky, and that she should go home and rest, perhaps make herself a pot of tea. And try not to worry. I found Frisky, who is part dachshund and very overweight, sniffing his way around the park. He didn't come when I called, in fact when I finally got close enough to pick him up, he took a nip at my hand. Freedom went to his head I guess. Poor thing doesn't get walked much anymore."

The ornate clock on the wall bonged eleven. Isabelle looked at the time, colour rising on her cheeks. "Oh my. I didn't realize . . . "

Edward touched her arm lightly, started toward his not-quite-office. "Fashionably late," he said. "And how nice of you to help a neighbour."

He hadn't really noticed when Annie was around, but Isabelle was pretty in a quieter, growing-on-you kind of way. Her hair, unlike Annie's silky blue-black, was shades of browns, her eyes a mix of bronze and green.

"She must have been relieved." He didn't add that he was pretty damned relieved himself.

"She was." Isabelle smoothed her hair, breathed a deep breath. "Frisky is really the only company she has now that Herbert is gone. Of course, I had to help. Still, I'm not one to be late for appointments."

He opened the folder on his desk, his hands only slightly trembling. "I figured that about you," he said. "So I haven't really been worried."

She picked up his silver pen.

"Sign here," he said. "And here." He slid another paper across the desk. "Nevertheless, I am sorry."

Her voice was soft, and eventually, he found, so were her hands.

5.

Edward and Isabelle
Ottawa

Lamps were lit in their snug little house on Saunderson Street, circles of yellow pooled on tables and on the burnished floor.

The smell of fresh-baked bread lingered in the front hall and he could hear soft music from the gramophone. When he thought of the eight hours he'd just wasted behind a desk at the airless and eternally boring bank, he squared his shoulders and put the whole day out of his mind. He began to whistle. Not an entire song, just snatches of this and that. It was good to be home.

Supper was beef stew with plenty of carrots and onions and not much beef. Still, it tasted as good as it smelled.

He began to stack the dishes but Isabelle shoed him away. "I know you're willing," she said, "but we really can't afford any more broken plates. We're down to six as it is. Mother's best china too. We shouldn't be using it, really."

He had to admit that more often than he could account for, dishes leapt from his hands. "I'll replace your precious plates, when I get my raise. Until then, I guess I'd best stay clear of the dishpan."

He straightened his armed oak chair at the head of the table, and then Isabelle's too, shook some crumbs from the tablecloth. He'd never been drawn to domestic chores, but he'd found if he did even the smallest thing, it seemed to please Isabelle immensely. She hadn't been pleased about much of late.

"Maybe we could afford an everyday set if only you hadn't . . . " her voice trailed off to nothing but the snap of her dishcloth spoke volumes.

She had been about to bring up the dwindling balance in her chequing account, and ask again why Edward had tied up all of their ready cash. And when she might look forward to getting some of it back. Or even, God forbid, if she was.

She'd like to buy a sweater of fine cashmere for Annie, something in a bold colour, plum purple, or a rich dark red. She knew the size, just a little larger then she. Or maybe Annie would rather have a shawl, a fringed length of fine wool to wrap around her in the night, an extra layer to keep out the cold.

But she had vowed to leave that tired subject alone. Arguing with Edward about the "missing" money got her exactly nowhere. Edward would slow the pace of his words, and raise the volume too, as he explained that the funds weren't really missing, just invested elsewhere and not accessible at this time.

She hated it when he talked to her like that, as if she didn't have the capacity to really understand.

"Don't worry your pretty little head about such things," he would say, as if handling money would be entirely too difficult for anyone but him.

In the quiet of the parlour, Edward savoured the ritual of his evening pipe, pinching his tobacco from a soft leather pouch, tamping slowly on its sweetness, making himself wait for that first puff, deeply drawn.

"I could smell your tobacco," Isabelle said, wiping her hands on her checked apron. "So I decided to leave the pots and pans. Let them soak for a bit."

She sat in her tapestry chair. "All your careful tamping reminds me so of Grandpa Henry," she said. "Now there was a man who really loved his pipe."

"Mmm." He finally struck the match, the smell of sulphur floating above the sweetness of his tobacco.

He didn't want to talk of Grandpa Henry, a quiet, cautious carpenter who'd never cut a corner, not even once, so he had been told.

"Nasty habit really. But at least my smoke's going up in the world." He glanced at Isabelle. "More than I can say for myself."

Isabelle picked up her knitting, always near at hand. "Please, Edward, don't start."

"Come north with me. We could file a claim. Sift sand through our fingers and eventually come up with handfuls of gold. You wouldn't be peddling your bread at the Saturday market or cleaning for the women up on Sentinel Hill."

"We both know those jobs are only temporary, until you get our account straightened out, so I really don't mind. You said I shouldn't worry, so I haven't been."

∾∾∾

Isabelle crossed her fingers, asked forgiveness for the lie.

She loved a clean house, so the cleaning job at Estelle Wigmore's elegant house didn't seem like work at all. It amazed her, how little care Estelle took, and amazed her too when Estelle paid her absolutely no mind, dropping her pay casually on a side-table as she left. Sometimes, far more than her agreed-upon wage.

"I'm off to lunch," she'd say. "Whenever you're finished, feel free to go."

For all Estelle knew, Isabelle could have spent the rest of the afternoon reading elegant magazines, maybe buffing her nails.

But she scrubbed the unused kitchen until it shone, lovingly polished the heirloom silver, arranged crimson roses from the gardens in a heavy crystal vase.


"You're miles away." He hated it when his wife seemed absent.

"Not far." Isabelle smiled. "Just at Estelle's, polishing the silver."

"Bad enough you work for her. Now you're bringing her home." He pointed at Isabelle with his pipe. "Next time I see her, I'm going to tell her you don't need her piddling little job anymore and . . . ."

Isabelle raised a hand to stop his rant. "Relax, Edward. The job is easy. And I think it makes her feel important, having hired help. And we can certainly use the cash."

She resumed her knitting, cast off another row. "We should be grateful to Estelle. She's been nothing but good to me."

He cupped his warm pipe in his right hand, pointed its ebony stem. "You're right," he said. "And at least when you're over at Estelle's, you're doing things you love." He lifted the pipe to his lips, took a deep draw. The wind began to pick up and the eyebrow window above the piano rattled. "At least you're not bored. Now boredom," he said, "can kill your very soul."

Isabelle didn't look up, continued knitting and pearling, her chestnut hair glowing in the golden light of the lamp.

"Things are so very slow these days. We're supposed to get out there and hustle, bring in our own accounts and I hear talk of instituting a monthly quota, for God's sake. Not so hard if you are connected. A brother here, a father there, an old friend from school. But for me? Not knowing the 'right' people can cost you, certainly when you're working in a bank." He drummed his fingers on the worn arm of his chair. "Bastards," he said.

"Edward!"

"When I think of Annie and Trapper out there, doing something grand, well, it makes me realize even more clearly that I'm wasting my time. And, all of us, really, have only so much time."

The clock in the hall bonged as if to emphasize his point.

Isabelle stuck her needles into her knitting, set it aside. "Some less than others," she said. "I'm thinking of my father. It's a good thing we don't get to know."

Edward shifted in his chair, drew again on his pipe. "Listen to that wind howling. Such a drastic change. The equinox party seems ages ago. What was it, two weeks now? Or three?"

His boss was a star-gazer and arranged the staff parties according to the summer solstice, the fall equinox, anytime the earth was poised for change.

"That was a lovely evening. You know, your boss recognized me, from when I used to go with Papa to the bank. Not so many people remember Papa anymore."

Edward reached for her hand. "And did you speak of me as well?"

"No, not really, but I do think he was interested to know that you are now handling David Olson's accounts."

He sighed. The man had been dead for a long time and God knows, you couldn't wield influence from beyond the grave no matter how important you once were.

"Your father's been gone now for what, four years? Five?"

"Five. But it seems like yesterday to me."

How much things could change in even one year. He exhaled and a cloud of blue smoke obscured the room. "Out of sight, out of mind. That's the way of the world. Even for a well-respected man like your father."

Isabelle reached for the basket of wool, tidied her needles and her yarn. Out of sight, out of mind? She never felt that way about her father, hoped she never would.

What if Edward got his dream job at the Bay, and was away for months at a time? Would he forget their life together, just like that? She swallowed hard.

"Out of sight out of mind doesn't always work does it?" she said. "Hardly a day goes by you don't mention Annie and Trapper. And they've been gone for almost a year."

The rising wind moaned and Isabelle felt a small draft, harbinger of the approaching winter, a time of year that she'd come to dread. Mostly because of Annie living God knows where, maybe not warm enough, maybe short of food or company. It pained her to think of her sister, so far from home and perhaps alone.

"Can't we just be happy where we are? Bloom where you're planted, like my mother used to say."

Edward crossed his legs, dangled his ankle up and down, up and down. "Well, I know for sure I can't."

She studied her sweater, found where she'd changed colour one stitch too late. She ripped the stitches back to the miniscule mistake. "Can't what? Bloom? Or be happy?" She took up the needles again, began a rhythmic click, click, click. She could usually knit without ever looking at her stitches, and she never tangled the wool. A knitting mistake on a simple pattern was uncharacteristic for her. "I, for one, think you must be in line for a raise soon, after all of your dedication, the extra hours. How many times are you late to supper? Certainly more than is reasonable. Someone at that bank is noticing. There's no doubt in my mind."

6.

Out of Sight ·

Oh God, he thought, I hope she didn't mention my long
hours to the boss. I really hope she didn't. What's wrong,
at the end of day, with one small drink? The Penny
Farthing, where smoke was thick, and the smell of beer
ripe and lush. He ordered a mug, grabbed a stool at the
bar and nursed his drink, fondling the bowl of his pipe.
He reached for his tobacco pouch, but it was painfully
thin. Save that for later, he thought. One indulgence at a
time. At least Isabelle approved of his pipe.

He couldn't say the same about his taste for a brew.

The hum of low conversation loosened his hunched
shoulders, made his head feel light. He drew a circle in
the wetness of the bar. From his pocket, he pulled his
marbles. Two steelies, nothing special, just ball bearings
polished with use. Still he liked the heft of them in his
hand. Then the pride of his collection, a clear marble
encasing a purple heart. Bartered away on the docks
by a foreign fella who'd had too much whiskey and was
desperate for more. Edward hadn't noticed until the next
morning that the interior had a major crack. Oh well, it
was his favourite still.

He rolled them under the flat of his palm, felt their
perfect shape. Wondered if Joan had given the rest of his
collection to Ward. He squinted at the heart, glowing in

the low light. Should have been Ward's. A man should leave something special behind for his son.

Bethany had laughed when he showed her his marble collection.

"To tell the truth, I never thought I'd be marrying a man who still played marbles. On the other hand, why men want to cluster in stinky old pubs and play silly games is beyond me, but at least darts I can sort of understand."

He was sorry, then, that he'd shown her. The marbles were more than just marbles to him, but he found there was no way for him to explain.

She picked up the crystal one and held it to the light. "This one is flawed," she'd said. "In case you haven't noticed."

When he arrived home late, smelling of beer, she would stir the stew in the pot, plop it onto a plate and set it in front of him. She'd bring the breadboard, with no butter and no knife, so that he had to tear pieces of bread to mop his plate.

She never berated him, but went to her rocker and picked up a book, ignored him for the rest of the night.

Sometimes, he wished he'd stayed longer, perhaps until closing time. Bethany's frozen silence was a shock after the cosiness of the pub and he wondered why he'd bothered to hurry home. Might as well be hung for a sheep as a lamb.

Isabelle ripped open the envelope, read Annie's letter through quickly the first time, thirsty for any kind of news. The second read, she savoured Annie's every word. Her own private hoard, a few letters she felt were written more to her, sister to sister, were tucked under a stack of white cotton panties in her underwear drawer. Sometimes, she paused, re-read them as she was putting freshly laundered clothes away. Sometimes she just ran her fingertips across the envelopes, comforted by the fact of her sister's words, nestled safely in her drawer.

She pressed the precious letter to her cheek, as if seeking the familiar touch of Annie's hand. She considered hiding this letter too, but instead, she folded it neatly and tucked it beneath the doily that protected the wide velvet arm of Edward's easy chair, and waited for him to come home.

"We finally got a letter."

Edward straightened, leaned forward in his chair.

"A letter? Where?"

Annie's letters seemed to stir something in Edward, and his restlessness lasted for days. He would go for long walks, alone, and he smoked more, talked more, fidgeted more. Everything more.

"Right there," she said. "Under your hand."

Edward spied the torn envelope and his fingers curved. Really, how could he have missed it? At the very least, he should have felt Annie's words near.

He tossed the doily aside, picked up the envelope, caressed its creases and stains, disgusted by the softness of his palms, as he'd been the first time he shook hands with Trapper John.

Postmarked Dunvegan.

Although he wanted to tear into the letter, he also wanted to anticipate, like a boy with an unexpected gift on Christmas morn.

"Dunvegan," he murmured. "Dunvegan." The word felt smooth, like toffee on his tongue.

A trading post? A settlement tucked between towering pines and shivering birch on some distant rocky shore? Was Annie alone in camp, keeping the fires banked for Trapper's return, maybe picking berries and drying them for winter when food might get scarce? And just for a bit of fun, trying her hand at panning gold? Other than himself he couldn't think of anyone he'd rather have find a nugget of serious size.

Or was Annie in Dunvegan too, following Trapper John?

He leaned toward the light, opened the envelope and smoothed the pages covered in Annie's familiar hand. Not dated, of course.

It might have been months, he thought, or if they were close to a trading post, it may have been written only weeks ago. So like Annie, he thought, full-tilt ahead and to hell with the details.

*Dear Ones,*

*I am writing by the light of a snapping birch fire and my long hair, of which, I must admit, I was just a smidgen proud, now smells like old moccasins and looks much worse. The first thing to go is vanity, which may not be so bad.*

*This land is so beautiful and so incredibly vast it's hard to imagine it, back home, where all you can see is another house across the street and a little patch of the sky. It's the stars I would stay for, dotting the huge black bowl of the universe. Silence so absolute you could hear the beat of an angel's wing.*

*Johnnie has the knack of trapping for sure, instinctive maybe? Somehow, his traps whisper a siren song, and every night, those poor sleek beavers paddle their way to their own doom. Although I do mind the sight of their lifeless bodies and the putrid smell of drying pelts stretched on racks, I don't mind the money we get when Johnnie sells them to the Bay.*

*I have learned a thing or two about bargaining too. I now know what a made beaver is - the perfect specimen against which all other pelts are measured. Of course, the agent almost never finds a perfect pelt, so his initial offer is always low. Thank God Johnnie is a good trader and at the end of negotiations, he usually gets a passible price.*

*However, I do fear for the Natives. They don't know the language like Johnnie does and often, I think they get much less for their furs than is fair. The Hudson's Bay agents are a cut-throat lot. I hear they are like that because head office says they have to be, and profit is everything, but really? I think they are often downright unfair, to say the least.*

*After Johnnie sells the pelts, it is my turn and I do all my shopping for staples, so the Bay ends up getting plenty of their money back. They keep a satisfactory inventory of essentials, although I have to say that shopping here is nothing like shopping at home.*

*Isabelle, please stop worrying for I know that you are. I am happy and healthy and fine.*

*We have spent some time in a Dene camp and the women there were amazing. It seems to me that although the hunters grab the glory it is the women who keep things going. I have even learned to make dried caribou meat pounded into a powder, an essential, I am told, for the*

58

*lean season, when the caribou are gone. The making of achees has taught me a bit of patience and you should see my muscles now!*

*Living up here is not quite as I'd imagined. There have been times when I questioned my own sanity but I've come to love the peace of it, with only the company of Johnnie and of course, millions of stars. I wish I'd paid more attention in school. At least then I might recognize more than the Big and Little Dipper and the North Star. And of course, the northern lights. They are entirely glorious, the most intense of pinks and pansy violets, moody blues, a shimmering emerald green that changes to purple and then back to green. And they move so sensuously across the sky, like a belly dancer swaying behind a silken shawl, although really, how would I know anything about that? Having never seen a belly dancer myself!*

*I'd like to know what causes those lovely lights. Some celestial event so far away that no one on earth could guess, or something more mundane?*

*I hope there is no logical reason for their beauty. I like to think that God has his hand in that.*

*If you can find a good book on astronomy, I would love to have it. You can send it to me in care of Twelve Foot Davis in Fort Saint John. He is good and dependable, which is not a given with a lot of the traders here. He travels incessantly, or his agents do, and he will make sure the book finds its way, eventually, to me. The man has his fingers on the pulse of the north, and he's taken a liking to Trapper, so although we are entirely alone out here, I have the feeling that Twelve Foot knows exactly how to find us.*

*We are about to break camp and head for Sagitawa. Trapper tells me it is the most beautiful place, at the conjunction of the Smoky River and the Peace.*

*I am surely seeing the breadth of this land, as Johnnie is not one to stay too long in one spot, as we both well know.*

*Have you and Edward thought any more of coming? Opportunity is everywhere.*

*I would love to see you again.*

*Much love — Annie*

*(Johnnie too although just now he is out somewhere moving his trap line again)*

*Here is food for thought — Johnnie somehow got his hands on an Edmonton newspaper — thought you might be interested.*

THE MCDONELL DOMINION SURVEY PARTY ARRIVED IN EDMONTON YESTERDAY, AND BROUGHT WITH THEM A STORY OF A DISCOVERY OF GOLD IN THE PEACE RIVER COUNTRY, WHICH, IF IT ANSWERS TO SURFACE INDICATIONS, WILL ESTABLISH A NEW RECORD IN THE HISTORY OF MINING . . . . THE CRUDEST ASSAY WILL GIVE A VALUE OF FROM $7 TO $2 PER TON. THE DISCOVERIES WERE MADE 37 MILES BELOW FORT ST. JOHN, ABOUT 17 MILES FROM ALBERTA. EACH MEMBER OF THE PARTY STAKED A CLAIM IN THE DISTRICT.

Edward held the letter for a long while after his reading was done. Then he slid it back into the envelope, smoothed the address with his thumb. The news clipping he slipped into the pocket of his shirt, right next to his racing heart.

"Nice newsy letter," he said. "But still, it would be nice if we could see her, despite how optimistic she seems."

Isabelle tidied her skeins of wool, cobalt blue and gunmetal grey, and stuck her needles into the half-finished sweater. She sighed, tucked her project carefully into the basket. "You know that's not likely to happen anytime soon."

He blew out a noisy breath. Even the promise of seeing Annie didn't seem to light any kind of fire in his wife. "There is a way if you would just think about . . . "

Isabelle stood, and lifted the lamp. "It's time I finished the job at hand. I don't suppose those pots and pans have jumped up and washed themselves."

He felt as if he'd just had a conversation with Annie, and when he closed his eyes, he clearly saw her standing on the shore, her head thrown back, magnificent black hair glinting in the hard-working midnight sun. Her letters might arrive irregularly, but she was a faithful writer. Sometimes two or three were dropped in their mailbox in a single day, like a feast.

He, on the other hand, had failed miserably at his promise to keep in touch with those back home. When he'd left England and the familiar shores receded, his life there also receded and in no time it all seemed a dream.

Out of sight, out of mind.

Except for the damn marbles of course, bringing the whole mess back. He should have left them behind too. Sometimes, when his fingers itched to feel their smoothness and he longed to be soothed by their click, click, click, he made himself stay away, and he had managed one letter to his wife's sister.

*Dear Joan,*

*I am now in Montreal, working for the Bank of Montreal. Easy to remember, at least, although I don't plan to stay long. I am looking for a transfer to Ottawa, as I know no French and so I am finding it hard to navigate here.*

*The Hudson's Bay Company is not hiring just now, although I still have hopes. Their wages are much better than wages at the bank and it seems adventure would be part of the package too. They have a string of trading posts established out west, although their headquarters remain in England.*

*(Maybe you could go down there and tell them what a good chap I am! Ha, ha.)*

*You'd think they might give preference to hiring a real Englishman, someone from home. But until they see the light on that, I will remain at the bank, totting up columns of figures for a less than adequate wage.*

*The money order I am sending is smaller than I'd hoped. Getting ahead in the land of opportunity isn't quite as simple as I'd been led to believe and plum jobs are not falling off trees and right into a chap's open hands. I have also heard that homesteading, which was touted as an easy way to riches, is harder than anyone could imagine and that some are giving up and others have died out west with their dreams unrealized.*

*Sure there is a lot of land available, but the winters are rumoured to be a frozen hell, and the summers the exact opposite. Mosquitoes, sudden storms, relentless heat, severe droughts and wind, wind, wind. All manner of peril that wasn't mentioned by the recruiters in the town square. I think many a man would like a few minutes alone with one of those chaps, but they will no doubt be long gone with their pockets full of finder's fees.*

*How many men, including me, have left England with the highest of hopes, only to arrive to a life harder than the one they left behind? Someone should hunt down those blathering buggers and give them a thrashing.*

*Thank God I knew that being a farmer was definitely not for me. Those poor sods invested all their money in a few crude tools and a couple of good oxen only to find the prairie the most inhospitable of places.*

*Really, living in a sod shack with the wind blowing and the icy cold winters going on for months on end. The poor women who followed them there. No wonder so many have gone home, or gone crazy. Whichever came first.*

*I am lucky to have found myself a job. My little bed-sitting room is outfitted now with all I need to be perfectly comfortable and I am hoping the next time I write I will have more cash to send.*

*I miss Bethany still. She was your beloved sister, and you knew her much longer than I, but I miss her too.*

*Please kiss my son for me.*

*With fond regards,*
*Edward*

## 7.

Joan Spencer
Brighton, England
September 19, 1897

Joan stood at the sink, the baking dishes soapy and piled high. The red and white gingham curtains ruffled in the breeze, and she could hear sparrows quarrelling in the oak trees outside. She checked the clock. One more hour of blessed calm before the boys came home. Ward was up from his afternoon nap and out in the garden, doing what she had no idea. He was a dreamy boy and didn't need much to keep him entertained.

The house smelled of buttery biscuits.

She scrubbed the biscuit pan, grabbed a towel to give it a quick dry. When she heard her son's quarrelsome voice, she pushed the window open farther, looked down the lane. Collin was walking fast, pulling Ward forward faster then he could walk, so that every once in a while his feet left the ground. Even from this distance, she could see smudges on his dear little face.

She ran to the gate and Collin shoved Ward toward her. "He's been at it again," he said.

He had a scratch on his cheek and his knees were scrubbed. She took a fresh hankie from her pocket, brushed some gravel from his oozing skin.

"We've talked about this, sunshine. You aren't old enough yet to go to school with the others. Your time will come soon enough."

He sniffled, turned away.

Joan took his face in her hands. "You're not to leave the garden without letting me know. You promised."

"It's the bloody marbles," Collin said. "He thinks he can just walk into the yard at recess and plunk himself down in the middle of a game."

"Don't swear, Collin." Joan swatted her son's behind with an open palm. She turned, looked hard at Ward. "I thought we agreed to keep the marbles just for home."

He swiped at his smudged face with the back of his hand.

"I just wanted to show them to a mate. But then he wanted to try them. And he didn't listen when I told him no."

Gently, Joan checked his jacket, retrieved the marble bag.

"We'll just put these away for now," she said. "When you get a little bigger Collin will teach you to play. Then you might win a few more of your very own. Wouldn't that be fun?"

He nodded and Joan vowed to hide the marbles somewhere safer, somewhere that he would never think to look. Mostly, they were nothing special. A few steelies and three not-quite-perfect clays. But there was one she admired. A lovely cobalt blue, glazed so it shone. Collin knew his marbles, and when he'd told her it was a Jasper, she'd been truly amazed. A marble? With a name?

She tightened the drawstring, tucked the bag into the pocket of her apron. Ward was such a good little lad, mostly, but the marbles seemed to rile him up.

And she had never told him that they came to him from his father's hand.

She'd had good intentions to keep Edward informed, but letters took so long to get to Canada and after the first, and Edward's discouraging reply, she'd decided to let sleeping dogs lie. It wasn't as if Edward was writing her and asking after his son. Or sending money as had been the plan.

She and Tom had decided that for now, the less Ward knew about his father, the better off he'd be. And really, he'd been with them so long that he truly had become one of their own.

"Come," she said, taking Ward's grubby hand. "I've got fresh-baked biscuits inside."

She looked at Collin and then at the clock. Not much use sending him back to school with only a half hour left and a ten-minute walk to get there.

"You might as well call it a day," she said. "Have a glass of milk and a bicky while they're still warm."

A grin split Collin's face. She knew he didn't love school and an hour off at the end of the day would suit him just fine.

She was dead-tired. The boys had raced through their tea and gone to bed without one bit of fuss. Sometimes bedtime could get to be a handful, with the three of them, but not tonight. The kitchen was spit and polish, all ready for the morning. But still she tossed and turned, flipped her pillow to the cool side, which didn't help at all.

Sometimes, when she hugged Ward, she felt a mix of grief and guilt. For her sister, who had died so young. For herself, trying too hard to make a new family for the boy. And then falling in love with him. Loving him as fiercely as she did her Collin. And James now smack in the middle. Was she being fair?

She got up and drew the shade tighter to the sash.

"Quit your fussing now and come to bed." Tom drew the covers back and when she lay down beside him, she fitted herself to the curve of his back. His steady breathing soothed her and finally she drifted into a troubled sleep.

I am shocked to see him walking up the lane and I have an urge to grab Ward and run. But as if I have no free will, I open the door, stunned to see how much older he looks.

"Hi, little man. It's me. I've come back for you, just as I promised. For sure you won't remember me, baby that you were. But no doubt you've heard lots about me."

"No." Ward drops his gaze. I put my arm across his bony shoulders, pull him close.

"I always meant to tell him, but the time just came and went and before I knew it . . . well. And it has been so long since we had any kind of word."

Edward bends forward, as if I've just kicked him in the gut.

"I never forgot about my son. Not for a minute." He reaches for Ward. But the small tow-headed boy evades his touch, takes refuge behind me, his fist kneading his eyes. "No need to be afraid. It's me, your father. Come for you at last." Edward stands stone still. How he must long to touch the boy.

My hand lingers on Ward's hair, stroking it, and my eyes will not meet Edward's.

## 8.

Ottawa

The bank was stuffy, and quiet as a tomb. Edward doodled. Idly, he wondered what Joan had told his son. Maybe Ward had no idea he had a father who'd high-tailed it to Canada seeking his fortune and a mother who died bringing him into the world.

Probably all for the best.

He ran his fingers through his hair, pushed away the thought of Ward's first steps, his first word. His son would learn to ride a bicycle with another's hand steadying the wheel; someone else would show him how to kick and dribble a ball.

He doodled some more, began a fresh sheet. Dear son. But then he lifted his pen. He was quite sure that his son could not yet read. All well and good to send a letter, but there was really no way to confirm that it arrived. Or that anyone would read it to him if it did. He opened his desk drawer, slipped the paper inside.

His marbles clicked in their compartment. He picked the clear one with the purple centre, rolled it in his palm.

Maybe when he gets older, I'll send him a nice long letter. Send these along too. He might as well have them all. And so far, the damn things haven't been one bit lucky for me.

The thought of a loving reunion, sometime far, far in the future, made him smile.

Isabelle dried the last china plate, held it for a moment before she placed it carefully in the cupboard with the remaining five. Next to the pretty little cups and saucers. The leisurely ritual of afternoon tea that she and her mother regularly shared brought a smile. The most she'd ever managed with Annie was a quick chat over a cup of fresh-brewed Red Rose, often cut short because Annie had places to go. She wiped her hands on the tea towel one final time and hung it on the rack to dry. In the kitchen window, Edward's reflection wavered. She watched him draw again on his pipe and smoke wove braids of silver through his hair, so that she saw how he might look when he grew old. The wind rattled the window, ruffling the faded roses twining up the limp curtains. Satisfied that her kitchen was once again pristine, she slipped into the parlour.

Annie's letter lay on his lap. Twelve Foot Davis and Dunvegan and Sagitawa, the Smoky and the Peace. His lips were moving as he savoured the words.

With her foot, she pushed a multi-coloured rug closer to her chair. "It's a work of art, this rug," she said. "I could sell it at the market. Probably for a pretty penny too. But I'm afraid I love it too much. All those hours of cutting the fabric and braiding it, getting the colours to coil just right."

"If we do decide to go, you could roll it up and take it along. Show Annie your handiwork." He took her hand. "Come north, like she's asked. Maybe Annie needs you, have you thought of that?"

She pulled her hand away, adjusted the neat bun at the back of her neck. "Annie? Needing me?"

Annie had always been at ease in the world, and she had never needed anyone. Isabelle wondered sometimes if that's why she had been her father's favourite. Because she was the lame duck, the one who needed extra care.

"It's not such a ridiculous thought," he said. "You're her sister, after all. And sisters will always need each other, so I've been told."

She picked up a needle, threaded it easily, even in the fading light. Edward's best blue shirt was missing a button. "Really. Who told you that?" She positioned the ivory button perfectly, pushed the needle through and back.

Edward frowned. "Don't try to change the subject, my dear. We're talking here about changing our lives."

The needle slipped through the buttonhole too quickly and Isabelle felt it prick her forefinger. No blood, thankfully. She tied off the thread, clipped the ends with her teeth.

"I don't want our lives to change. And if Annie gets lonesome enough, maybe she'll come home. And bring John too."

He sighed, tucked Annie's letter into his breast pocket, next to the clipping, stroked it absently as he blew out the lamp.

"Time for bed," he said.

Later, in their bedroom silvered by the three-quarter moon, she whispered into the curve of his collarbone. "I'm afraid to leave home. I could die up there all alone."

"You won't be alone." He encircled her with his ropey arms. "I'll be there. And Annie will too. Trust me, we'll find Annie for sure." He tightened his arms around her. "Have a little faith, Isabelle. I'm as good a man as Trapper John."

She slid from his arms, rolled to her right, farther away. "Why do you constantly compare yourself to John?"

"Because Trapper acts," Edward replied. "He doesn't just dream."

She sat up, fluffed the pillows to support her back. "Well, I think he rushes into things. Look at how fast he married Annie. That, no doubt, will turn out well, thanks to her. But heading north? And taking Annie too? Irresponsible, is what that is."

And as he drifted, Edward thought of Annie and Isabelle's dwindling account at the bank and how he'd never admitted to Isabelle the scope of his ill-advised trades.

Trapper had no corner on irresponsibility, not by a long shot he didn't.

How would he ever get Isabelle to leave? To agree to the sale of her childhood home? If, God help him, it should come to that.

All those endless hours spent attending Sunday School in the cool dank vestry, while above him, his mother prayed, sang the dreary old hymns they favoured in the Church of England. About the only thing he got from all of his mother's religious zeal was his badge of perfect attendance, which he'd kept for years.

He'd been forced to memorize the Ten Commandments, to think about the many ways a person could sin, but at the age of eight, he was pretty sure that none of that stuff would ever apply to him.

He remembered that sins of omission were sins all right, often of the worst kind, but he'd never mentioned his first marriage, nor his son, to Isabelle.

For the life of him, he couldn't figure it out. It wasn't as if he'd done a single thing wrong. If he'd told her at the beginning, Isabelle would have been full of sympathy for him, a young widower forced to start a new life and to leave his beloved son behind. A tragic figure is what she would have thought. But now? A damn poor time to mention that he'd had another life, a wife he had loved, and an infant son.

He pulled her to his chest, inhaled the faint lemon scent of her hair. She washed her locks in dish soap and rinsed with clear water to which she added the juice of one lemon. The scent was heavenly and Isabelle's hair had a lovely sheen.

The wind rose and the shutters began to thump.

When she finally became heavy with sleep, Edward eased himself away. The moon shone through the stained-glass transom above their window, and splintered into a kaleidoscope on the wall. The shattered light painted Isabelle's shoulders pink and violet. He tucked the blanket around her, gently, so she wouldn't wake.

The light seemed otherworldly, coming from everywhere, the room so bright he couldn't settle. He tossed and he turned, the magical rays wrapping him in a fragile rainbowed web.

He stilled, felt himself slip through the thin membrane that held him in his world with Isabelle, so quiet by his side.

9.

Joan
Southhampton, England
May 1893

"Oh, my poor little Bethany wanted this baby so badly. I told her. So delicate, so fine, not built for bearing children. But she wouldn't listen and look where's it's taken her. Six feet under, that's where."

She blinked back her tears, furiously sweeping Edward's floors and tidying his cottage as if restoring a semblance of order might make everything right again.

She'd just got back from market, laden with food. "Really, Edward," she told him. "You have to pull yourself together, for the child."

She floured and seared the stewing meat and dumped it into a pot of stock simmering on the back of the stove.

When the baby began to cry, Edward didn't move, and it was she who lifted Ward from his cradle. "You poor little thing," she whispered and patted his bottom, appalled to find it so heavy and so wet. "For goodness sake, Edward, he needs his nappy changed. And probably has for quite some time. You might have noticed the stink."

She laid the baby on a flannelette cloth on the countertop, washed his soiled bottom and applied a thick layer of cornstarch to his raw-looking rash.

"There now, you'll be a lot more comfy, poor boy."

She folded the child into her shawl and began a rhythmic rocking on the edge of the bed. "How long has it been since the wet nurse left?"

"I'm not sure," Edward said, "but it's been a while. She comes and she goes. She has a little one of her own and a two-year-old who seems to hang on her legs almost all the time. So she's doing double duty, what with her own children and Ward, and sometimes it seems she's hardly in the door before she's gathering her stuff to leave."

Joan continued her rocking, thinking that maybe a new wet nurse was in order. But how to find one when she wasn't around to attend to the search? Obviously, Edward wasn't thinking too clearly about how his household should be run. "Edward, you need to pay more attention. You are paying this woman? Correct? That means you are the boss."

"I know I'm supposed to be . . . " he replied, shame flushing his face.

"How often do you leave him like this? Sleeping in his own filth? It's a shame. A real shame."

The baby belched a large, noisy burp and then settled against her bosom.

"The wet nurse changes him, before she leaves. At least, I think she does. And I've managed it myself in a pinch. Although it is most certainly women's work. Maybe I haven't been tending to him as often as I should."

Joan turned away, stiff with indignation for the child. "If he's used to this, things are worse than I'd thought."

Edward rose, poked at the dying fire. "Things have got pretty bad. I just thought the wet nurse would be, you know, here a lot more. And I know she counts on the money she gets from me to keep her own family afloat, so I don't feel right about letting her go."

"I could take him home with me for a bit. Just until you pull yourself together."

"Yes," Edward replied, as if he'd given the matter careful consideration. "That would be good."

She gathered Ward's blankets and greying nappies and the two woollen sweaters that Bethany had knit, one yellow and one green.

"We'll have to leave soon," she said, packing nappies and salves and a brown bottle of anti-colic tincture into her bag. "Tom and the boys will be wondering what's keeping me. But you can rest easy. Ward will be fine with us for a while."

"Thank you," he said, adding another piece of birch to the fire. He picked up a paper, fanned the coals until the wood burst into flame. "I can tend a fire all right. But tending a baby? The wet nurse started out fine but she did seem to lose interest and . . . well. I just didn't know what to do."

"Obviously," she said. "Tom might be a bit surprised when I bring this fine fellow home, but he'll see the logic, I know he will. And it's only for a bit."

But the days turned to weeks, then weeks to a month and he was surprised to find he didn't miss the baby. He didn't miss the stink of soiled nappies soaking in the pail, didn't miss the overwhelming smell of puke.

When he still had Bethany, he'd read the posters, listened to recruiters extolling the glories of Canada from the speaker's platform in the town square. Men were excited, talking of the wonderful opportunities for those who decided to leave their bleak lives in England for a chance to make a new start. How a man could get his own land just for the asking, and good paying jobs were everywhere. He'd been only mildly interested, anchored in England by his wife and a decent job. The fellows leaving in droves were the desperate ones, the ones with nothing to lose.

But with Bethany gone, he too began to dream of leaving. He gave his notice to the landlord and in two days, before he'd had time to rethink his plan, the place was let.

He could have gone to see Joan, he'd had the time, but he'd sent her a letter instead. Plus half the money from his last pay.

*Edward,*

*I can see the sense of your plan. They say Canada is full of promise. Perhaps you will prosper there.*

*Ward is a right lovely little fellow with a good disposition and I've already grown very attached. And he does so look like my Bethany, with his blonde curls and his blue, blue eyes. But despite the fact he favours our side of the family in looks, and I do believe, in temperament, I know that a son belongs with his father.*

*Godspeed on your voyage, and please, get yourself established and send for him soon. For in my mind, I am already calling him Ward Spencer.*

*If you wait too long, giving him up will surely break my heart.*

*Your sister-in-law,*
*Joan*

The next day, he booked passage on a freighter bound for Halifax.

He sailed early one morning. Leaning against the rail, gazing at the shore as if storing up the green of England, he was surprised when he drew his sleeve across his face to see a dark stain on his khaki arm.

"I'll be back, Ward. I promise."

A fog suddenly dropped, coiling across the deck, poking icy fingers up the bottom of his pant legs. The shore dissolved and he shuddered as he made his way below the deck, seeking the chatter of strangers and what little warmth he could find in the small flat flask he'd tucked into his vest.

10.

Edward and Isabelle
Ottawa
May 1896

Market day, Edward's least favourite day. Ridiculous to think that Isabelle would be out hustling so hard for a buck. And at such a demeaning task, although he had seen the pride she took in her baking, how she admired her racks full of golden grainy loaves.

Once she'd had money, enough to be comfortable at least. And now? Since the cash had been in his care?

He was desperate to recoup.

He'd walked across the park on his way home, maybe to put off the moment he would find her counting her column of coins, figuring what cheap cuts of beef they could afford for the coming week. Or maybe it was because the grass had been neatly mown and a slight shower had freshened the air. He sat on a park bench, watched as two young girls passed by, schoolbags swinging in unison, their arms linked. Chatting and laughing, seemingly carefree. He hardly remembered that.

Isabelle sat the kitchen table. The yellow-checked gingham was covered with her specialty breads, whole-grain, oatmeal, and even the molasses loaves, which usually sold out right away.

"Three," she told him. "I sold only three. And Estelle will soon be gone to the shore for the summer. So no cleaning till fall. And when my days are idle, I find I miss Annie more and more. Maybe you're right. Maybe it is time for us to leave."

11.

The Peace Country
June 1896

Edward patted his vest pocket, felt his lucky marbles move and heard their small soothing clicks.

He found and extracted the crumpled paper he'd picked up at the Hudson's Bay in Edmonton.

Suggested supplies: one waterproof groundsheet, two Hudson's Bay blankets, a pillow if absolutely necessary, one granite cup and saucer per person, a knife, fork, and a spoon. Flour and sugar in bags, coffee and tea in tins, butter in a covered tin, a frying pan, a tin or copper pail with lid for making tea or stew, one water pail, hobbles for the horses, matches in a waterproof tin, oats, if you can get them, for the horses.

He re-folded the list. When he'd tucked it into his vest, the little list had made him smile, and he'd meant to share it with Isabelle. Imagine heading out on such a rigorous trip with so few supplies. But he wasn't smiling now.

He surveyed all the goods Isabelle had so carefully packed. She had crammed so much into each container that it had made his back truly ache. Just think of how many boxes and crates he had lifted and carried, first into the boxcar at the station in Ottawa and then onto the platform when they finally reached Edmonton.

She had tried to pack their entire life and bring it along, He, with just a few tools and some sturdy new work clothes, was travelling light.

It was she who had insisted he bring at least one suit. "For what?" he'd asked.

"Funerals," she'd said.

He didn't know much about horseflesh and the two sturdy-looking horses he'd purchased had faded amazingly fast. He was beginning to sense he'd been had.

The first time they bogged down it was in an innocent looking little draw, surrounded by willow. Only much later would he learn the willows were a clear warning sign. What he should have done was fell some sturdier pines, lay them parallel on top of the sinking trail until he'd made it passable at least.

He swore when the hubs of the wagon mired in the mud and as much as he yanked on the reins, even resorting to whipping the poor horses, the wagon would not budge.

Eventually, after his efforts became more than half-hearted, an outrider scouting a route for a group of six wagons happened upon him. Between the two of them, and a third horse pulling, they freed the wagon from the sucking mud.

"Name's Smith." They were sitting beside the fire, waiting for the coffee pot to boil. "You'd be amazed how many Smiths you'll meet up here. But I really am one, not a wanted man with my face on a poster. Want to thank you for showing me where not to go. Master of the train I'm scoping for don't suffer fools gladly."

Edward's head snapped up. Fools? he thought. He's calling me a fool? But really, I guess the man is right.

The jettisoning was painful, with Isabelle choosing what she absolutely had to keep, and what to leave behind for someone else to scavenge. A tall armoire, the head and footboard of their bed, carved walnut and beautiful, but also weighing a ton.

The oak chairs that had been her grandmother's. Crystal vases and heavy crystal serving trays and one beautiful fluted glass bowl. All that crystal looked exquisite in the china cabinet back home, but put it in a box it just seemed ridiculous and it weighed up, that's for sure. The resulting pile was indicative of the refined life that Isabelle had lived, a life they were leaving behind. Edward shrugged. He rearranged the wagon, folded their bedroll, and tucked it down. At least they still had that.

The gramophone remained, tall and dark, solid walnut. It had been her mother's pride and joy and it was Isabelle's too. He remembered the soft sound of music when he came home after a day at the bank. How the sound lifted his heart. How Isabelle might sometimes be found swaying to the music, dancing alone in the living room.

As they jolted along, he thought of those carefree times. But he also thought of how heavy the gramophone was. How hard to load, even with the help of two strong men.

The horses strained and sweated their way up yet another rise. The ruts were deeply grooved, throwing the wagon sideways and back again. His tailbone hit the ridged seat hard and he winced. Damn this rutted road and all the ads that he'd read, touting the wonders of the Peace River country. No mention of sudden soaking rains, hordes of hungry mosquitos, the sheer lonesomeness of the hard travel. They had talked about a road, not an almost invisible trail, appearing and disappearing at will. Did the grooves jog west or was that a faint trail heading true north? It was a guessing game, but the consequences of taking the wrong trail could be deadly.

And the hordes of flies, the stubborn horses refusing to move sometimes, preferring the safety of the smudges. Wiped down and hobbled, having preserved just enough energy to find fresh grass, they became untrustworthy.

Edward watched their every move. Stubborn, wilful beasts.

Isabelle, at his side, was not moving with the motion of the wagon, as he had finally learned to do. She sat upright. Eyes forward, with not one glance for him.

The trees seemed to be crowding the trail, some of the smaller blackened poplar trunks fallen so he had to get out and pull them aside before they could pass. He held his temper, but really, he could have used a little help.

Only the aspens remained upright, like high-minded aristocrats, seeming to look down on the rest of the forest.

He saw a slinky shadow weaving its way through the trees. Perhaps a wolf? He dropped the small poplar from his hand, hurried back to the wagon.

If you see one wolf, others will be lurking somewhere near. A wolf is a communal animal and the packs live by a strict set of rules. They care for each other's young, and are monogamous. So perhaps there is something noble about wolves?

Not wanting to test his theory, Edward whipped the horses, and slowly the wagon moved ahead.

Rain had fallen, and the rich black earth did not suck the moisture in, as he had imagined it would when he first saw the richness of the soil. Instead, it pooled on top. That bit of water in his way seemed like nothing; the draw didn't seem dangerous until he tried to cross.

Dammit, stuck again. But at least this time not so deeply, and he now knew what he had to do.

"I know you love your music but the gramophone's got to go. We need to lighten our load again and we might as well do it right now. If you take the emotion out of it, it's just a huge heavy piece of furniture. The last thing in the world we need is to have one or both of our horses come up lame."

He leaned into the gramophone, tried to push it out and onto the side of the trail, but eventually, he had to ask for Isabelle's help.

They'd seen other pieces of fine furniture, ridiculous things, a grandfather clock, a large carved settee uphol-stered with flowery petit-point fabric, a full set of china spilling from a walnut box, most of it broken, sometimes bags of flour, split and gooey, full of grubs, and damaged boxes spilling crystal and silverware jettisoned along the side of the trail.

At least they weren't the only ones who'd over-packed, not really having any idea of the difficulty of their journey. It had looked fairly straightforward on the map. The trail however, was much tougher than he'd ever imagined.

As he and Isabelle pushed on the gramophone together, he felt her eyes on his face and he felt the unfamiliar heat of her hate.

84

Edward made camp early and started a fire, although they didn't need it yet for warmth. The hobbled horses soon found a small stream trickling nearby. He dipped a coffee can into the clear stream, filled the kettle and set it on a tripod of willow above the fire. A good strong cup of tea might help. But Isabelle refused to look at him, to reply to his nervous chatter.

He added two logs to the already healthy fire and then set off toward the horizon at a brisk pace. A walk might do him a world of good. And Lord knows, some time apart was a necessity right now. Sometimes, talking got them exactly nowhere. Today was one of those times.

He found and followed a faint trail through the spindly aspens, and worked up a good sweat. The land was rolling, small knolls and dips. But as he crested a rise, he came upon a natural bowl, with a steep slope.

There, like a hidden jewel, he saw a small lake, clear aqua, surrounded by black slate rocks slippery with moss.

He worked his way down to the edge of an overhanging rock and knelt to dip his hand into the crystal water. It was cold, much too cold for a swim. Shadows moved in the depths, and thinking of supper, he wished for a fishing rod.

But any kind of killing, even a fish, would seem wrong in this perfect place. He could feel it in his bones. He stayed there for a long time, mesmerized by the filtered green rays of light striking the aqua water, by the sun on his back, the birdsong that came in bursts and then trilled away.

If only Isabelle had come.

It would be hard to stay angry when confronted by such breathtaking beauty. He took one last long look before he turned toward their camp, toward Isabelle and the anger held tight in her rigid spine.

The peace of the place stayed with him and somewhere along his walk back to camp, he forgave Isabelle her inflexible ways.

Change is hard, he thought. For all of us.

They neared the Peace River on a sunny day in early June, a glorious day, Edward thought, to be alive. Small grey birds with yellow breasts and black striping on their crowns swooped, warbled an unfamiliar song; the sun shone warm on his back and the sky was vast and achingly blue.

They topped a rise and he saw banners of grey smoke wafting, it seemed to go straight up to God. His breath quickened.

The river, far in the distance, was wide, curling like smoke around obstacles in its path. Water so deep must surely be cold, but just now it looked like silk shot through with jagged bits of silver.

But silk, Isabelle had told him once as she cut a fabric for a dress, was cold on the skin and hard to work with. Every needle mark showed and if not sewn perfectly, it wasn't nearly as beautiful as it seemed.

A meadow lay before them, dotted with clumps of blue-grey grasses, grass so thick it was tangled and flattened in spots, downed by its own weight. Bright yellow flowers, and what looked like purple puffballs were scattered everywhere, like confetti, and behind them, tall spikes of amethyst, an intense hue he had never noticed in a flower before.

The edges of the plateau dropped down to the river, not gently, but as if pulled there by a strong force. Filings to a magnet, and he felt the pull.

A thin dirt road meandered across the meadow, and he counted four small clapboard shacks. One of them, painted a startling blue, stood aloof, but the others, with their greyed siding blended almost into the landscape, looked as if they had always been there.

"Hiy-aah," he clucked, and as he lifted the reins, Dolly and Dexter dutifully leaned into their harness and the wagon lumbered forward.

Poor old nags, so very close to spent.

"Look Isabelle," he said. "Prairie, pure prairie everywhere. I never expected that. I was thinking steep riverbanks and sheer rock, pure forest and busy little streams. How is it that the farther north we come, the flatter the land? More open too. Maybe years from now, when we are old, this place could turn into some fine farming country. But right now, this piece of paradise is all about the gold. I just have to find the perfect place."

Isabelle didn't reply.

"Have you ever seen a person divining for water?"

She shook her head no.

"Well I have. It's an amazing sight, the Y of a willow bending to the ground and a man's arms straining against the pull. But the willow bends to the water and the man's arms must follow. I have a feeling that I have that affinity for finding gold. I'll know the best place to find it, just by the feel."

She swept her gaze across the landscape, and then she rubbed at the spot between her eyes where she'd developed a deep vertical crease, perhaps from seeing too much space for too long. No orderly streets, no shops, no people bustling along wooden sidewalks. No banks or restaurants or factories.

No peaceful little cleaning or baking jobs, where her hands were busy but her mind was free. The chitter chatter of other women in the market, comforting to the ear.

Just the overwhelming silence.

The clearing was so vast it made her want to hide her face.

Edward was standing now, the reins loose in his hands. "It looks like we've finally reached civilization. Or a close proximity."

Yes, here, at least, there were the shanties to stop the eye, pull it down to the rolling prairie, dotted everywhere by yellow and purple and the faded blue of sagebrush. Along the narrow paths that crisscrossed the waving grasses like stitches on a quilt, she spotted a new kind of flower, vibrant orange, some of them edging to red. Their tall stalks leaned east, blown by the prevailing wind. Lilies? she wondered. Really? Here?

She felt as if she'd walked into a painting, the clear blue sky so high and vast and, beneath her feet, the field of vibrant flowers.

For the first time since she'd left her home, excitement bubbled in her belly. Maybe this strange and remote part of the world would reunite her with Annie. Maybe someday, it might actually start to feel like home.

The door of the nearest shack swung open and Edward saw a woman there, hefting a large tin pail. She set it down, waved them closer.

"Stella Douglas," she said. She was scrawny and sinewed, her skin creased and dry. "Ain't seen a new arrival for many a month." She eyed their wagon, still heavily laden despite the pieces they'd been forced to leave along the trail. "Kind of lonely here lately." A fit of coughing racked her thin body. "Since the Johnson's left. You thinking to squat?"

"Squat?" Edward climbed down from the wagon and stretched his stiffened limbs.

Stella leaned against the doorframe, watching with brightening eyes. "That one's empty," she said, gesturing to the shanty across the road. "Old Johnson's place. Why don't you take a look-see. Around here, it's first come, first served."

Edward climbed down and crossed the ruts. He opened the door of the abandoned shanty and sunlight spilled in, painting the windows, the sills, and the scarred plank table pushed against the far wall with a blanket of gilded dust. Two wooden chairs, one painted yellow, the other one red. Seems one of the Johnson's had, at least at some time, been full of good cheer.

A place just sitting here waiting is a piece of luck, he thought. And I think we can use a little luck just now. The house looked solidly built, its door swung easily. How damn lucky, to find a house when all along he hadn't been sure of how to find a place to rent, never mind how to afford the payments.

"Isabelle! Come look. I think we've found a home."

"It will be nice to have another woman close enough to share a cup of tea or coffee or a place I can borrow a bit of sugar or a dab of milk when I've run short," the thin woman said. "Amazing how often that happens when you're far from town."

Another fit of coughing shook Stella's thin frame. When it passed, she offered Isabelle a calloused hand. "Welcome. And don't think twice about squatting. It's the norm around here. I'd offer to help you get settled, but I'm only starting on my laundry. Got to get the whites done while my water's still nice and hot. And getting water heated up is no small task hereabouts."

Across the trail, Edward was shifting a smooth round rock to prop open the sturdy door.

"If we truly can just move in, easy like that," he called, "I'm sure we'll manage just fine. Everything seems to be falling into place. Finally."

Stella turned to her shack, leaving Isabelle alone on the buckboard.

Edward climbed into the bed of the wagon and wrestled Isabelle's black leather trunk to the ground. Be damned if he knew what she'd packed inside, but the thing weighed a ton.

Isabelle was removing her gloves, finger by finger, and when she had folded them and laid them, pearl buttons up, on the seat beside her, she folded her hands, her eyes gone glassy and far away.

"Are you going to help?"

She didn't reply.

"At least you've got the gloves off. I guess that's a start."

Isabelle turned to him then, a flush of red rising on her cheeks. "We're really moving in? Like we own the place?"

"It won't be for long," he said. "You might be doing the real owner a favour if you start with lots of hot water and some good strong soap." He moved closer, offered her his hand. "I'll find a way to contact the guy. Pay a little rent. And don't worry, we'll soon be moving to something better, something of our own."

By mid-afternoon, he had their bedroll supported by boards and blocks of wood he'd found on the north side of the house, tucked under the eaves, so the boards were still straight and true. The head of the bed he positioned to true north, which he was sure would bring luck to their life, or at least a good night's sleep. He threw the pillows on top of the pile of rumpled blankets, hoping Isabelle might pitch in, but she sat on the makeshift bed and watched as he unloaded the rest of the crates and boxes, all of their worldly goods.

"There now, that's the last of it," he said. "I'll leave it to you to decide where you want the kitchen supplies."

## 12.

Isabelle stood in some stranger's abandoned kitchen, her gaze pulled to the dust-glazed window. So much beauty outside. At least it was a start.

She opened the first box at hand, and then stood transfixed. Her six remaining china plates, with their twining yellow roses. She lifted them out, carefully, one by one and ran her fingertips around the golden rims, checking for chips.

It had been so long.

Edward picked up a tin half-full of oatmeal, thinking that he wouldn't be surprised if it contained a grub or two by now.

He walked to the doorstep, his eyes drawn to the horizon. Pure azure blue, with a tinge of gold.

Stella was pinning a greyed sheet to a line strung across her yard and the smell of boiling coffee wafted in the still air.

"We're officially squatted," Edward called. "If it weren't for you, we'd still be on the trail."

She took a clothespin from her mouth. "Got a fresh pot of coffee I'd be happy to share if you're interested."

"Interested?" he said. "I'd give my left arm for a hot cup of coffee right now."

"No need," she said. "Cream? Sugar too?"

Stella went inside and returned with two brimming cups. Eagerly, Edward crossed the short distance and reached for the one with cream.

She sat down on the step, settled her faded flowered dress around her and drew a cigarette from the pocket of her apron. She struck a match, drew hard on the cigarette. "Got an almost full pack if you're hooked like me."

"The pipe is my vice. But thanks for the offer."

They sat in silence, sipping the coffee. Edward sighed. "Lots to do before we lose the light."

"You've hours yet," Stella said. "June in the Peace? You'll be wishing for darkness soon. Which, as I'm sure you've seen, is only a very thick dusk that lasts about three hours. Kinda hard to get the urge to sleep when it's never really dark. You have to guard your rest this time of year. Or you'll stay up all day and more than half the night. Burn out fast, like fireworks."

"Really?"

"Really," she said.

Edward looked at the wide, blue sky, tried to imagine working a twenty-one hour span with only three hours of semi-dark for rest.

"But if you last till winter, the whole thing switches around. Dark all day and all a body wants to do is sleep. Kind of like the hibernation cycle of bears, only, God knows, it affects us humans too." Stella glanced at the shanty across the road. "What about your wife? Perhaps she'd be ready for a cup of coffee by now." She peered into the battered enamel pot. "Might have one cup left. Stove's going, so it'll be quick to heat."

"Isabelle pretty well sticks to her tea."

"Oh damn," Stella said. "I think I'm all out of Red Rose."

She went inside. Minutes passed, and Edward was lost in the raw beauty of the place. Tiny field flowers hiding in the lush grass, the blue of the sky, random clumps of silver-grey willows and farther back, near the horizon, taller trees, poplars and pines.

He started when Stella returned with her blackened aluminum coffee pot, steam rising from its spout, and topped up their cooling cups.

"Couldn't find a tea bag. Not a one."

"I could get you some tea when I go to town. I have to assume there's a town somewhere near. That there's some sort of store."

He looked over the vast expanse of cloudless sky, at ruts grooved in the prairie grass. In the distance, green hills and a smoky smudge of trees.

"There is a mighty fine store," she replied. "Davis Mercantile. Twelve Foot Davis owns the place."

Edward had been lost in the landscape but at the mention of Twelve Foot Davis his head jerked around. Twelve Foot Davis? He knew that name.

Annie, he thought, where are you now?

"Well, I've business to attend to. And we're down to the bottom of the barrel when it comes to supplies."

Stella inhaled deeply one more time, reached down and snuffed out the glowing stub of her cigarette. "You staking a claim?" She looked again at the silent shanty across the road, its door firmly closed.

"I aim to. How far is it to town?"

"Just over the rise and follow the ruts. What passes for a road around here. I'd say about four miles, maybe five. Once you're in town, the government office is hard to miss. Only decent-looking building in the place." She took a pencil and piece of paper from her apron pocket.

"I was wondering if you're not too busy . . . well, if you could maybe pop over and check on Isabelle tomorrow?" he said. "Seems kind of quick to be leaving her alone. But I'm chomping at the bit." He picked up the blue tin, peered inside. "Looks like we need some fresh oatmeal for sure. A few grubs in here I sure don't want my wife to lay eyes on."

Stella's pencil was scratching the paper, her pressure hard and constant. "Just making a bit of a list myself," she said.

He upended the tin. "Supper for your blue jays. I hope you don't mind."

He'd seen a pair of them swoop through Stella's yard. Bigger blue jays than the ones he'd known, but no mistaking them.

"Those jays will soon take care of any grubs or edibles, camp robbers that they are. And they're not my blue jays. I don't encourage them and I advise you to do the same. Stellar jays are petty thieves if you ask me. They're scooping my hen's scraps right out of the dish, bold as could be. Seems they really prefer potato peels. And dried bread too." Stella reached around her thin hips to untie her spotted blue apron and slung it over her shoulder.

Edward wasn't listening. Why, exactly, had the Johnson's left? Maybe the man had left a few usable tools behind. A sharpened pick, perhaps a sluice-box tossed aside, gently used, easy to repair. Hopefully, out back, a pile of wood, dried and stacked.

"You're another one," she said, "with gold dust in his eyes. If you notice how many of these shacks are sitting empty, you gotta wonder. God knows Gordon spent enough time scoping out the most likely place to stake our claim, tramping the river's edge and making notes for days on end. Probably just as likely to pick the perfect spot by closing your eyes and jabbing a finger onto the map." She waved at the vista of the sky. "Might look like heaven to you. But all I remember 'bout the day we came was how small I felt, and how awful alone."

"I'll get that tea you mentioned," Edward said, rising. He handed her his cooling cup. "Anything else you need?"

Stella handed him her list. "I'm good for that. And if you run into a red-headed man about five foot ten, with blazing blue eyes, and a scar on his left cheek, tell him to get on home. Tell him it's been too long."

Edward's conscience was clear as a mountain stream as he stood at the door of the Dominion Land Office and despite Stella's warning and the empty shanties, he felt a certainty that this was the place.

"Feeling lucky?" the man behind him asked. "That is, if there's any luck left, after Twelve Foot's been around."

Edward remembered Annie's request for an astronomy book and her trust that Twelve Foot Davis would surely deliver it to her. He'd found one in a second hand store and although it was almost new, he'd bought it for a song. He'd spent hours engrossed in that book, studying the stars, but he'd never gotten around to putting it in the mail. He'd thought about bringing it along, placing its well-worn pages straight into Annie's waiting hands. But after all his harping to Isabelle about packing light, she just might have wondered why he managed to pack a large astronomy book for Annie and not much else.

"Twelve Foot?" he asked, as if he'd never heard the name before.

"A gold-miner with a brain, a damn sight more than I can say for most."

Edward eyed the scrawny man, eyes stark white in his dust-caked face.

"First he finds himself a shitload of gold on an impossibly small strip of land, only twelve friggin' feet wide, and then instead of gambling it away, he buys supplies. Turns around and sells them to the rest of us stupid enough to be out here still, looking to find the mother lode." The man adjusted his bulging backpack, rubbed his left shoulder. "No gold here," he said. "Just beef jerky and canned beans. But thanks to Twelve Foot's honest trading, at least I can eat. Trapping is my business now. Darn sight easier than panning for non-existent gold."

With a wave of his hand, he shuffled away.

The sun was getting hotter. Edward wished for water, wished that the sign hanging inside the door might give at least some indication of how long breaks might be at the claims office. The sign read only 'Back Soon.' What in hell did that really mean?

"Looks like not much happenin' here."

A bow-legged man dressed in chaps and a fringed and beaded vest had sauntered up to the hitching rail, leaned there while he rolled a cigarette. He eyed Edward with unabashed curiosity. "Waiting for my horses to get shod. Blacksmith likes to take his own sweet time." He sniffed, grabbed the side of his nose and threw a glob of yellow mucus to the dust near his boot-clad feet. "McLeod," he said, and fortunately for Edward, pulled his hand back for a moment to wipe his grimy palm.

When Edward took the leathered hand, he was exquisitely aware of the softness of his own. "Armson," he said. "Edward. I'm hoping someone shows up soon. I'm here to stake a claim."

"Gave up on gold myself. Now I'm packing supplies." He took a small tin from his back pocket, pinched a bit of snuff and chewed vigorously. "Mostly for Twelve Foot. Or anyone else who can pay."

Edward shuddered, for he'd come for much more.

"Twelve Foot's got horses too if you're looking for a good one."

"Thanks," Edward said.

He was sorry to hear that horses were plentiful, as he'd counted on selling one of his own, now that the lush grass had fattened him and his coat was once again shiny and sleek. His stash of cash was running low and there was no bulging bank account to fall back on and, as of yet, no pending sale of the family home to shore up his dwindling reserves.

"I got a couple of horses I bought in Edmonton and they made the trip in fairly decent shape. They're looking real sleek now they've spent some time resting and filling up on all that plentiful grass. Never thought to see so much prairie here."

Edward could almost see the waves of grass, light catching the blue and the grey clumps that wavered above a carpet of green.

McLeod spat out the last of his chew, and reached for a tobacco pouch, meticulously rolled a cigarette and lit it with a sulphur-stinking match. "More horses than people around just now. Partly because May last year, I trekked up a bunch of good-looking Appaloosas. There's a shortage of places to overnight and load up on food and water but they're tough little horses and we made it. Damn right we did."

Edward looked up and down the empty street, uneasy with this flood of information from a stranger. Perhaps the man was daft.

"One night I almost made a fatal mistake. I was pushing 'em too hard, trying to make just one more mile. When it started to snow, I kept on going, right past an abandoned cabin where I could have found some shelter for the night. Could've hobbled the horses and let them forage for their supper. Damned stupidest decision I ever made. Eventually, I had to get off, walk behind the horses, whipping them on through a hellish storm that dropped down out of nowhere. It's dangerous for man or beast if you get caught in the open and get the notion you'd like to lie down."

Edward shivered even though he felt the warmth of the sun on his back. "Snowstorms? In May?"

"You might be safe in July. But I've seen snowstorms in the middle of June. Real snowstorms that can erase the horizon, so a man has no idea where he is." One last deep draw on the dangling cigarette and McLeod pinched the butt, dropped it in the dust. "Busted my ass bringing those fine horses here and then Twelve Foot turns around and gives the lot of them to the Indians. Can you figure that? But he said the breeds wouldn't be of much use

99

to him unless they had good, strong packhorses. Not to complain, but the bastards are already cutting into my business."

Edward was silent.

McLeod retrieved his pack from the ground. "Goin' to talk some business with Grey Wolf so I guess I better run."

"Grey Wolf?"

"Twelve Foot's ceremonial friggin' name. Don't mean squat to me but he got it from the breeds and he acts like getting it was a goddamn priceless gift. Goddamn those Indians. I got a real bad feeling about them and Twelve Foot setting up in business together. Don't bode well for me."

He was about to give up on staking a claim, at least for this day, when the door finally opened at the government office. Maybe he'd be a lot smarter forgetting all about gold and looking for an easy office job in there. He entered and walked over to the wall map, faded from the sun. Lots of open land. Eyes wide and glazed, he let his fingers hover. The water diviners could do it with water, so why not he with gold? Finally, he felt a pull and he jabbed his forefinger down. This would surely be his lucky place. He got his claim slip from the sleepy clerk. Outside, the day seemed exactly the same. He flipped himself over the hitching rail and let out a whoop. Yee-hah! When his boots hit the dust, his exhilaration faded. He had a list from Isabelle and one from Stella too. It wouldn't do to have two women mad at him, no matter how anxious he was to get home to share his news.

He stopped for a moment to admire his reflection in the sparkling windows of Davis Trading and Mercantile, Twelve Foot's store. His hair was longer than it had ever been, but it was neatly combed. His face was browned, his waist trim and shoulders wide and he didn't look at all like a banker anymore.

The windows fronted a full array of tools and blankets and pots and pans, perhaps once artfully arranged, but now looking as is if someone had flung them there in a hurry. He stepped inside, saw shelves stacked with canned goods and staples and a slump of burlap bags leaning beside the counter. Boston beans, flat white limas, blood-clot kidneys. Beans of all kinds. He gave them a wide berth, pondering a pork roast, and some crisp orange carrots and yellow onions too.

Finally, he compromised. Carrots and onions and a piece of salt pork. As he made his choices, he thought longingly of golden gravy, studded with bits of crispy meat.

He counted his money carefully as the pile had seemed to shrink daily since they'd left their home.

A silent woman took his cash and packed his purchases into two small burlap sacks.

"I'm new to this part of the country." Edward picked up one laden bag and smiled wide. "Glad to be here too. Edward Armson's my name. And you might be . . ?"

The woman lowered her face, her black hair falling like a curtain across her eyes. She pushed his remaining bag toward him and almost ran from behind the counter back to the bowels of the store.

Edward was disappointed, as he'd been about to ask her about Twelve Foot's whereabouts. Surely if she worked for him, she would know about his comings and goings. Had he said something to offend?

He stopped by a clump of willows, leaving Dexter's reins loose, thinking the horse was too old and tired to run away. A cloud of mosquitoes rose around him. The little clumps of willow that dotted the prairie usually ringed a swampy area, a place where the mosquitoes thrived. He waved his arms, and grabbed a few of the nearly dried sprigs of pussy willow as he ran.

I'll pop these into a jar. Put them on the table. Something pretty for Isabelle to admire.

He had his claim slip tucked safely into his inside pocket. He felt like waving that paper, grabbing Isabelle, and dancing around the cabin as if he'd truly lost his mind. If only she were a little more like Annie. He imagined that with such exciting news, Annie would be over the moon.

"Look," he said, pulling out the paper. "The keys to our kingdom."

She glanced at the paper briefly and then she slipped it between the pages of the family Bible, on the shelf near their bed. She was still sure Edward's plan was reckless but she hoped their future might have some small chance if it was resting next to the word of God. Feeling so small and alone in this vastness had set her to thinking about God more and more. Even talking to him out loud.

She watched him dig through the kitchenware box and find the cast-iron frying pan, rank with old grease, and then he stoked the stove.

"I'm sorry," she said. "I meant to start supper but I . . . "

"Shush," he said. "I'll give this a try. After all, us pioneers have to be able to do most anything."

Over a supper of mealy over-boiled potatoes and bacon that smelled slightly off, he described the settlement.

"Not much to see. Calling it a town is a bit of a stretch. Davis Mercantile and Trading is a greying, false-fronted building. Not very big. There's a small livery stable and then the government office, the only brick building in town. A few houses with gardens in the back and chickens scratching in the front yards. No streets and sidewalks laid out like we're used to. A wooden one here and there, but nothing organized, nothing on the square. More like someone has just thrown down the whole town helter-skelter."

Isabelle was still picking at her supper. "Is there a post office?"

"Yep. Saw the sign at the back of Twelve Foot's store, but we both know from Annie's letters that there's nothing regular about the mail up here. The postal service could use a damned good enema when it comes to that."

Isabelle dropped her fork onto her plate and it clattered to the tabletop.

"Edward," she said. "You're not going to start talking like that are you, just because we're nowhere near civilization?"

He flushed. He'd spent just a part of one day away from Isabelle, in the company of roughened men. He had no intentions of turning into a man like that himself.

"Sorry," he said.

The wind was rising, the flour sacks tacked above the windows billowing inward. He closed the window to shut out the sigh of the wind. He pulled his chair closer to the fire. Suddenly, he wasn't so eager to get to his claim.

13.

Edward had been panning for ten days straight. No gold nugget to show for all of his hard work, just cracked and bleeding cuticles, sore muscles across his shoulders and down his arms and the beginnings of chilblains on his feet. The little creek he'd chosen was ice cold and it seemed no amount of insulation could keep the cold from seeping into his soles. Hordes of mosquitos and black flies tormented him and he'd taken to wearing two neckerchiefs — one to protect his neck and another to tie over his face, like a bandit might. At least with his face covered, he could breathe without inhaling a black cloud of buzzing no-see-ums.

He checked his smudge pot, a metal pail with a lid that he filled with embers from their dying fire each morning. The pail had holes poked in its sides and when he added grass to the embers, he had a portable smudge. The contraption helped with the insects, if only a little. He added a few dried sticks and some more green grass to his pail and smoke billowed around him as he walked. Kind of like a priest.

When the sky lowered and turned molten pewter, he paused. A fork of blue lightning speared the horizon and he counted until he heard the rumble of thunder. Not so far away, and he hastily gathered his tools.

The gentle summer rains back home in Ottawa only enticed people to step outside, and from his vantage point at the front door, he would watch the brightly coloured parade, a sudden blooming of umbrellas bobbing along the rain-slicked street. Even if you found yourself stranded, without the ever-present umbrella, a walk through the misty rain would barely get a man wet.

Ragweed pollen, which made his eyes water and itch, was floating thick on the air. He sneezed, then sneezed again, searching vainly for his hankie as clear fluid steamed from his eyes and his nose. Perhaps a good strong rain might alleviate at least one problem. But add moisture, and a fresh hatch of damned hungry mosquitoes that would surely find their way to any gleaming strip of exposed skin, and you've got trouble.

It was a hard country, this one.

When it rained in the Peace, it was like the rain was being shovelled in huge scoops from the sky. It came in blasts, it sluiced down your neck and shoulders, soaking through any protection you might have counted on. Muck flicked up behind as you walked, so that your pant legs were wet and splattered too.

When he encountered his first big storm, he'd tried to take cover beneath a thick stand of poplar and wait it out, but soon found he ended up too wet and too cold to go back to digging and panning and that no amount of kindling would start a rain-drenched log on fire.

Rain was a reason to head for home and, more and more, lately he was looking for reasons to leave his claim.

Today, however, he'd unearthed a few shiny flecks that he'd tucked into an empty tobacco pouch.

Gold or fool's gold? He wasn't sure and until he found someone he could trust, he wasn't about to ask.

"How about a trip to town? Maybe you can find something pretty. Gingham for curtains, or lace, something nice and thin. These flour sacks seem cozy at night but come sunrise, they keep most of the light outside." Edward was sitting in the gloom, sipping his last bit of cold coffee.

Isabelle wiped the breakfast crumbs from the table. "I don't care much if I buy anything right now. This place is temporary, after all, so I don't see putting too much work into fixing it up."

She piled the dishes into the dishpan for later. She didn't feel up to filling the kettle from the rain barrel outside and feeding the fire. Every little task was so complicated. Maybe a trip to town would be a good excuse to shirk her duties, something she had never dreamed of doing in her own home.

She was hopeful that her house in Ottawa would sit forever on the market, as she was quite sure Edward had it overpriced. She was hoping the bank would soon send a letter, telling them the place just wouldn't move, the market being too sluggish, as it seemed to be. Six months now, just sitting there, empty and cold. Perhaps they should take it off the market, for a while at least.

In her dreams, she returned, and found it just as she'd left it. Waiting for her.

"Maybe there will be a letter for us, Edward. Perhaps from Ottawa."

Twelve Foot might help find her sister. Annie was a rolling stone, but even she might be unhappy to hear that their childhood home was for sale. Tell Annie everything? Or just a hint?

106

Isabelle shook her head. She'd been with Edward too long. Deciding which part of the truth to tell, or if she should tell any of the truth at all.

Edward shifted in his chair. He had been sorely missing the mail, but it wasn't news from Ottawa he longed for. It was Annie's hurried downhill scrawl. But she had no way of knowing where they were, nor did they have any idea where she and Trapper might be.

"Maybe," he said. "Twelve Foot's scouts have picked up some mail along their way. What if we've gotten a letter from Annie? Maybe Trapper has heard we're here. News travels fast up here, the moccasin telegraph I believe it's called."

She brightened. "I never thought of Annie finding us. I had thought of writing to her until I realized John and Annie are somewhere between here and the shores of the Lesser Slave. What kind of an address is that? If that's where they are."

"You'll be amazed," he said, opening the screen door for Isabelle. "Twelve Foot's place is a real treasure trove. There's bound to be something here that catches your eye. Not real organized though. You've got to be patient is all."

She stepped over the scuffed and oiled sill, stopped for a moment as her eyes adjusted to the gloom. "You said he's not around much, so how does he manage to run a store?"

"Honour system lots of days. A breed woman once in a while. Seems I was lucky to actually meet him so quickly. He's a busy man. And he comes and he goes."

Isabelle picked up a yellow onion from a wicker basket. "Breed woman? What does that mean?"

"Half Indian, half-white. Seems to me that puts you square in the middle of nowhere up here."

She dropped the onion back into the basket, sighed. "Kind of like me."

❧❧❧

Twelve Foot was standing on an apple box, arranging tins of tobacco on a shelf. As he moved, Edward caught a sniff of strong body odour and tobacco and maybe a hint of campfire too. When he noticed Edward, he stepped down from the box and offered his hand. "Armson. Good to see you again. Thought maybe you'd moved on. Like most seem to do."

"No, not me," he said. He turned to Isabelle. "This is my wife. Isabelle, meet Twelve Foot Davis, sometime gold miner, thoroughly dependable guide and sole proprietor of this fine establishment."

Twelve Foot nodded at Isabelle and blushed a deep tomato red.

"Our neighbour has already filled Isabelle in about how things run in these parts. Who's to be trusted and who's not. Never said one bad word about you."

Isabelle offered her hand. "I've never shaken the hand of a famous man before."

"Charmed, I'm sure." Twelve Foot said. "And I'm not really famous. Just got luckier than most when it came to finding gold. And a bunch of tall tales told around a campfire and added to again and again have made me richer than I ever dreamed."

Twelve Foot reached into a vest pocket, pulled out his knife. He cut a plug of tobacco, stuffed it into his ruddy cheek. "Excuse me, ma'am," he said. "But I'm a slave to this nasty habit so I'll be stepping outside for just a moment. Pile your purchases on the counter and give a holler once you're done." He swept his arms wide. "Got most everything in here," he said. "If you need something you don't see right off, it's probably here anyway — you just need to know where to look. I hate to leave you, but I'll be back to help in a spit or two."

When Twelve Foot returned, he stacked Edward's canned beans and buckwheat honey and three cans of stewed tomatoes into a small cardboard box, added the potatoes and three yellow onions. Then he reached into his ice-box, pulled out a package of greying meat.

"This meat'll be fine," he said. "Trust me, it'll taste better than it looks. And it's half price today. If you're interested, that is."

Isabelle was still wandering the aisles. Twelve Foot raised his voice. "Find anything you're hankering for, Ma'am?"

She came to the till, shook her head no.

∾∾∾

Twelve Foot studied her face, the way the fractured light from the window fixed flecks of gold in her neatly braided hair. He wondered how it might be to loosen that tidy braid, spread her hair until it flowed, like rivulets of light.

He blushed again, and stopped his imaginings. What was he thinking? He'd given up on women long ago.

"I've got some linens and lace on order. They should be arriving within the week. If I get something I think is really fine, I'll set it aside so you can have first look. No pressure, of course."

He reached behind him for a small bunch of limp spinach.

"I was kind of saving this for my own supper," he said, looking directly at the woman. "Greens are mighty scarce up here, depending on the time of year. And if your garden thrives or not. But you have probably been too busy settling in to have the time to till and plant. And growin' a garden in this country is something else entirely. But if you decide to give it a try come spring, I'll order in the right kind of seeds. Weather hardy and such. And some vegetables thrive in this black soil and some don't at all. Apparently too rich applies to soil as well as people." Twelve Foot ran his forefinger down the spines of the sorry spinach before tucking it quickly into Edward's box. "Here you go. A gift from the management. Your wife being a first-time customer and all." He ciphered the total, his lips moving as he added the sum. "Two dollars ten," he said.

Edward counted out his coins, acutely aware of his dwindling cushion of cash, then took the full box of groceries from Twelve Foot. The man was a salesman, no doubt about that.

When they arrived back at the shack, Edward stoked the fire.

Isabelle thought of her rich loamy beds in Ottawa, full of irises and tulips in the spring. Roses later on. Flowers she knew how to grow.

Then she was thinking of finding Annie and how she might get a moment alone with Twelve Foot. Perhaps he would be the one to ask.

"Isabelle?"

"Twelve Foot, Stella told me, casts a very long shadow, so I was surprised to see him so small. He seemed a very nice man."

Edward washed and steamed the greens. The meat would be fine once he fried it with a little salt, and maybe some garlic too. Maybe lots of garlic, he thought.

He felt the tobacco pouch on his inside pocket, sorry it had been too late to run down to the assayer's office. If it really was gold, he could probably get a quick opinion of its worth. At least that way, his little stash of wealth would be official.

"Dinner is served," he said, with a sweep of his hand to their cheery painted chairs. "Although I never did sign on to be chief cook and bottle washer too."

Isabelle chose the yellow chair, as she usually did. She picked up her fork, pushed the meat around on her plate. "Are you sure this meat is safe to eat?"

"Aged to perfection," he said. "So Twelve Foot said."

She took a tiny bite. "Then I somehow think that it might be true."

Should have asked Twelve Foot, Edward thought, his hand straying to his tobacco pouch. He obviously would recognize real gold when he saw it and he didn't seem the kind to mock someone who couldn't. The man obviously knew how to keep his counsel and no one else need know if he turned out to be just one more greenhorn fool.

After their simple supper, he swept the hard-packed floor with their new straw broom, opened the door and swished out the worst of the dust.

"Isabelle," he said, "starting tomorrow, I'll be spending all my days at the claim. Seems like we have all the time in the world, but really we don't. In this county, summer's barely started before winter's coming on. Sooner than we're used to I hear, and harder too."

"All day? You're just going to leave me?"

He hung the broom on its hook behind the door and opened the curtain on the small window that faced the trail. The sun was finally setting, but the heat was still fierce. It would help cool the place if he could catch a bit of a breeze.

"I'm not exactly leaving you. Looking for gold and laying up a store of wood for winter is enough to keep any man out of trouble, and that's a fact."

Isabelle was washing a small blue saucer, and it slipped from her hand back into the basin. "It's brutal here alone."

"If you don't cotton to Stella, there's got to be someone around who needs a friend. There're two other shanties an easy walk from here."

He was thinking of Stella's steady warmth, her offer of coffee on that very first day, the old codgers in town who'd told him all kinds of gossip, some of it helpful to a greenhorn like him. The people he'd run across had been open, friendly, offering their assistance before a man had to ask.

It was not yet fully dark. They had stayed up very late. The immensity of the sky made her feel so very small, while Edward was awed by the brightness of the stars, always saying how close they seemed here. He liked to sit outside the shanty, study them at night.

Isabelle moved to their bed, closed the curtains there, she and Edward at cross-purposes as they often were.

She straightened her braided rug by the hearth, its muted colours a reminder of home. "You mean I should just drop in on people? Without an invitation?"

Edward sighed. "Why not? There is no standing on ceremony here."

She hadn't had anyone to really talk to since Annie left Ottawa with Trapper, but she was becoming used to solitude, to spending her days alone.

"I've already had one caller. Mary Ellen Hartley. Said she'd come over to check on Stella and saw our shanty was being used."

Edward smiled. "That's nice. You never mentioned it before."

He topped up his coffee, stood near the sink as he slurped. And nibbled a heel of bread, slathered with Stella's home-made blueberry jelly.

She sighed. "I couldn't think of much to say, other than hello and yes, we are new here and yes, we are managing just fine."

Edward set his cup on the table, took her hand. "Sometimes people just want a little distracting, to hear something new. And everyone knows we've just come from Ottawa." He grinned, as if just struck by an amazing idea. "You could describe Estelle's beautiful house. Pretend it's yours. Talk about fashionable clothes, the fancy places you go to lunch. Embroider things a bit, make the story your own."

"But Edward, that would be telling a lie." She screwed the lid back onto the blueberry jelly and put it on the shelf where the staples belonged.

"What would it hurt? Sometimes, you've got to give people a little of what they want."

She crossed her arms and looked closely at her husband. She'd begun to have her doubts about his way with the truth, but she'd never realized how far he was willing to go. In her books, a lie was a lie.

She wiped crumbs from the counter top. As she did, she noticed cobwebs hanging from the rafters, above the open shelves.

The lowest shelf held her cooking staples, the higher, safe from harm, her beloved china, twined with yellow roses and sunshine and memories of her mother. Memories of Annie too. Thank God she'd not had to jettison that on the side of the trail. Now that would have been a disaster of epic proportions, worse than anything she'd endured so far.

Sighing, she reached for the duster, always close at hand.

She caught sight of Edward and herself in the mirror above the washstand, Edward with his boyish good looks, his sparkling eyes, and herself, looking plain and sad. She shook her head, turned away.

Edward opened the door, leaned their new broom against the outside wall. The stars were out, perfect pins of light against the inky fabric of the sky.

"Remember that night we went walking? When the moon was so bright it lit our way better than a lantern would?"

"Yes, I do."

He kissed her forehead. "Let's do it again. If you won't go anywhere alone, then the two of us will go." He picked up his still warm cup, rolled it in his hands. "We will make it here, Isabelle. I've got the feeling our big break is just around the corner."

The claim took over Edward's whole life and his focus narrowed to the sluice box and his gravelly piece of stream. Shovel and wash, shovel and wash. Shovel and wash again. Sometimes, when he couldn't face one more shovelful, he took his rock hammer and a lens and when he found a likely looking outcrop, he'd try a split or two. He never found a rock laced with gold, but at least it gave him a break from the endless searching on a barren riverbed.

His hands were raw from the water, from the wind, from the handle of his shovel.

Where in hell was the gold that was supposed to fall so easily into his sluice box? For all his labour, he'd found just a few flecks and a not-quite nugget or two. Not exactly riches. Not even close.

And where was the adventure he'd dreamed of? Rough and ready men, the kind who'd offer the last drink of whiskey in the jug?

He'd never dreamed that gold mining could be such a lonesome job.

"Isabelle?"

She was sitting by the fire, leafing though the Bible, and she didn't reply.

Edward closed the door, hung his shirt on a hook. He came closer, ran his fingers across her brow and through her silky hair. "Taken to praying now have you? I didn't think it was quite that bad."

She smiled, touched his palm.

"Sometimes the silence overwhelms me," she said. "Reading seems to help."

14.

Isabelle

I had a home in Ottawa. It was a perfect size. Two generous bedrooms tucked under a sloping eve upstairs, the twin dormer windows offering a view of the park across the way.

I grew up watching people meander in the park, stop to sit for a while on its many benches, chatting with one another and with the passers-by.

I used to love the dappled sunlight on the earthen paths, the beds of irises, purple and green like bruises, and the yellow daffodils cheerful on a cloudy day.

The kitchen was large, with whitewashed pine cupboards everywhere, and solid maple counters for cutting and chopping. There was a linoleum floor, grey and blue squares, shiny with years of washing, and waxing, and care.

In the living room, a wide door to the lush, green yard in the back, two floral tapestry armchairs pulled close to a small tiled hearth. A loveseat and a long, low couch of a caramel-coloured corduroy fabric that hugged your back on cold winter days. And in winter, there were shivery days aplenty. The cold in Ottawa is wet and it seems to freeze your very bones. Thank goodness for a fire crackling in the fireplace on winter nights, the coats and mittens hung on a nearby wooden clothes rack to get perfectly warm and dry. As we always were in my cozy home.

It had white clapboard siding and a wide veranda across the front, with four wicker chairs, two on each side, with puffy cushions of cream and green.

The pillars were square, sturdy, painted forest green, and in the front door, four small vertical panes of glass to let in the light, but not the view of who might be knocking on your door.

My father left this perfect place to mother, and we lived there with her quite contentedly. At least I did. Annie didn't have a contented bone in her body. Not even back then.

Mother joined our father too soon and left everything to the two of us.

How I loved that place, the place where I was born. I wonder now how I was ever persuaded to leave and I think it was because I was missing my sister. I thought a lot about our times together and got just plain lonesome for how things used to be.

I was my father's favourite. It was plain for all to see, but Annie was too busy frenetically living her life to fret about such things. She was a whirlwind, touching down, wreaking havoc, and then spinning away.

I used to go to the mill with my father on a Saturday afternoon. The mill was quiet then, and my father would sit behind his desk and read his papers, sort them into piles. He would make me a cup of tea and sometimes one for himself. He used to say he could accomplish more in two hours on a Saturday than he could all week, with people coming and going all day, asking questions, requesting holidays or days off to attend a funeral or a wedding or just needing to settle into one of his deep leather armchairs and be still for a while. So when we were at the mill, I kept very quiet, mesmerized by the sound of a bluebottle fly battering the window panes, the scritch-scritch of my father's pen.

Annie wouldn't have lasted half an hour there. She'd be twirling around father's office, disturbing piles of papers, flipping through files, checking for a treat in the top right drawer, where oftentimes peppermints were stashed.

There would be no lovely quiet if Annie was around.

I would watch my father's hands, so slim, his fingers long and smooth on the ivory shank of his pen. The smell of raw wood was everywhere, and it was a scent that I loved. It didn't matter how often or how long he bathed, the lumber scent lingered on my father's clothes and in his hair, a scent that always told us when he was home.

My father worked at the McKay Mill his whole working life. He called himself a clerk, but he was much, much more.

Working the mill was good money for unskilled men, but the shifts were twelve hours and it was noisy and dusty, hard on the lungs and the work was dangerous too.

He must have hated some parts of his job — the times he was told to lay off those who'd cut off a finger or two, perhaps an arm, and who were no longer productive enough to earn their pay. The owners never stooped to such unsavoury tasks, but my father had to.

All the years he organized the McKay summer picnic, lists would litter our kitchen table for weeks, the small table beside his easy chair or be tucked into his shirt pocket or his pants pockets, so you had to be very careful to check before you put them in the wash. White paper and black pants can make a real mess.

He drove himself crazy with details, with setting up the large blue and white tent rented for the day, arranging the folding chairs and buffet tables, digging up the horseshoe pits, measured once to regulation size and then measured again to be absolutely sure. Mac and James McKay usually showed up at least a half-hour late, hearty fellows, shaking everyone's hand, pouring lemonade and coffee, cooking the sausages and chops my father had ordered and picked up early, encouraging everyone to take seconds on the salads.

They joined right in with the workingmen for the horseshoe tournament to see who would come out best. Although often as not, Mac and James took their own trophy home. I was never sure if they really were expert players or if perhaps the men knew better than to best the bosses in front of a crowd.

The McKays always remembered to praise my father for his organizational work in their never-ending speeches that wrapped up the day. And then they thanked everyone for their hard work, their dedication to their jobs, for bringing their families out to enjoy the glorious weather.

It was a point of honour for my father that he was the one the big bosses chose to arrange the big company event. My mother, I'm sure, would have preferred a little cash.

"All fine and good to get a pat on the back, but you can't eat compliments, or use them to pay bills."

"Shush. You don't want Mac and James McKay thinking we're a pair of ingrates, do you now?"

After the speeches, when the men began to clap, first quietly and then ending up on their feet, the McKays waved and took their leave, as if embarrassed by the accolades.

One of our regular, easy Saturdays, my father opened the deep bottom drawer of his desk, pulled out a small flat flask. It gleamed like silver, but there wasn't a bit of tarnish anywhere, so I think it must have been silver plate.

I knew all about silver because my Sunday job right after church was polishing our Canterbury silverware, my mother's pride and joy. If left unpolished, real silver turns black. She said I should be honoured to polish the silverware because holding a newly buffed silver spoon was a bit like holding moonlight in the palm of your hand.

Father poured a little brown liquid from the flask into his cup. Next he pulled out a small printed pouch, and from the pouch he pulled a short cigar, thick and stumpy. He licked its surface, rolled it across his lower lip. Then he struck a match. As the smoke began to curl, he winked at me.

"This will be just between us," he said.

The McKay mill eventually worked itself out of a job, and so did my father. The trees surrounding the mill had all been logged, and no one had thought to plant replacements. The shifts were first shortened to only eight hours each, and then the night shift was gone. Soon the mill was mostly silent, with no logs to feed the great machines.

The devastated forest looked like a giant wave had crashed through the trees, carrying most of them away, leaving only spindly saplings and flattened grass.

The entire area was eerily silent, not a goldfinch or a blue jay to be heard.

When he came home on the last day of operation, my father seemed shrunken, smaller somehow, and quieter too.

"Mac McKay asked for my keys," he told mother, "as if I wasn't to be trusted. After all these years, he didn't even shake my hand. And I'd barely cleared the gate before he clicked the padlock shut."

It was the end for the mill, and the end for my father too.

He took to sleeping in regularly, sitting most of the day in his easy chair, watching the world go by. Long before his body gave up, the essence of my father was gone. It was almost a relief when he died.

My mother followed him within the year.

Sometimes, I thought of making a change of two, to sort of make the place my own. Small changes like a new trim colour outside or sanding and re-staining the kitchen cupboards, maybe a rich chocolate stain. But I never did because I always thought things over too long, thought them to death.

After I was done missing them, and it took me a very long time, I eventually became entirely content.

And when my husband slid three ordinary-looking papers, from many in a pile, across our kitchen table, and handed me a pen, I signed them all. Every one.

I did not read them. Not a one. Shame on me.

I hadn't even begun to clear the supper dishes yet.

And now I know my little home is for sale and that this has been wrought by my own carelessness, my failure to take a firm stand.

So I left my lovely house. And I have not just failed myself, but I have failed Annie too. I am still searching for news of her in this godforsaken place. But if I do find her, how can I ever explain?

Although knowing Annie, she'll think it all a great adventure if we stay here, in this vast unsettled land.

The thought I may never return to Ottawa, to my cozy little home on Saunderson Street, is almost more than I can bear. Sometime I cannot even look at Edward. And so I turn away.

When I was living in Ottawa, I did not realize that I am deathly afraid of the dark, for when I went to my room at night and looked out from my dormer window, there was always a light flickering somewhere, perhaps a neighbour reading, a lamp left lighted to guide a latecomer home. Streetlights here and there. Never blackness like here, where the sky is pressing itself down on me, taking my breath away, smothering, a thick woollen blanket wrapped too tight.

The stars are so far away, mere pinpricks in the inky fabric of the sky. All of my fears rush to the fore in this endless darkness and I have to remind myself to breathe, just breathe. But my heart is hammering and I am so, so afraid.

My house is now a one-room cabin. It is not Edward's and it is not my own.

The walls are rough-cut logs, with grey chinking in between. Inside, it has two plaster walls, badly done, as if smoothed by a drunkard's trembling hand. Lumpy and cracked and painted a depressing putty beige.

The cupboards are basic boxes, fastened to the wall and there is one wood-burning stove to keep us warm. I keep a pot of water on the back of the stove, and sometimes, when I forget to feed the fire, I cannot even make a cup of tea.

There are two small windows, to let in the light, or the cold, and only one door. If I ever really need to escape, there is only one way out.

## 15.

Sarah Louise
1896 – 1897

Edward held the needle to the light. His khaki shirt was missing two buttons now. He'd told Isabelle twice, finally draped the shirt on the back of her chair. He needed this shirt. It's long sleeves protected his arms from inclement weather, from the scrape of rock, from the never-ending hordes of black flies and no-see-ums that swarmed, drove themselves into his hair and hovered around his ears and under his nose, trying to find a way inside. Sometimes he inhaled so many he felt he would drown.

He'd continued to wear a bandana always, looking, he figured, like some kind of outlaw. But at least he'd not, in the last week, breathed in any little black bugs.

He tried one more time, licking the thread like he'd seen Isabelle do, but the light was waning and he had never threaded a needle before.

"Isabelle, can you please help me with this?"

She was reading the Bible. Again.

"Hmm?" she said.

Isabelle lit the lamp, for the days were much shorter now, the darkness dropping suddenly, like a velvet curtain at the end of a play, and she was uneasy until Edward finally came in the door. Sometimes she wondered if he'd stopped somewhere, at one of the other shanties for a shot of whisky, and maybe some company other than her, but she was never sure.

Her fingers knew how to knit without her seeing, but she needed the lamplight to feel safe and not so alone.

She reached for a new ball of purple yarn. It was thick, soft, and nubby.

The first time Twelve Foot dropped by, she'd assumed he was looking for Edward. But it wasn't so.

He was a shy man, and when he handed her a bag containing three skeins of fine grey wool, his face had flushed.

"Just thought you might be running low," he'd said. "And this stuff isn't selling like I thought it would."

She'd invited him in for tea and served it in her china teacups.

Thankful that she had a box of soda crackers on hand, she served up a small plate of crackers and jam. She hadn't served that since she and Annie used to play tea party on their front porch. Twelve Foot ate only four crackers, fastidiously, so there were no crumbs on the table or the floor. He left the others for her.

"Really," she told him. "I apologize for the crackers and jam. I'd have baked some biscuits or some cookies if only I'd known."

She smiled when she saw his leathery fingers curved around the delicate handle of her mother's china, how carefully he set down the cup after each small sip.

"Crackers and jam suit me just fine."

She'd come to look forward to Twelve Foot's sporadic visits. After the first utilitarian grey, he'd brought her scarlet yarn, and sunshine yellow, Irish green. And sometimes, he brought her a sweet — some hard lemon drops, green peppermints in a small tin, and once a whole bar of dark chocolate, so shiny and fresh she could smell it in the cabin for days.

She never mentioned Twelve Foot's visits to Edward and she was not sure why.

His list was short. Mundane things. Flour, yeast, sugar, lard. Isabelle had used the last of their grub-filled flour, straining it with her sifter in a determined way.

A grocery list written in Isabelle's careful hand seemed a precious thing and he folded it in half and tucked it into the inside pocket of his jacket.

The screen door snapped behind him. "Twelve Foot?" Deep silence filled the store.

He pulled the list from his pocket, rubbed it smooth with his cracked hand, then dropped it on the green counter. "Can you fill this when you get a minute?" he hollered. Twelve Foot was no doubt in the back, deep in some important job, or maybe outside, enjoying the sun and a chew. "Gotta catch the smithy before he closes shop."

An hour later he returned to find the list still on the counter and Twelve Foot nowhere to be seen.

Slowly, he filled his own order, wondering what emergency had called Twelve Foot away. He hoisted his bags to the counter, pondering what to do next. Write up his own bill?

He heard some cursing and Twelve Foot appeared.

"Inventory today," he explained. "It's a sad day when I'm too busy to wait on my customers. Counting goddamned sacks of beans, no less. No shortage of those."

He quickly scanned Edward's hard-to-come by produce, the eggs, the yeast and flour, and the usual six cans of beans. "Sorry for the lousy service," he said. "That will be one dollar, fifty cents."

"But," Edward began, about to protest the deep reduction on the actual cost of his order. Twelve Foot's reputation for being fair had been well-earned, but neither was he a fool. Twelve Foot could tote up figures in his head faster than most men could write them down. "Don't know why you're giving me such a deal," he said.

"Big sale," Twelve Foot said, scuffing his boot against the oiled plank floor. "Clearing out some stock. I'm thinking it might be time to move on. If not right now, then sometime soon. Gettin' prepared. You know, just in case."

Twelve Foot? Planning to leave? Slowly, Edward hoisted his packages. "Sure hope you stay," he said and then instead of pounding Twelve Foot with questions about why and where, he turned and left the store.

The familiar smell of baking bread filled their little shack and a wave of warmth hit him as he stepped inside. He handed over the flour and the yeast, but he didn't hand over the news of Twelve Foot's tentative plans. The very idea of Twelve Foot's leaving filled him with dread.

"Taking a couple of loaves over to Stella," Isabelle said, as she wrapped warm bread in flour-sack towels. "She's been so helpful. It's about time I gave something back."

Thank you, God, he thought.

Isabelle gritted her teeth as she cleaned. Dust all over everything. How she hated it. Half an hour later, the water in her basin was a slough of grey, so she swished it around the enamel rim and threw it out the door.

I wonder, she thought, if Annie has a house of her own.

She searched the shelf above the washstand until she found a piece of creamy paper, and her favourite pen, fine-nibbed. She opened the inkpot and dipped the pen, began to write.

*Dear Annie,*

*We are here! Where in the world are you? I thought surely we would find you and John or at least hear fresh news of you but no one seems to know where you have gone. Twelve Foot has been keeping an ear open and he was kind enough to ask his Indian guides to look for news of you. But even those skilled hunters have found no sign.*

*Edward is eternally optimistic, so full of plans. And I, well, sadly, I now know some things. For instance, our bank account, which you left in my hands, and Edward's, was sorely depleted, even before we began this long journey. God knows what the balance was by the time Edward purchased all of the required supplies. And I cannot even write of our snug little house in Ottawa.*

*My husband says the shortfall in funds is temporary and he has set things in motion to correct the problem. He says there is absolutely nothing to worry my pretty head about. There was a time I'd have believed him.*

*Oh dearest Annie, I am praying for your safety, not only for you, but for myself, for I really need you now.*

*Your loving sister,*
*Isabelle*

She re-read the letter, then tore it into pieces. She would use them to feed the fire.

She shook a cupful of rice from the bottom of the sack, and chopped a single onion. When she lifted the frying pan from its hook on the wall, it was surprisingly heavy, but when she slid it onto the stovetop, she found no hint of warmth.

She'd forgotten, again, to stoke the fire.

Maybe canned beans for supper tonight? Or maybe no supper at all.

She opened the blackened door of the pot-belled stove, placed the pieces of her letter under a tipi of small kindling, and lit a match. She watched the pieces burn, one by one, until they were ash. But the kindling never caught and the smell of burned paper filled the room.

Since her first missed monthly, eating seemed a chore and she was almost glad the fire had died. The smell of food frying, bacon, cabbage, and especially onions, had lately made her feel like throwing up.

She took down the Bible, and let it fall open in her lap. She sat in the near dark and prayed. That her period would miraculously arrive, please God, even tonight.

Soaking and scrubbing stained bedding would be a welcome chore. Perhaps her monthlies were only delayed by her failure to eat a healthy amount. Her deep unhappiness. Maybe she wasn't really pregnant at all.

She bargained with God. She would leave heaps of seeds on the windowsills to attract small birds, especially the flycatchers, which she used to love, even let spiders have a corner in her shanty, if they really wanted one. Plan a garden, turn the soil and turn it again until she had a rich black garden patch, like Stella's. She would plant her seeds tenderly, and pull the encroaching weeds with something close to regret. Be mindful to His wonders every single day. Anything, she thought. Anything You want if You can answer my prayers just this once. She flattened her abdomen with the palm of her hand, felt no movement.

"Please," she whispered, "please."

Edward found Black Dan and Twelve Foot Davis out back, dismantling Black Dan's small cook stove. Wolf Runner was there too, statue-still in the shadows.

They'd lit a birch fire and the fragrant smoke drifted in the evening air.

The days had shortened, the darkness creeping in on padded feet, folding itself around the trees and the houses, obliterating detail until the yellow circle of the campfire was all that was left of the world.

"Something broken?" he asked.

"Nope, stove's working just fine but I'm starting to pack," Twelve Foot said. "I think the boom really is bust. In six short months my customers have dwindled from a river to a pitiful trickle." He nodded at Wolf Runner. "Can't just leave 'em high and dry though so Wolf Runner's wife is going to run things. You've seen Dyani in the store. Awful quiet. Always dusting and straightening. Knows the place like the back of her hand."

Black Dan's teeth were rotted stumps, like a picket fence with the slats broken and some of them gone, and when he smiled, Edward had to look away.

"We'll find a us new vein," Black Dan said. "Richer than the last. Twelve Foot's a wizard on that. Maybe we'll consider takin' ya' with us. For a fee, of course. We can negotiate. Especially seeing as there's some talk you might have found a nugget or two." Black Dan's voice dropped when he spoke of the gold, a kind of reverence there . . .

Edward imagined Isabelle's panic if he told her they were about to move on.

"Don't know what you're hearing, but a fee of any kind is beyond me just now."

He downed the last of the whiskey that Black Dan and Twelve Foot had been kind enough to share, savoured the fire in his throat, the warmth in his veins. The northern lights licked the edges of the sky, flickers of emerald and purple, shifting and swaying like curtains billowing in a breeze. He was mesmerized.

"We could find a way," Twelve Foot said. "For you and for Isabelle. If you decided to come."

Black Dan, his voice raspy with cigarettes and whiskey, snorted, threw his spent rollie into the fire. "Three's always a crowd. Not good on long hauls, that's for sure."

"There'd be four," Twelve Foot said. "Counting Isabelle. A good woman can make all the difference. Make the longest trail at least tolerable. Or so I've been told." He picked up a stick, poked at the coals, and sparks sizzled and died. "Can't say I've ever travelled with a woman, but there's a first time for everything. Edward did it and he got here didn't he? Against all odds. And remember, my friend, I'm the one who makes the decisions around here." He smiled, to take the sting from his words.

"You sure you got all your marbles?" Black Dan threw another bit of cedar on the dying fire. "Never took you to be one to travel with a woman. Nothing good about that idea. Nothing at all."

For the life of him, Edward could not figure out why Twelve Foot kept Black Dan around. His hand went unconsciously to his vest pocket, to his lucky marbles. Something had surely guided him to this beautiful place. Lucky marbles? God? Who could ever know?

Twelve Foot finished his drink. "Strength in numbers they say."

Wolf Runner slid closer and squatted near the fire. Twelve Foot refilled his cup, handed it to him. The four men sat silent for a long time, the fire burning down to ashy embers.

Black Dan finally spoke. "Twelve Foot's right as usual." He looked hard at Edward. "Green horn like you don't have a hope in hell if it turns out you have to leave here alone. Especially with winter coming on. So I'll guide you from the goodness of my heart. Food is plentiful in the bush, if you know how to hunt or trap, and sometimes a belly full of meat can be worth more than a pan full of gold."

Black Dan picked up a stick, drew a map in the dirt of the planned route, showing Edward landmarks and the spots where they planned to portage.

"Can you draw that on a piece of paper for me?"

"Sure I can."

But Edward had seen the way Black Dan looked at Isabelle and he was unsure about the goodness of that heart. Black Dan was a man to meet where men played cards and told lies and drank rot-gut whiskey, not one to bring into the close company of your lovely young wife.

"Isabelle," he said. "I think she's finally feeling settled. I just don't see her wanting to . . . "

There was Isabelle's pregnancy to consider, although he was quite sure it was only him and his hawk-eyed neighbour who knew for sure.

"Women get a certain look," Stella had said to him one morning. He'd been lifting his pack to his back and she lifting soggy laundry to the line that sagged across her yard. "It's a blooming not everyone can see, especially with the first. But I've got the eye."

"You do for sure," he said. "For she told me only last week. She's not ready to tell anyone else," he admitted. "I'd like to tell perfect strangers, anyone I meet."

Isabelle was all but hibernating inside their cramped cabin, as if being with child was an affliction and not something to celebrate.

Black Dan pulled again on the bottle, grunted when he realized the damn thing was dry. "Women," he snorted, "should never have a say in any kind of decision. Up here, gettin' it wrong could mean life or death."

One night, coming home from panning to the cold and darkness in their little cabin, he'd grabbed a short piece of birch, stood it end on the cabin floor, and swung the axe aloft. He brought it down sharply, splitting it in two.

"See this," he said as he grabbed the piece, chopped it in half again. He threw the kindling toward the stove. "Not much effort required."

"Edward, calm down. You know I don't like to handle the axe. It's razor sharp. And that I have no idea how to . . ."

"No idea because you haven't once tried."

He shoved the kindling into the stove, lit shavings with a match. "It would be nice to come home at night to some small hint of supper, and perhaps a welcoming fire."

He remembered his grandmother, who as often as not forgot to start the evening meal. She'd been reed thin, a reader and a dreamer. But she'd had a practical bent.

Just fry up some onions, she told her daughters. The smell of frying onions makes men think that supper is not far behind. So brown the onions slowly, but hurry with the rest.

Browned onions would be a luxury right now, Edward thought, as he fed the feeble fire.

After a supper of cold beans and sourdough bread, he brought the axe to Isabelle, showed her where to place her hands on its handle for maximum effect. It's easy, he said, anyone can learn to chop a little kindling. But although she stood beside him and placed her hands correctly on the handle, felt the heft of it, she flat-out refused to swing the axe.

Maybe some other time, she said. I just don't feel up to it right now.

"Isabelle?"

Edward dropped his pack inside the door, hurried to her side.

She was sitting on the red chair, one leg elevated on the yellow. Her right foot was bandaged and bloody.

"I told you I couldn't do it," she said.

He unwound the bandages, relieved to see that the wound on the edge of her foot was slight and that the bleeding had stopped. He applied some of Twelve Foot's all-purpose healing salve from a round green tin and then re-wrapped Isabelle's foot.

"I'm so sorry, Isabelle. From now on, I'll keep a good supply of kindling inside, where it will be dry. And I'll build a new woodpile just outside the door. All you'll have to do is bring it inside and keep the fire fed."

He pulled her close, something he'd not done for quite some time and he smelled the oily odour of her hair, the pungent scent of her unwashed armpits. Lord knows, bathing was a chore. Hauling and warming the water, pulling the tin tub into the circle of warmth beside the hearth. The first time, he'd thought her refusal to join him in the Saturday bath was punishment for some transgression he didn't know one damn thing about.

He ran his fingers gently through her hair, stopped by a nest of tangles. With infinite care, he straightened the knots, working his way back to smooth.

Edward grabbed the poker, broke the skin of ice that had formed on the water pail. His feet felt like chunks of ice too, and he wished for the luxury of staying in bed, next to Isabelle. All he could see of his wife was her reddened nose.

Outside, the wind howled and explosions of snow obscured the landscape. There wasn't a sign of human habitation anywhere. How long could a storm possibly last? For the first time, he felt a glimmer of understanding for Isabelle's fears. They were entirely alone.

He struggled into his coveralls and a striped Hudson's Bay parka and stepped into the cold. Frost seized the fine hairs inside his nose, and he felt suddenly short of breath. But he knew better than to open his mouth and breathe

the freezing air straight into his lungs. He'd done that once, and once was enough.

He checked the woodpile by the door, grabbed an armful as big as he could manage. The pile had shrunk alarmingly, but it would have to suffice for a day or two. Until the storm blew itself out. It was bone-chilling cold and the wind howled, snow obscuring the landscape and even the outlines of his little shack.

Weak sunlight struggled through the wavery windows, panes lacy with crystal frost. Inside, amazingly, tiny black spiders survived, and even managed to spin an intricate cobweb or two. They'd probably come in on the wood he'd chopped and he felt a twinge of guilt as he swooshed the fragile webs with a wet dishcloth. They dissolved, gone for the time being, at least.

He cut two slices of bread, checked the frying pan to see if the water was boiling.

"Got three eggs from Stella's chickens yesterday. A sure sign of spring. Table scraps and a little barley and those stupid chickens made it through a hellish winter."

"Just like we did," Isabelle said. "I'm not sure which is the bigger miracle."

She patted her Bible, sitting on an apple crate by her left hand, and pulled her purple shawl closer as she rocked.

"I'm surprised they survived. Thought they might miss Stella, a little at least, and go off their feed. Kind of like you."

"I'm not really hungry for food," Isabelle said. She scratched the taut sides of her immense belly. She looked like an over-ripe melon and said she felt like she might burst. "What I am hungry for is a good long talk with Annie. For I really need her now."

He cracked an egg against the black of the pan, gently dropped it into the bubbling water. Another, and then one more.

"Isabelle, no one seems to know anything about Annie and Trapper . . . and believe me, I've made a pest of myself asking. Besides, neither of us can travel right now, even if we knew where to start. We're managing just fine here and maybe we . . . "

She turned her foot, so he saw the fading scarlet scar. "We surely aren't," she said. "See this mark? It says I'm doomed."

"That's crazy talk," he told her.

Finally, the eggs rose to the surface, pale gold and white. He took a flipper, lifted the soft eggs from the simmering water and set them on two pieces of slightly stale sourdough. He handed a full plate to his wife. He'd given her two of the eggs.

Annie, he thought. I need Annie too.

Thank God for an early spring, and for sunlight. The cruel clutch of winter was finally losing its grip. The willows were swollen with buds, ripe and ready.

Every day he walked the two miles to the riverbank, sat on a flat-topped rock and watched the growing trickle of the springtime stream. When the snow finally lost its battle with the strengthening warmth, the stream would be a river again. Maybe the rushing water would stir the black sand, throw a nugget or two.

In the meantime, fitfully, he panned for gold.

On the day that his daughter was struggling to come into the world, he was glad for the excuse of his claim.

He heard again Bethany's anguish, heard the loud ticking of the clock, felt the heat building in the cramped room. Bethany's even, determined breathing giving way eventually to hoarse cries, and then to cursing God and her husband and the midwife too.

He remembered his own helplessness, his inability, finally, to stay. How he'd fled to the corner pub, sat with total strangers, drinking beer after beer.

How he had lingered for hours, afraid to go home.

For Isabelle, he'd fetched the midwife early on. Had gotten proper help right at the start. Pauletta was proficient and kind, and when she'd shooed him out the shanty door, he was grateful.

When the sun finally began to fade, he found a nugget, bigger than the end of his thumb. He'd been idly combing through a patch of warm black sand with numbed fingers and, like magic, there it was. He tucked it into the small purple bag that contained his three lucky marbles. A bag he kept in the inside pocket of his vest, close to his heart. Suddenly he was sure. All would be well.

When he opened the door to the shanty, he was comforted by the smell of chicken soup or maybe a stew bubbling in the blackened pot on the back of the stove. The lamp was flickering, soft yellow shadows danced on the walls. Isabelle was propped in their rough wood-block bed, holding a bundle in her arms and he saw such raw love in her eyes that he felt like an intruder who should back out slowly and close the door.

"Come say hello to your daughter." Isabelle unfolded the edge of the flannelette bundle so that he could see a skiff of black hair and one perfect little hand. "I hate to admit it, but right now, I don't really remember the moment she was born."

Edward kissed Isabelle's hot cheek. "What matters is she's here." He held out a blunt forefinger, and the tiny fingers curled and clung. "Aren't you the impatient one?" he said. "Couldn't wait to come into the world." But privately, he thanked God his daughter had arrived a little early and that Isabelle had been up to the job. "She's perfect," he said. He tucked the loose end of her blanket and straightened Isabelle's tangled hair.

Pauletta was re-packing her bag. "She is perfect," she said. "Makes my job worthwhile."

"Thank you," Edward said.

Her hand swept toward the shanty door, to an enamelled pan covered by a snowy white cloth. "Take that outside," she said. "Bury it tonight by the light of the moon. Bury it deep. Walk around the hole three times." She lifted her bag. "Counter-clockwise," she said.

"Why do I . . . ?"

"It's the placenta. It's extremely important that it, too, find a home."

The midwife sat down on a kitchen chair, as if suddenly exhausted. She lifted a foot, pressed her arch with her thumb.

"It's sustained and protected your daughter for months. But it offers protection for all. There's more to birthing a baby than any man can know."

"You can count on me," he said as he helped gather her supplies. "If you're sure it's important."

When she left, he closed the door behind her, leaned his forehead on its roughened wood. Pauletta was good

140

at birthing all right, but the other hocus-pocus she came up with made him wonder if she'd been alone in the bush too long.

"Suppertime," he said. He found a ladle, dished up full bowls of soup — it was soup — one for Isabelle, one for himself.

At least Isabelle's done something to earn her supper, he thought as he spooned soup from the warm white bowl, grateful to the midwife for not only bringing his child safely into the world, but for preparing his supper too.

Isabelle sipped only three full spoons before she pushed his hand away. Life is good, he thought, as he refilled his own bowl, took a spoonful of the steaming broth. He had time for only one more bite before the baby began to cry. He looked at the tiny bundle in amazement, as her howls seemed loud enough to raise the roof. He rose then, went to the sideboard where Isabelle's Bible lay. He found a fresh, white page near the front and took up her pen.

He wrote: *Born this day, April 30th 1897, a baby girl with vocal cords in fine working order. Underneath he signed their names, Edward and Isabelle Armson*

*Baby: Sarah Louise*

Then his hand strayed to his pocket, to his lump of gold. Not a bad day for the entire family. Not bad at all.

He awoke in the night when the howl of a wolf erupted from a struggling stand of birch. He shivered, pulled the blankets closer and made sure that Isabelle was snugged up too. As he rolled over, he saw the basin, the edges of the white cloth gleaming, the centre drooped and now a clotted red.

Tired, and a little bit cold, he didn't get out of bed. I'll bury it in the morning, he decided. Who's ever going to know? The sound of the wolves softened and died.

Edward stoked the fire so that the little shack was as hot as an August afternoon and he drew warm water from the reservoir at the side of the rust-specked enamelled stove. He checked the temperature of the water on the inside of his wrist.

"Water's perfect now."

He poured a cup of good strong coffee, and leaned against the doorframe, watching as Isabelle un-swaddled their child.

Sarah lay naked on the table, and he admired how tiny she was, how like a doll. Her hair blue-black, like Annie's, her round eyes so dark they seemed like bottomless pools.

As Isabelle examined their furious, squalling daughter, Edward saw the colour drain from her face, heard her quick intake of breath. She lifted Sarah's foot, then sagged against the table, sloshing water from the small tin dishpan.

"She's marked. Sarah is marked."

He moved closer, took his daughter's dainty foot and held it in his hand. Slowly, he ran his rough finger over the miniscule scar of silver on her middle right toe.

"You're right," he said. He checked her other small toes. "But it's a good sign. A daughter born with a tiny touch of silver probably means that gold's not far behind. I think my girl is telling me I'm about to strike it rich in more ways than one."

142

"Really Edward?"

One look at his wife's white face told him he'd better come up with something more to calm her fears. "It's a sign from above."

He took the baby from Isabelle's hands, lowered her into the bath and swished warm water across her silken skin. Then he wrapped her in a soft blanket and carried her close to the stove so the warmth of it would seep into her tiny bones. She was so delicate, so very, very small.

"I don't really believe in signs from above," he whispered. "But I will do everything in my power to make your life good."

When she nursed their child, Isabelle's eyes strayed to the window, watching the passing clouds or sometimes a lone raven circling in the empty sky. She didn't bury her head in the sweetness of Sarah's baby smell or hold her close and hum old lullabies.

Isabelle ate so very little, Edward was quite sure her milk must be thin, and in short supply. He began to worry about Sarah, wondering how she could possibly thrive.

When he bought a baby bottle and cans of condensed milk and syrup too, and brought them home, he felt a little guilty. But the baby had to eat.

"How do you mix this stuff?"

Isabelle was sitting at the table, sipping tea from her yellow roses cup. Sarah was content in her cradle, entranced by the movement of her hands.

"I have no idea. You could read what it says on the label I guess."

He measured the creamy mixture into a blue granite bowl, added water and sugar and then began to stir. "This is only to tide her over for a bit. Until you get a little stronger and can feed her yourself."

"Here," Isabelle said, picking up the baby and thrusting her into his arms. "She won't eat for me."

He pulled closer to the fire, and ever so slowly, he began to rock.

He offered the nipple to Sarah. At first, she turned away. He shook the bottle so that two drops of the sweetened milk fell onto her bottom lip.

She ran her tongue over her lip and began to smack. Then she latched onto the nipple and began to suck, long noisy draughts.

A great wave of tenderness washed over him then, and he was almost glad that Isabelle seemed totally uninterested in their child.

Isabelle heard the knock, considered ignoring it, but Stella was already opening the door. She was carrying a large basket, full of lacy lettuce, crisp green beans and baby beets, with the greens still attached.

"Harvesting the garden," she said. "And really, with nursing the baby, you're still eating for two."

She set the basket on the table and peered inside Sarah's cradle. The baby was sleeping soundly and Stella ran her fingers down her silky cheeks.

"I'll miss this," she whispered.

Isabelle knew that Stella's garden was her pride and joy and the basket was full to overflowing. "How generous," she said.

Stella's face was grave. "I'm leaving. Soon as Black Dan gives me the word. He's promised I can ride along next time he goes south."

Isabelle gripped the arms of the rocker. "But Stella, where will you . . . ?"

Stella drew a deep breath, balled her apron with her fist. "Rocked four boys in this chair," she said. "Now it's time for me to part with some other things. My time is over here and it's time for someone else. I'll get a job in Edmonton, a restaurant somewhere, maybe a laundry or a store. Finally figured out my old man ain't coming back. And my boys are gone now, with their own lives to live. By bad luck or by design, seems I'm on my own."

When Stella turned to leave, Isabelle took both of her hands, held them tight. "Godspeed," she said. "I'll keep you in my prayers." She knew Stella didn't put much stock in praying, but she continued to hold both of her hands.

"There's lots of stuff in the garden still," Stella said. "It would ease me to think you and your family would take care of it now."

Isabelle nodded, unable to speak. A friend, she thought. I finally have a friend. And now I'm losing her too.

∾∾∾

Most days, Edward came home to find Sarah in the cradle sucking on the bottle Isabelle had propped with a tea towel, so he took the baby in his arms and held her close, held the bottle too.

He patted her back until she burped, wiped milky bubbles from her bow-tie lips with the satin binding of the blanket before gently tucking her in for a nap. He thought of Ward, and how he'd been too preoccupied with his own grief to take care of his son.

Isabelle, at least, kept Sarah's diaper changed.

You can't go back, he told himself, but this time, you can do it right.

He threw back the bleached sacks that shadowed the shanty, whistling as he boiled the coffee. Maybe the smell of coffee would start the day off right. When he heard Isabelle sigh, he went to their bed, took her limp hand.

He was startled by its heat and when he touched her forehead, it seemed to be on fire. He picked up the mewling baby, laid her on her mother's breast, but Isabelle turned away.

Sarah had quieted, her head heavy on his chest, and he wondered if she was calmed by the steady thumping of his heart. It worked that way with puppies. If the bitch deserted, and the puppies were mewling, you could put a clock into their bed and the steady tick-tocking sounded to them like the beating of their mother's heart. The puppies would grow quiet, and soon they'd be asleep.

But he didn't know about babies. Didn't know if such a thing could work.

It was Stella who first suggested there was something more wrong with Isabelle than just being lonely and a little depressed.

"I feel double bad about leaving right now," she'd said. "But I got no choice. Black Dan's nearly ready and I have to jump when he says the word. He don't take kindly to waiting on a woman."

Edward smiled, for he could not really imagine how Stella and Black Dan would manage, travelling together for weeks on end. Probably Stella's idea and nothing to do with Dan. But Stella was a resourceful woman. She'd find a way.

Stella's brow was creased, the deep vertical line between her eyebrows reddened slightly too. "I'm worried about Isabelle. Only three days since I've last been. I can hardly believe how quickly she's failing. So thin and such poor colour too."

He berated himself for not noticing Isabelle's quick descent, for not feeling her jutting hipbones or seeing the yellow in her eyes.

He found Pauletta at home, thanks be to God.

"Please, Pauletta," he said. "Something's wrong. Isabelle either can't or won't get out of bed. And she looks awful. I'll pay whatever you ask."

"It's not the money," she said. "Although I hear you're good for that."

He wondered what she had heard, and from whom. He'd carried his thumb-sized nugget for weeks, zipped into the inside pocket of his overalls, right next to his heart. And he hadn't told a soul. Except Isabelle, of course, and even that piece of wonderful news had failed to excite his wife.

Strangely, it seemed gold attracted gold, and now his stash had quadrupled in size.

Pauletta was stuffing herbs and seeds into a little cheesecloth sack. "I don't understand. The birthing went so well. How long since Isabelle took to her bed?"

"Four days now," he replied, "since she's been up at all."

He saw her quick intake of breath. "I'll do what I can. But I've another birthing six miles the other side of town."

He kneaded his knotted hands.

"But it's a first child coming tonight," Pauletta said, touching his brawny shoulder. "And the first one usually takes its own sweet time. So I can probably spare a little time. For Isabelle and for your perfect little girl."

To her bulging bag, she added a bottle of tincture, tinted purple. She began to rummage in her pantry, muttering something Edward could not hear.

"Can we get going?" he said. "Please."

"Patience," Pauletta told him. "There's a thing or two more that I might need. Although hopefully not."

Edward exhaled, bit the inside of his cheek.

When she was finally satisfied, they hurried down the shadow of a path trampled in the scanty grass.

When he saw his front door swaying open, he broke into a run.

"Isabelle," he called, his heart thumping in his ears. She was propped up in bed, the Bible open on her chest. The cabin was cold and she must be too.

She tried to get up and he hurried to her bedside, supported her with his sun-browned arms.

"Is someone here?" She was shivering, so he pulled the blankets closer, tightened his arms.

"It's Pauletta and she's going to make you well."

When he looked at his wife, really looked at her, he was startled by the fine translucence of her skin. He kissed her brow, then eased her back down. He turned to Sarah's cradle and tucked the blanket around her too, took her warm little hand. At least the chill in the room hadn't reached into the cradle, hadn't touched his child.

When he saw a sudden flutter of wings in the corner of his shanty, he quickly turned. But it was only shadows from the flour-sack curtains fluttering in the breeze.

He thought of the red and white gingham he and Isabelle had talked of. How she might sew up new curtains to make the place more cheery. I should have just bought a yard or two, he thought, and brought it right home.

"Sometimes new mothers take a fever."

He saw tears roll down Isabelle's waxy cheeks as the midwife pushed on her swollen abdomen, felt the lumps along her groin.

"Milk fever it's called." She handed Edward a cheese-cloth bag, tied at the top. "This is the most potent medicine I have," she said. "Known to work wonders. Brew her a good strong tea and add some whiskey if you have it. Make sure she drinks every drop."

Edward thought, for the first time, of the enamel basin, his failure to follow Pauletta's orders on the day that Sarah was born. Surely most of this was just smoke and mirrors, a way for Pauletta to convince people she had some real magic in her bag. But for a moment, he felt a flicker of doubt. Maybe if he had followed instructions? Done exactly as she'd said?

"But Pauletta, I was hoping you'd be able to do something more . . . "

"Sometimes things are taken right out of our hands." She nodded her head towards the family Bible open beside Isabelle on the bed. "Do as I tell you. And it wouldn't hurt one bit to pray."

He could feel moisture gathering in the corners of his grit-filled eyes as he prepared the tea. From the locker beneath their bed he retrieved the whiskey Twelve Foot had given him, partly because he couldn't carry all of his secret stash through the bush, but mostly because he'd told Twelve Foot of Isabelle's pregnancy.

It had felt so good to finally say it aloud.

The whiskey was a parting gift, Twelve Foot had said. "Someone will no doubt need it sometime soon. Either Isabelle or you. Possibly both."

Edward took a chipped green mug from a shelf above the sink and poured himself a large portion of Twelve Foot's whiskey, which burned his throat at the first swallow, but after the burn, he felt the welcome warmth, the taste sweetening as he drank again and again.

When he offered Isabelle the tea, she turned her face away.

"I'll leave it here, beside the bed. Please, drink it. It smells kind of nasty with the whiskey but Pauletta said it would help. I can add a little maple syrup if you'd like." He took the cup to the cupboard, added two tablespoons of maple syrup, stirred it well. "Try this, my love." He was relieved when she took a small sip. "Here, just a little more." He held the cup to her lips but he didn't press when she shook her head no.

He folded back the comforter, and slipped into bed beside his wife. He drew her closer, curved his firm body to the jutting thinness of her bones. Her fever raged against the icy coldness of his skin.

"Rest," he whispered. "Just rest and you'll be fine."

He was tired, and so damn scared and he did not leave their bed that night. Not even when Sarah whimpered, when she outright cried.

Nor did he try to wake Isabelle again, make her finish the drink.

All night, he held her, awake in the glow of the waxing moon.

Sometimes he felt a burning gaze, saw a pair of reddened eyes, a slide of silver fur. A wolf, he thought. Too much whiskey for sure.

As the golden sun cracked the horizon, he finally joined his wife and daughter in a trio of fitful sleep.

And when Isabelle's spirit slipped from her body, he did not feel her go.

16.

Ka-thunk. Ka-thunk. The sound of soil hitting the lid of Isabelle's simple pine coffin was torture to his ears. The earth was rich and black, crumbling as it landed in the newly opened grave.

"Ashes to ashes, dust to dust," the minister intoned, clutching a handful of soil and sprinkling it into the grave. "Go in peace my brothers and sisters. God's blessings on us all, here and forever after."

Isabelle would hate this place, he thought. No white picket fence surrounding it, no black granite headstones, nothing to mark the boundaries between the people buried here and the never-ending sky.

Nothing but waving grasses, the forest a dark smudge encroaching, the only music the steady hum of insects, clouds of them, disturbed by the presence of humans, and as always, even on such a day as this, out for blood.

Two blue-black ravens landed on a leaning cross to the left of Isabelle's mound and began their raucous song, their voices hammering his ears. He grabbed a clump of clay, threw it hard, but the birds ignored him, continuing their noise. Not the celestial choir Isabelle should have, with her love of fine music.

He hoped she was somewhere else already, that she couldn't hear.

The minister handed him a shovel for the ceremonial first shovel of earth but he kept working after the first pass. He helped with the burying, shovelling faster and faster until the metal of the spade was a silver blur and sweat ran down the sides of his face and onto his white collar.

He finally stopped when he heard the snuffle of a woman crying in the crowd, the whiney complaint of a small child.

Leaning on the shovel, he looked around. For a moment he had no idea where he was or how he had come to be there. He was glad when Sarah began to cry hard and the clutch of mourners turned to leave.

His eyes searched for Sarah, found her held tight by a neighbour. He took his daughter, clasped her to his breast as he stumbled across the windswept graveyard, its staggering rows of wooden crosses silvered by the sun and the rain. Such a large graveyard for such a young settlement.

Someone took his arm, led him home.

The shanty women, four of them, came to the house after the burial, dragging reluctant husbands in tow.

"Thank you," he told Helen, the only one he really knew. "Thank you for helping me with Sarah today."

"Of course," she said. "Of course. Anything to help you get through this dreadful day."

The men lounged outside, smoking and talking together in low tones. Soon they found reasons to leave. Chores. Watering the horses. Checking the chickens. Running away. That part, he understood.

The women stayed too long, watchful over the rims of their china; teacups that Isabelle had eventually unpacked and set on a wooden shelf above the kitchen table, so she could glance at them as she cleaned and cooked, perhaps

153

taking pleasure from the twining yellow roses she loved so much.

It was he who had lifted them down from the shelf, wiped them clean. Perhaps if he lent a hand, the post-funeral ritual could be speeded up and the women would feel free to go.

He supposed they were fearful of leaving him alone with a baby, but all he wanted was quiet and the soft sound of Sarah sleeping on his chest.

He fed Sarah her evening bottle, settled her beside him in the bed. He had no trouble falling into a deep, sound sleep, for he was exhausted by the events of the day and he longed for the oblivion of sleep. But he was not to be blessed by sleep without dreams.

Twelve Foot hunkers near the campfire. Edward scrapes charred bits of caribou from the bottom of an iron pot suspended on a tripod above the glowing coals. He banks the coals so they will glow long into the night.

"I loved her too." Twelve Foot says. Sparks erupt into the blackness of the sky. "She was soft-spoken, with a quiet kind of beauty that made a man notice, not right away, but after a bit. You know, she never bought extras. I added a head of lettuce or fresh corn, if it was in season. I wish that I'd given her sweets instead. Or maybe Irish lace or shiny satin bindings. Something really fine." Twelve Foot's face is flushed from the heat of his fire or his crazy confession. "She was your wife, I know, but she was a lady, and I loved her too."

He almost punches Twelve Foot then, but there is something oceanic and sad in Twelve Foot's hooded eyes.

154

Each night, week after week, he bathed and fed Sarah and laid her next to him on the bed. He never worried about rolling over on her, about not feeling her breath as he soundly slept. He didn't like to put her in the cradle, out of his reach. Even with the strange presence of Twelve Foot in his dreams, he never moved, kept still beside her, guarding her from God knows what.

He'd never hurt Sarah, even locked in the deepest of sleep.

When they've eaten all the caribou and the fire is only glowing embers, Twelve Foot takes a stick and draws a map near his feet.

"This way. Same route Black Dan showed you months ago. Take the North fork in the river and be prepared for one set of rapids. It's a rough one, so take it slow. About halfway through, the riverbank drops off sheer and spray from the rapids makes the rocks like glass. Once you travois your supplies around that, you're done the hardest part. Float your empty canoe down the rapids. If it comes out at the bottom, all the better. If it doesn't, there's a canoe hidden in a stand of willow beneath those rapids. And when you reach the Lesser Slave, you're almost back to civilization. Or somewhere close."

Annie steps like a shadow from the clumps of birches that flutter on the shores of the Lesser Slave and takes the baby from his arms. She peeks beneath the blanket, and her face goes soft with recognition.

"She's beautiful."

Edward looks from Annie's black hair to Sarah's. Same glowing curls, same black curved lashes, even the same dusky skin.

"I see the rightness of bringing her to you. It's what Isabelle would have wanted." He touches her hand, and wants to do much more.

"Trapper has gone north to set his winter trap-line somewhere up the Smoky River and I've been awful alone, until now."

Annie watches the baby by day, but at night, she offers Sarah to his arms. The baby sleeps the sleep of angels tucked beneath her father's chin and the father needs the fresh smell of the baby to clear the stench of his scorched sorrow.

Together, they tend the child and they are content.

Edward studied the large map tacked to the wall at the Bay outpost, had even thought to suggest that maps such as that might be made smaller and sold to customers. But he didn't pursue his brilliant idea, not wanting to help the Bay in any practical way.

The Lesser Slave was drawn large, an awe-inspiring lake. How sad to be so substantial and still considered lesser.

He'd begun his preparations to leave. He already had a canoe and he had practised the art of paddling, and he'd hired Black Dan's kid brother to help him cut boughs of lodge-pole pine, show him how to lace them tightly across long white birch poles to make a travois, light and strong. Practice for the real thing, somewhere down the road.

Wolf Runner was leaning in the open doorway, smoking, and Edward inhaled the sweet drift. "You have come for supplies," Wolf said. "First let us walk."

Edward followed him across the scrabbly grass and into the tree line, the day getting darker.

Wolf Runner upturned a half-rotted stump. "Mushrooms, edible kind." He pulled up a purplish vein-leafed plant. "Strip it and eat the flesh." Showed him which of the shade flowers were delicacies and which ones to avoid.

Edward felt ashamed for his failure to make this man a friend. A quiet man, and easy to overlook with Black Dan around. But now? Sharing his survival skills? He really had a heart of gold. Easy to miss the gold, so goddamn easy to miss the gold.

They walked back and Wolf Runner pulled a large package from his pack. "Achees," he said. "Full of good stuff to keep a man going for a good long time. The little one too."

Edward smiled as he imagined Sarah sucking a bottle of milk fortified with powdered caribou, lines of drool dribbling down her chin. He guessed he might give her some if it turned out she needed something extra, but he had no intention of running out of supplies. Certainly not when he had Sarah in his care.

"One thing," Wolf Runner said, sitting on a bench in front of the store. "The rapids are too dangerous for a newcomer, especially with a baby aboard. So above the rapids, set your craft free. Pack the baby and your supplies." He lifted his moccasin, the soft leather moulded to his foot. "You will need your own. To make your footsteps sure."

Edward mentally added moccasins to his list of supplies.

"If your craft does not squirt through the rocks and the rapids, there's Twelve Foot's hidden canoe."

Edward wondered why a man of few words would have so much to say. "Everything alright with you, Wolf?"

"Me and my woman leave tomorrow. On the fullness of the moon."

He stooped, picked a small dried pod from a bushy plant. "Edible, good for aches and pains." He tucked the pod into his cheek. "You would be welcome. Dyani has always been good to care for babies."

Edward reached for Wolf Runner's hand, clasped it hard. "Thanks, but I have a few things I have to do first," he said, thinking of the slumping mound of Isabelle's grave, covered untidily with flourishing weeds, the lack of even a plain white cross. He would never forgive himself if he left her in an unmarked grave.

He had found a trapper with a real talent for whittling and had ordered up a four-foot cross, with flowers and birds twining around its stem and Isabelle's name engraved on the crosspiece. Paint would soon fade, but her name would be preserved there for a while at least.

The marker would take a little longer than most, the trapper had said. Not the only thing he had to do at this busy season. Also Edward felt a need for a small ceremony of some kind when he erected the cross. Isabelle had stood on ceremony for sure and he was determined to give her this final gift.

Wolf withdrew his hand from Edward's grip. "We will meet the Dene. Before they follow the caribou if the Creator wishes it so." He touched Edward's shoulder. "May the Creator watch over you and your baby as well."

"Thank you, Wolf. But Sarah and I will be just fine. And we'll run into you someplace down the road. I know for sure we will."

He missed Stella, the way she used she to give one quick knock and then a "Yoo-hoo anybody home?" as she stepped inside. Isabelle gone from the world and he with no way of letting Stella know. Sad.

Right now, hers was the only face he'd care to see and he knew there was precious little chance of her coming back.

He was almost done packing, had pared his possessions to just a precious few. He held Isabelle's crystal sugar bowl in his hands, sure it was too fragile to make the trip, but wondering too if it might bring solace to Sarah when he told her of her mother's short life. Something beautiful and sparkly, something to gather and fracture the sun. Rainbows, he thought. Rainbows from her mother. Now wouldn't that be fine.

He heard an insistent rapping on the door.

The knock came again. With a sigh, he rose.

The preacher stood on his doorstep, a Bible in his hands, and looked around at the disarray of boxes overflowing with dishes and blankets and clothes.

"Are you going somewhere?" Thomas asked.

The preacher knew full well that he was planning to travel with Sarah to the banks of the Lesser Slave and find Trapper and Annie. For a week it had been fresh fodder for the gossips in shantytown. A man alone, travelling with such a small child?

Word was that grief had caused Edward's mind to unhinge.

All summer, Twelve Foot had warned him in dreams about the meddling of others, how he'd need a plausible story when he was ready to leave or they might take Sarah from him and then he'd have to stay.

"Tongues are wagging. Nothing but trouble once the women get involved. So move careful and move fast."

The words had stayed fresh. Edward could not imagine walking past Isabelle in the graveyard every day and taking Sarah there to visit her mother for the rest of her life. And his life too.

"Step in for a moment, Reverend, although I'm busy, as you can see."

"I just thought we could have a little talk . . . "

"I know there've been concerns," Edward said. "Well-intentioned, I'm sure. But the plan is to meet up with my brother-in-law, Trapper John. And Annie, of course. Isabelle's sister will surely want the child if for some reason I cannot cope. Although I don't see that. Not at all."

The preacher cleared his throat. "Well, some things don't come natural. Like a man raising a child and sometimes it might be best to . . . "

Edward held his palm up, then passed the back of his hand across his brow. "My goal all along was the gold. But Isabelle so wanted to see her sister. It's the reason she consented to coming up here in the first place. And now, here we are." It was the first time he'd admitted, even to himself, that his plans hadn't turned out the way he'd

160

hoped. "Our meeting place is to be halfway between here and the Lesser Slave." He pulled the wrinkled paper from his right front pocket, smoothed it on the table so the preacher could see. Black Dan's line drawing was small, but neat, and dated in the corner. "Should be fairly easy," he said. "Even for a greenhorn like me."

He felt no remorse for what he knew was a lie. But not all that he said was untrue. He had sent a letter to his sister-in-law, care of the Dunvegan post, to break the news of Isabelle's death and suggesting they meet on the shores of the Lesser Slave in early September. Hopefully, long before another hard winter set in.

He'd used Black Dan's simple line drawing to choose a suitable meeting place.

*I will make camp on the north shore near the big white rock,"* he wrote, *with the straight-up massive face. Not far from the Dene camp. I will await your arrival for as long as it's feasible. I surely look forward to seeing you, and Trapper of course, for with Isabelle now gone from this world, I feel so very alone.*

*And I can't wait for Sarah to meet you. She is my reason for being just now. A lovely little girl.*

No answering letter had arrived.

He imagined the perils of travel so late in the season, and he knew he might miss Trapper and Annie by a day or an hour, a stand of papery aspens, or even a bend in the trail. Assuming of course, that they even knew of his plan.

Winter had not sent up its shivery warnings, wilted grasses and crispy, turning leaves so he had a little time. Wolf Runner had assured him that until they left to follow the caribou, the Dene camp would be a welcoming place.

If not Trapper and Annie, the Dene would do.

Sometimes, at night, he thought of Trapper John. Trapper would have known what to do, wouldn't he? A man used to making his own way probably did his own doctoring too. He'd have seen the signs of Isabelle's decline before it was too late.

Annie wouldn't blame him, would she? After she read the letter, would she have time to grieve and then to forgive?

But what if she didn't already know, if he had to be the one to tell her?

He dreaded the sorrow he would see in her doe-brown eyes. Anger too.

"I know you have her best interests at heart, but the baby is fragile for such a journey," the preacher said. "It might be prudent to leave her behind, just until you get settled. You could send for her. Actually, my wife and I thought . . . "

Edward pictured Thomas's wife, a prune of a woman, with pursed lips and the sickly smell of violet talcum billowing in her wake. She hadn't come to see Isabelle, as most of the other camp wives had. There'd been no pots of homemade soup or kindly words from her.

He turned abruptly, pulled the cradleboard from its resting place against the shanty wall. "Sarah will be snug as a bug in here," he said. "I don't mean for anything to happen to her and I certainly don't mean to leave her behind."

Once, he'd left a child behind. He didn't intend to make the same mistake again.

The Reverend cleared his throat, his eyes slithering from Edward to Sarah and back again.

Edward stepped forward and blocked his view. He didn't like the longing he saw in those preacherly eyes. Then he thrust the cradleboard out, so Thomas could see. "Papooses seem to like travelling in them. Never heard one cry." His hands itched to shove the man across the threshold and slam the door but instead, he smiled and offered tea.

"You're busy," Thomas said, his eyes once more darting around the mess in the shanty. "My wife just thought . . . you know, she's always wanted a child and that on such a treacherous trip maybe you didn't want to be burdened by . . . "

"I'll not be taking even one step without my girl strapped to my back," Edward said as he flexed his shaking hands. "She'll never be a burden to me."

"Then I wish you Godspeed," the preacher said. "May the heavens protect you and your precious cargo. I will tell Adelaide that I tried. Really, I did."

After he was gone, Edward lifted the crystal sugar bowl again to the light, but as he did, his eyes fell upon his Bible, so he set the bowl aside and instead, tucked the Bible into his pack. So much for rainbows, he thought. But truly, Isabelle took solace from the word of God. Maybe someday, in the unknowable future, it would help Sarah too.

The river cradled his craft and beneath his body, he could feel the swiftness of the feather-light canoe. His recollection of Black Dan's map was clear and true. And the crinkled original was tucked in his pack, easy to check if need be. The unusually fine fall weather was holding, and other than a few unscheduled stops to attend to Sarah's needs, he had made good progress.

The rugged beauty of the north dulled his ache for Isabelle, and every day, as he paddled, he felt stronger, hopeful that better times were soon to come.

His intention had been to rest for at least two days before he began the final portage. He'd planned to shoot some game, fill his belly with simmered doe or duck, thick gravy with soft berries floating in the mix, for cranberries were plentiful in the underbrush. Or maybe a fish-fry. That would be a nice change. And for dessert, maybe mashed blueberries with a bit of sugar?

He thanked God he'd constructed the sturdy lean-to before his accident. At least they had a roof over their heads. What food he had left was stashed in a footlocker at the back of the natural bowl he'd used as a base for their temporary home. He blessed Black Dan's lessons in choosing and felling suitable trees and he was pleased to see that with its dappled green canopy, his dug-out was nearly invisible, except of course, for the remnants of his fire.

The waxy needles of the jack-pine were well suited to the north, letting moisture slide off in wintertime, preventing branches overburdened with snow from breaking to the ground. Thankfully, the needles also filtered the warm afternoon sun, and he and Sarah slept beneath its fragrant boughs, quiet and cool.

So far, the skies remained blue and bright, and there was no threat of rain or snow.

He settled on his bedroll, unwrapped the red bandanna he'd used to bind his leg. Sarah watched with her wide violet eyes. The cut was deep, the flap of flesh loose on the right side of his thigh.

"Bad for both of us, little one," he said. "Looks like your father has no real skill with a filleting knife. Just one little slip. And of course, that slippery damned jackfish. Too bad I didn't hook a pickerel. Easier to handle for sure."

He pushed gently at the edge of inflamed flesh, winced from the spider web of pain.

"Sorry for the language. Not a good example, I know. Here's hoping you'll have no recall, as well you shouldn't."

He'd been leaning into the knife and when the fish slipped from his makeshift cutting board, the razor point had stuck deeply into the long muscles of his thigh. It was all he could do to pull the blade from his flesh and when he did, stars burst and he saw the familiar shadow of a silver wolf slip from the clearing and into the trees.

He'd shaken off his vision, if that's what it was, as he washed and cleaned the wound as best he could.

But that night, as he lay in his bedroll, he felt the throbbing and knew before he even looked that angry red streaks were reaching upward from the base of the gash.

He rolled over, groaned as Sarah stirred.

He gritted his teeth and hobbled to the river's edge to search the overhanging willows for some cool, clean moss.

Twelve Foot shakes him awake, holds his finger to his lips and gestures to the sleeping Sarah.

"Better get some fine straight birch rounded up tomorrow, just in case."

"Just in case of what?"

Twelve Foot doesn't answer. He is busy drawing a diagram of a raft, indicating how many logs Edward needed, how he should position them just so. Two logs placed about three feet apart on the diagonal atop the little craft. The rest of the logs lashed beneath. When Edward questions the design, Twelve Foot's face grows grave.

"Build it like I show ya. Do as I say. And as quickly as you can."

Edward pokes the coals. He doesn't want to provoke Twelve Foot. This new Twelve Foot is nothing like the easy-going guy he remembers.

In the dirt at his feet, Twelve Foot drafts a pattern for the lashings. "Check them twice, once when you're finished the raft and again the next day, when the sun is high in the sky and the bark has dried. If they're not tight, get some water from the river, soak 'em really good. Then let nature do its work. You don't want them lashings giving out. For damn sure you don't."

Heat rises in his face, and it isn't heat from the fever. The old Twelve Foot would never speak to him like this one. "I'm listening," Edward says. "Listening and taking heed."

Twelve Foot leans back.

It is pretty damn hot near the campfire tonight and Edward doesn't care much if he eats any stew. He has only a small portion left, and three stale biscuits.

Edward was surprised on waking at the emptiness of the iron pot held steady by a green willow bough staked above the nearly dead fire.

Building the raft was no easy task; it took him almost three full days. Why was he compelled to build it? Just because Twelve Foot said he should?

Dragging even small birch limbs from the brush to the clearing was torture, his swollen leg screaming with every move he made and the whole idea seemed as foolish as his dreams of hauling in nuggets of gold, enough that someday, he would finally be someone. Although he now had the gold, he didn't feel one bit different. There was not one soul around to impress and he regretted the loss.

Alone in the bush with his stash of gold and his little girl.

Sweating and shivering, he persevered with the birch limbs and solemn little Sarah, hanging in her cradle-board on a low birch bough, watched his every move.

Strangely, when the sun was high in the sky, and she should have been hungry, she didn't make a sound.

But he put his work aside, stoked the embers to boil some water and syrup, and added a careful handful of dried milk powder. His supply of canned milk was gone and even the powdered was running dangerously low.

"Here you are my girl," he said. "It might taste a little different, but it's all that we have."

Sarah sucked noisily and when the feeding was finished, he somehow found new strength to trim and bind the logs.

When his work was finally complete, and he dragged the little raft to the water, it floated on the icy river like a cork and he saw that it was good.

Spent, he staggered toward his bed, Sarah on his arm. He held her close to his chest, feeding her the last of the milky mix. Her petal lips smacked as she tugged on the nipple.

Blackness washed over him and slowly receded.

He looked at Sarah's dear little face, her strangely knowing eyes.

Twelve Foot rises from a clump of birches beside his leafy dugout and Edward suddenly remembers Black Dan's promise the night they'd sat beside the campfire, how there would be food enough for everyone on the trip, how a bellyful of beans was better than gold.

Black Dan is right, although he is not hungry and hasn't been for three long days. But Sarah, without milk powder, without her sweet syrup.

Twelve Foot has never come before when Sarah is awake. Her eyes widen as Twelve Foot touches her dark silky hair with the tip of a finger and her lips curve in a smile and all day they sit listening to the wash of the Peace against the pebbled shore, and as the last rays of light disappear beneath the silver skin of the river, Twelve Foot reaches for the bough where Sarah's empty cradle hangs.

Edward stares as Twelve Foot glides to the moon-washed water and positions the cradleboard between the diagonal logs on the top of the raft, wedges it in so tightly that he will surely have trouble freeing it again.

When Twelve Foot takes Sarah from his arms, Edward touches his flaming leg, feels the poison coursing through his veins and suddenly knows what Twelve Foot has known all along.

"My Bible," he says to Twelve Foot. "In the footlocker. Send it with Sarah. Please."

"It's time," Twelve Foot says and he lifts Sarah from Edward's arms. "It's best if she begins her journey in the night, away from the heat of the sun. Under a scatter of stars. God really does keep a night watch."

Edward reaches for Sarah. His leg screams but he clamps his mouth shut. No need to alarm his little girl. "Please, . . . not yet. Maybe you could go find medicine berries, some special ones that the Dene use? To make a plaster and pull out the poison? Maybe if you looked further into the tree line you could find some and then you could help me and we wouldn't have to . . . "

"It's too late," Twelve Foot says. "Say your good-byes."

Edward kisses Sarah's forehead and both of her cheeks. He dips his thumb into the icy ripples at the edge of the Peace, makes the sign of the cross. "Godspeed, Sarah." And he thinks of Moses and hopes that the stories in the Bible are true.

Twelve Foot bends to push the raft into the silvered water, his hand only lightly holding the raft. "She may seem fragile, but this child will surely survive the trials of life. Sarah will live to a wise old age. Count on it my friend, for I feel it in my bones."

Edward is stricken. "Stop. She can't possibly . . . " He tears away the bandana that binds his wound. "Use this for a flag."

Twelve Foot ties the red bandanna to a sapling and wedges it securely onto the logs then slides the raft into the swiftly flowing water of the Peace.

Edward watched in the bathe of moonlight until the breadth of the river swallowed the tiny raft. He waved one final time, although Sarah was already gone from his sight. When he turned to bid his friend farewell, Twelve Foot was already gone.

He fingered the doeskin pouch, heavy with gold nuggets and his lucky marbles.

He'd thought to send it with Sarah, but what would a baby want with gold? He shook the nuggets into his hand. Without Sarah, with Isabelle gone, the gold didn't seem to matter. It was never really meant for him. With his thumb, he pushed the nuggets, one by one, into the sand. Not the black sand they'd come from, but close enough.

The nuggets could find their own way home.

As for the marbles, he couldn't see that they'd brought him one bit of luck. He withdrew first steelie, the smallest one, and let it drop into the river, then the larger one, cool to his burning hand. He tried to throw it far into the rushing river, but his strength failed him and it plunked into the water close to the shore. An eddy rushed over it and around and it was gone from his sight. Like Sarah.

He rolled his favourite, the purple-hearted, in the palm of his hand, then let his hand drift down. But his fingers wouldn't unfurl, and the marble was so deliciously cool. He dipped it in the water, put the glass to his parched lips.

A man has to keep something, some little trinket to mark his passage through this world.

He reached for the soft pouch, tucked his marble safely inside. Time to get back to his bed. He struggled to his feet, looked for Twelve Foot but saw nothing but the sharp shadows of the willows and the glow of the moon.

His leg crumpled and he sat down hard, fighting the urge to scream.

Then, with his muscled arms, he butt-dragged himself back to his makeshift shelter. Sometimes, he felt Twelve Foot's hands beneath his shoulders, helping to pull him along. Sometimes, he felt entirely alone. But as he collapsed on his bed of cedar, he felt someone draw the Hudson's Bay blanket securely around his shaking shoulders and gently tuck it in.

His body is bathed in sweat, and on his fragrant bed, he tosses and turns. He flings his hot hand and it comes to rest on the Bible. Damn Twelve Foot anyway, I told him to send it with Sarah. I've no need for it now, no need at all. But he tries to take the good book into his hands. It is so heavy and he falls back onto his bed.

He rests and then fumbles for his pen. He pulls the Bible to his belly, and on the last page, beneath the notice of her birth, he writes:

*Godspeed to my precious daughter, Sarah Louise Armson. May God watch over her and keep her from harm on her perilous journey down the Mighty Peace.*

He reaches into his pocket, lays the doeskin bag beside the Bible.

Even that small effort exhausts him.

In the corner of the shelter, red eyes, unblinking, glow at him until he realizes there is more. Again he grips the pen and writes with a wavering hand:

*Sarah's special mark is an arrowhead scar on her middle right toe.*

He begins his final entry.

*And to my son, Ward Armson, now mothered by Joan Spencer, sister-in-law in England, I leave my fatherly love and a sea of regrets.*

*My dying wish is that my children will come to know each other somewhere, sometime.*

*If this missile is ever found, contact Barton and Beverly, Solicitors, Brighton, England. Signed this day, September 23th, 1897. Edward Armson — on the shores of the Mighty Peace.*

Save Sarah, he prayed, not quite willing to put all of his faith in Twelve Foot's assurance of a Sarah living to a wise old age.

If the word of God were riding beside her as he had planned, she might have a better chance. He laid his shaking pen aside and closed the Bible, forgave Twelve Foot his failure of that final request.

We do our best, he thought. We all do our best.

A wolf with silver-tipped fur that shone a full-moon blue wove in and out of his dreams. He did not fear it when the wolf moved closer to his bed, stared with red-rimmed eyes. The wolf sat on his haunches, unblinking. His sleep was pure exhaustion and illness too, but somehow, as the moon moved on its milky path across the sky, he began to fidget, rise from the deeps of his sleep and feel the steady gaze. He rolled over, groaned, and gazed into the unmoving eyes. When he struggled to rise, the majestic animal turned and slid slowly into the night.

Edward pulled himself to standing and followed the glint of silver light.

The wolf wove his slinky shadow through stands of ghostly birch, stopping to wait whenever Edward fell too far behind.

In a small clearing lit by the moon, he turned, and looked back long and slow before he trotted silently through the grass and melted away.

Edward's body glowed with a banked fire. Shadows morphed, moved closer in the pale light of the moon, their movements as familiar to him as the beating of his heart.

"Isabelle," he cried. "Isabelle, it's me."

He fell to his knees.

"Oh Dear Lord Jesus, you've brought Annie too."

# TWO

17.

The Other Mother

My breasts will not stop weeping, weeping for my baby, weeping for me. On my bed of fresh-cut balsam, I turn my face from the light and pray for gentle death.

My husband seeks solace in the caribou hunt, the loud company of men and he tries to ease his grief with firewater and sweet-grass smoke. And at night, when he comes to our tipi, he is hungry, hungry for food, and hungry for me.

Please, I cannot. Not yet. Not so soon.

I do not want my body to conceive another, to bring my weakness again into the world. And so I sleep, and I sleep.

The tent flap is pulled aside, the light like needles in my eyes. Adahay, an ancient one who has brought me soup and achees and talked with me of my son, walks softly to my bed, kneels.

"Look," she says. She holds a languid baby, her tiny fingers splayed open, not fisted as a baby's should be. "Summer is waning and I fear you are too. This little one is hungry. Thirsty too. See, her hands are already pushing on the spirit wall."

And in the fading light this baby fixes me with her violet eyes. I touch the centre of her palm and the little fingers begin to curl around mine.

"You must help her." Adahay opens my buckskin wide, hands me the child. "And also, help yourself."

I stiffen, but the baby folds herself to my unyielding body. She smells my sweet milk and begins to make the small snuffle sounds, so like music. Her lips purse as she nuzzles, then she draws back and holds me again with her eyes.

Milk glazes my swollen nipples. As the baby fastens on I pull the fullness of my breast away from her face and she takes her first firm suck.

Snuffle, snuffle. Slurp. The beautiful sound fills my tipi, drumming in my ears and even in my heart.

∾∾∾∾

Yesterday the first leaves began to turn. The pale yellow flutter at the top of the birches will soon be a tide of ochre and orange rolling across the treetops, across the entire land. Departing birds peck the face of mother sky. Sometimes, they glide down to the silver strip of river to rest and feed, squabbling like children who've been waiting too long for their dinner. At night, a crisp coolness creeps in, nibbles at the blankets and pushes icy fingers under the edges of the soft skins piled upon my bed. The baby cuddles closer, seeking my warmth.

Her bright smiles push back the relentless river of tears I have swallowed down. Such unusual eyes, with their deep violet hue rimmed with charcoal. Where did she come from? Why has the Creator brought her to me?

Her eyes are dark, but her skin is a little pale. In the gathering twilight, she is the Daughter of Strangers held to my bosom, and for the first time in many moons, I am content. A sweet-grass smudge breathes my thanks up into the ear of the Creator. See my gratitude and be pleased.

"She eats too much," my husband complains. "Always at your breast. And she cries too much."

"She is a gift," I say.

Pray stay late around the campfire, become tangled in your endless tales.

But too soon his sinewed body slides beneath our pile of skins. When he clumsily seeks my warmth, he is doubtless thinking of our son, and his hunter's heart is sore. But I cannot talk to him of such things. There is nothing left to pour from the empty vessel of my body into his, no matter how great his need, so I reach for the Daughter of Strangers, hold her close, a shield between us.

I do not like the name that Adahay has given her. As she snuggles her face into the curve of my palm, she does not feel like a stranger to me. She is Newana.

The caribou have been circling, fidgeting, sensing the change of season even before the leaves on the trees. The males push at each other with their stubborn horns, old against young, father against son, brother against precious brother. The females watchful, their smaller antlers intended only to defend their newborns. But sometimes they too rush into the fray, perhaps to bolster a battling brother, shore-up a faltering son. Perhaps to take their own stand in choosing the strongest one, the leader who will take them south.

Hunting them is not so easy at this restless time of the year.

Mother Earth has a finite amount of energy that flows between her creatures, in intricate balance. Every birth brings a death, sometimes a small one, like a spent blossom falling from a flower, and sometimes a big one, like my little Kwahu. And for every death a balancing birth, perhaps the unfurling of a small green leaf, the blue egg cracking to free a downy bluebird.

Our great Mother remains a circle, like the moon. Each animal killed leaves a small hole in the spirit wall. But those holes will be filled by the souls of our people when they die. Were there no people dying, there would be no fledgling birds or see-through minnows who will grow surely into rainbow-sided fish.

I, too, once believed in the way those who have lost nothing believe.

At first, when they took my son from my arms and I refused to believe his spirit had fled, my man would say this to me, in our tent, at night, "Perhaps our son is now an eagle. Perhaps he is a magnificent fish."

I do not want my little son to be an eagle, for then Brother Wind will swoop beneath his wide wings and lift him higher and higher, until the world is a tiny, mottled ball far below, and he will be so high he will lose the sight of us and he will drift away. And he will soon forget.

And I do not want my little Kwahu to be a magnificent fish, sliding all day through rivers until he reaches the sea, for then a fisherman's net may fold around him and his struggles will exhaust him and he will soon lie on the floor of a boat, and his gills will open and close, open and close, as they sing a farewell song. My son must not be a fish, swimming beneath the shadow of my canoe as I listen to the song of my paddle, and do not hear the soft crying of my lost boy.

I want my son, here, in my arms.

We are hungry, for in our pots there is much broth, but few berries and very little meat. The last successful hunt, its nights of endless feasting, waves before me like a mirage. In the pot is only sand grating my fingertips, the curve of the empty vessel. My belly clenches and hunger reaches even into my dreams. Caribou bunch up on the top of the cliffs. Sniffing the breeze. Our young men rush up from the bushes, screaming, waving their arms. The caribou panic, pushing, shoving, until finally the buck in front bunches his back legs and leaps into the churning water. The rest follow, their tails and their backs breaking the surface, their antlers a velvet forest on the blue river. The caribou swim to the opposite shore, and surge upward, to the plain where our seasoned hunters lie in wait, their spears at the ready. Three, four, five, soon a dozen caribou lie on the ground, but still our men raise their weapons and move in for another kill. And another. Each warrior trying to outdo the other.

The death throes and the cries deafen me, and I hold my hands over my ears, squeeze my eyes shut.

The carcasses are piled high, their velvet racks entangled. The ground is red with blood, its copper smell strong on the breeze. The hunt is not a dream.

"Come now," Adahay says. "Come with me. There is much to do." Unsheathing her knife and kneeling beside a sightless caribou, Adahay says, "The Creator has answered our prayers. The glory goes to the hunter. The gut work to women's hands."

She chooses a small caribou, pulls his head toward her knife, runs the blade around the eye socket. Fluid squirts. With one quick flick of her wrist, she cuts the tendons that hold the eye secure and pops out the eyeball.

She gives it to her waiting grandson, who flips the eyeball quickly into his mouth, as if it is a smooth round peppermint from the Bay. Quickly he chews, liquid seeping from the corners of his mouth, then spits the skin of the eyeball, the now useless lens, into the dust.

"Please," he says, holding out his hand. "One more."

I feel so piercingly the loss of my son who will never savour a caribou eye after a hunt.

We women slit the caribou bellies and roll the carcasses onto their sides, the steaming entrails spilling into the dust. Then we cut the meat from the bones, slice it into slabs and hang it on racks. The odour of raw meat is heavy in our tents for nights on end. The fly-blackened meat looks charred, although it has not yet seen a fire. But the inside is tender, like grease when we cook it.

I own a well-honed knife. This knife on my throat would end my unending sadness and allow me to join my son on the other side of the spirit wall. I can slip through a hunter hole with my well of sadness, fill two holes, maybe three.

I too will be an eagle and I will fly with Kwahu, far above the caribou hunt, and we will be together again, mother and son to see those magnificent animals stampeding into the water, and swimming towards death.

Once, I was the best at scraping the skin, rasping the hairs so gently that the skin is unbroken, soft and smooth and ready for stretching across new drums or to sleep upon or to trade. My tools have lain idle for my son does not need warm skins. When these new skins are ready, I will take up this knife again. Soft covers for Newana, to keep her safe and warm.

When Newana stirs, I set the knife aside and offer her my breast. She latches on, her cries quieted by the milk.

"Shh, shh. Shh, shh."

The hunters sit around the fire, boasting, lusting after the spoils, waiting for the first taste of tongue, imbued with power. My husband is always the first to grab a piece and he says the taste is rich and sweet only for the chosen. If the gods have not favoured you, the meat will taste rancid. He says he is the chosen in his generation. He does not think of Kwahu then. And I do not care who eats the tongue, and who spits it out. Because my Kwahu is not here. And our next generation is already gone.

The tongue does not have powers for my man, for when he talks to me, his words are rough, like the grains that cling to the meat scraped from the pot at the end of the night.

Tomorrow we must leave. The trek south is hard, for the animals, for us, even for our hunters, and we are all loath to leave our summer home, to spend days on the trail with only pouches of achees to hold our hunger at bay.

Every evening, I steal away from our fires to the spot where my son lies beneath the spreading birch, covered by his blanket of soil, and I put my forehead to the cool brow of Mother Earth. Oh my lost baby, Kwahu, can you hear me? Kwahu, please, peek through the spirit wall, let me see your face.

But in the still clearing, there is only the whisper of the wind in the fluttering leaves.

When Newana wails from her cradleboard, which I have hung on a nearby branch, milk surges in my breasts. Oh Daughter of Strangers, I have named you in my heart. And she smiles and knows she is my daughter.

"Tomorrow," my husband says, is the first night of fullness. Sister Moon will light our way." And he tells me to pack our belongings, to make everything ready. In her cradle, propped in the sunshine by the tipi door, Newana hears his voice and begins to cry.

"That one," he says. "Will slow us down."

I shake my head and free her from the mossy cradle and hold her. She looks so wise, and I wish that I could read what is in her heart. "She is no trouble. No trouble at all. And when she is with me, I am not missing Kwahu so much. I am of more use, to the tribe, to the other children, to you. So you must let her stay."

His glance rakes Nuwana. She stops crying, becomes as still as a mouse who has spotted a circling hawk. He strides away, long angry strides and I know that he has put Kwahu away from his mind and his heart, as if his son had never been.

I breathe in Mother's face, her smell, cedar and pine and smoke, her fingertips. Once, twice, then one more time. Her milk keeps me from harm. She loves me.

A white man strides into our clearing, his eyes raking our camp. "Yo!" His voice is loud, hammers at my ears like the woodpecker that has taken up residence in the tallest aspen. This trader is heading north, and we south. Luck is not with us because our paths have crossed. When he notices Newana, he chucks her under the chin. "Fine bambino you've got there," he says. "Nice light skin."

This man makes me uneasy, so I take Newana into the forest when my husband offers him a plate of our stew and folds a hide so he can have a place to sit.

Smoke is a sweet ghost that follows Newana and me to the bluffs and I pick small pink flowers, tuck one behind Newana's ear and hold her close, and we walk and we walk through the autumn afternoon.

When we return, it is already dusk, the magic time. Silver moon-fingers caress the skin of my husband's neck as he tips back a squat-necked brown bottle passed to him from the trader-man's soft, white hands.

There will be no magic tonight.

"Thank you," he says. "Thank you, my dear friend."

My man has a pile of furs. He promised them to pay off our jawbone at the Hudson's Bay. Those men we know. They let us take flour, and sugar. Coffee and tea. Pay later they say, the jawbone will carry you until the hunt is done. And my husband is an honourable man. He counts and stacks his furs, those that we own and those that already belong to the Bay. And always, he pays.

I do not like his loud laughter and the smooth voice of the stranger. I am afraid. In the circle of my arms, Newana feels the speeding of my heart and she begins to whimper.

"Shh, shh. I am here. I am always here."

The Creator has forsaken me on the travois, too tired, too heartsick to even lift my head. At the front of our pitiful procession, my husband brags of his skill at making trades, how he managed to lighten our load.

"It was easy to see he was thirsty for the child," he says to everyone. "For his barren sister. He offered me much money, three fine woollen blankets, and three bottles of firewater. Some very fine fabric and buttons made of polished horn. These, look!" He motions behind him. "Soon she'll forget."

And a blossom of hot hate opens for that tall and handsome man who once was my life. Who will hold Newana now? How long will her small body remember mine? Not even her ghost tugs at my breast, holds me with its wide violet eyes. And the hate blossom in my chest opens wide.

Tethered by only a thread, my body lies on the travois and I am sad, so sad. Always I will seek the hole in the spirit wall, and feel the breeze from the other side where my Kwahu lives. But my love for Newana will always pull me back down. For she is out there, my daughter, somewhere in the world.

Our trek south has turned lucky, for today the men have found the spoor of a herd of caribou. I see them, the doomed, from my hiding place in a thicket of scrub brush on the brow of a hill. Grazing the simple lines of the earth and the sky, the blue-shadowed ridges, the sand and the water, they talk to me, tell me where I am.

I study the caribou, the land. Looking for some sign meant just for me so I can find a way to be in this world without my Kwahu and with Newana gone.

The caribou are restive, milling about, sniffing the wind, each distinct. Some of the animals are almost blond, others shades of browns and golds, some have patches of black. There is wildness in their eyes and snot swings in ropes from their noses.

You are right in your restlessness. You are right. The hunters are coming soon. My man in the lead. See him rise above the grasses, waving his arms? Turn back or plunge. Die or come out, alive, on the other side. Jump. Run while you can.

The never-ending circle. Hunger, then feasting, hunger, then feasting again. The stench burns my nostrils, embeds itself in my hair as I strip meat from bones, lay long strips on sapling racks. The heart, the kidney, the tongue, go into a pot of boiling water hung above the fire. The water hisses, the heart, heavy, plunges down. The moon crosses the sky.

When I pull the precious organs from the broth, I serve my husband, as a good woman should. Then the others.

They grab with greedy hands and stuff their mouths full, the juices running from their lips and dripping off their chins.

The children are next. Hungry and whining and tired. Ready for their beds. I serve them too. My eyes linger on the children. Their startling beauty. Their very presence in the world.

Finally, we women fill our bellies with the caribou and when we are finished, we scrape the pot, burnish it with sand, throw in Sister Water, swish it round and round.

"We have done our duty well," Adahay says. "The Great Mother will be pleased."

∾∾∾

In my bed, I am kept wakeful by the loud voices of our men that rise and fall, like birds on the wing, until my husband pulls back the flap of the tent, his shadow wavering on the walls. He walks silently, as he does when tracking prey. He pushes against my leg with his moccasined foot. "What kind of welcome is this for the great hunter whose skills have found the caribou at this terrible time of year?"

My body curves into itself. His foot finds my back, not a kick, just pressure, then more pressure, increasing as I curl like a leaf.

He prods, harder now. "You have been a dutiful wife. But there is more you need do than cooking and bringing my supper bowl."

"No," I whisper. "Not yet. Please."

Suddenly, he is on me, under the supple skins, tearing at my clothing, tearing at his own. He yanks my arm, flips me over onto his hardened body.

"Enough," he says. "Soon I will be a laughing-stock."

They need not know. They need not, except for your loud and boastful ways.

I am afraid of the flare of his nostrils, the flush of red on his cheekbones, the heat of his quickened breath.

His hands are rough on my waist. "Now. Right now."

So I move against his hardness, hating myself. Hating him.

Finally he grunts, tosses me aside. I lie like a stone.

187

"Three full moons passed since I was successful in killing the caribou." His loud voice drums into my ears. "And other successes too." His shadow wavers and grows on the skin of the tipi. "On the night of the last hunt, I made her a woman again. For she was in danger of becoming a ghost."

Loud laughter and then murmurs of approval rise above the crackle of the fire.

"I saved my seed," he says. "Saved it for many moons. For another son, strong and brave. Much stronger than the last."

I hear the guttural tones of the elders and the high-pitched admiration of the younger braves.

"Begun in the blood of the caribou," he boasts. "A great hunter my coming son is destined to be."

I hope this swelling will be a daughter. A daughter. For me.

Because a son will always leave. I have seen other mothers, silver-haired and wrinkled, longing for their sons. They say the mother who does her job well will surely lose her sons. But daughters will stay. They will be a comfort to their sick mothers, feed us when we are hungry, listen to our tales. They will wash our soiled sleeping skins and wipe sweat from our brow. They will lift aged heads, hold rich broth to shrunken lips.

I hold the curve of my belly. Talk to this blossom of a child. This is not your fault. Not your fault at all.

18.

Ellie and Samuel
Edmonton, Spring 1895

Ellie looked up from her soapsuds, saw Samuel walking
briskly up their lane. The clock in the hall had just struck
two.

She'd spent an extra half hour lingering over a pot of
Red Rose tea, watching the greedy nuthatches fighting in
the apple tree outside, thinking she had the entire day
stretching before her like a blank canvas. She dropped
her dishcloth. Samuel never came home early: it had not
happened once in the twelve years they'd been wed.

The Bay was decentralizing, sending men off to
isolated posts and out into the wilderness to oversee their
vast holdings, even selling off some of their land, but she
hadn't been worried. Samuel was a company man through
and through, and a dedicated worker. Surely they would
need his expertise here, at the big office, where he'd
been for years. But she wondered sometimes, if the Bay,
and Edmonton as well, had grown too big, too fast.

She opened the screen door, shoulders pinched
against her spine. "Samuel, whatever is wrong?"

"Nothing's wrong." He carefully set his briefcase inside
the kitchen door and his dust-covered shoes on the mat
near the door. "In fact, things are looking up for us, I'd
say. I've been offered a promotion."

Ellie clapped her hands, but before she could say a word, Samuel went on.

"But there's a catch. I'll have to do a fair amount of travelling. Most of it to Fort Saint John. The store up there's in big trouble. The jawbone account is way out of hand."

She only vaguely knew about the workings of the jawbone accounts. Samuel had once explained that it was a way of offering credit to the Natives and securing their loyalty to trading their next year's furs only at the Bay. It seemed to her that the jawbone account meant the Natives could never truly get ahead, that they would always owe no matter how good the hunt. She'd thought to ask Samuel if that was really fair, but she didn't want to get him started. He loved his job, he truly did, but sometimes he had a tendency to go on and on. She didn't really want to know every detail of the inner workings of the Hudson's Bay.

"You still have jawbone accounts?" she asked. "In this day and age?"

"Yep, we do. Can't get rid of the damn things because they're right there in the ledger, plain as the nose on my face. More than a few have gone unpaid for five or even ten years and some will never be recoverable."

"But the Natives," she said. "The way they live, barely getting by. How can they be expected to pay old debts? And interest on top of interest?"

Samuel reached for the blue mug, his favourite, and filled it with water.

"I can make some fresh coffee," Ellie said. "Just give me a minute to fire up the stove."

Samuel went on as if she hadn't spoken, as if he hadn't heard. "The prices Watson's paying for pelts lately doesn't make sense. My job will be to go up every couple of months to straighten out the whole mess. Thing is, I'll be gone a lot. More than two weeks in total. It's not only the work. There's the travel time."

Samuel poured himself a cup of old coffee, kept warm in the granite pot sitting on the reservoir of her shining stove. He sat at the kitchen table, pushing his heavy mug back and forth across the red and white squares of the new oilcloth.

"It's a long slow trek to Fort Saint John. Even when the weather is good. And of course, they want me to go on a regular basis. Weather be damned."

She took a tin from the cupboard above the stove and put three oatmeal cookies on a plate. Her hands were shaking slightly as she set the plate in front of him. She didn't fancy being home alone, not even for one night, let alone the weeks on end that Samuel was talking about.

"That coffee smells awful," she said. "I'll throw it away and we can start fresh."

Samuel took her hand. "The thing is, it's a huge opportunity. "It could change our lives. Might even be able to afford that big house you've been mooning over in the Eaton's catalogue."

She hadn't exactly been mooning over the two-story house with its wrap around veranda and its wide windows, but Samuel had seen where the catalogue opened, almost of its own accord, to pictures of the stately home and descriptions of what was included in the package, right down to the number of nails. Really, she kept telling herself, the house they had was perfect for them, with just the right amount of room. "I'm not sure I want our lives to change," she said, hearing the wail of the train as it approached the crossing.

The rails were new to Edmonton and so were the hordes of people that had arrived soon after the inaugural train. It seemed sometimes her whole world shook as the train pulled into town.

"It'll be a challenge, and God knows I've been more than a little bored just pouring over figures. But the thing I'm really worried about, is leaving you alone."

"I don't know. I guess I could . . . "

Samuel rose, walked to the window and stared into the yard. "It would be different if we had a child."

She folded into a chair as if he'd punched her. She knew full well that things would be different if they had a child, but after twelve barren years, she'd pushed that pain to the back of her mind. She and Samuel could be a family, just as they were. She thought they'd settled on that.

His uncharacteristic reference to their childless state shook her. It was a subject they'd come to avoid, because talking about it was like picking at a healing scab.

She quickly rose and filled the teakettle, clanging it against the edge of the stove as she set it down. "Here," she said, taking his cup and dumping its murky contents into the slop pail beneath the sink. "That stuff looks like pure molasses. And it smells even worse. Let's have ourselves a nice fresh cup and figure out how we can make this work."

The hardest part of building the new house was arranging for tradesmen. Edmonton was growing fast, with pell-mell construction going on everywhere, and no clear plan that Ellie could see. She didn't mind that Samuel had paid a little more for the large lot they'd both fallen in love with at the edge of town. The money was flowing in. The view of the river in the distance was what had sold her, and the fact that the train yards were far away at the other end of town. The wail of the train, filtered through blocks and blocks of new construction, sounded like lonesome music now. She didn't miss the rumble that shook their old home when the trains slowed down, not one little bit.

"Excuse me, Missus, sorry to bother." The stonemason was squatting near the hearth, the mud he'd loaded on his razor-sharp trowel as thick as his brogue. "Do you have a signature stone? Because if you do, the time to place it would be right about now. Or at least I should have it close. It's a bit like making a puzzle. You need the pieces near so your eye can figure it out while your hands are busy doing the grunt work. Lots of people don't see it, but really good stonemasons have to have an artistic eye."

She knew that some of her neighbours were adding such extras, etched with their names or the year, or even going so far as to name their houses. Hanson House was on their left and across the street, Breckenridge Hall.

For her hearth, she'd chosen golden Tyndall stone, with random layers of grainy grey and gold, and if you were lucky, fossils embedded helter-skelter. The rock had come by train all the way from Manitoba and she felt guilty sometimes for her extravagance. After all, there was plenty of rock available around Edmonton. It seemed the rocks grew in fields, so that every spring they had to be picked. But the Edmonton stones were nothing like the buttery colour of the Tyndall stone with its imprints of shells and leaves and who knows what all long-gone creatures.

When she found a fossil, she would trace its outline with her fingers, wondering how it had come to be encapsulated there. She loved the feel of them and she could imagine the creatures moving beneath her fingers. Time without end, right there in her living room.

"We don't have a signature stone," she said. "Samuel and I are more comfortable keeping things simple. Nothing fancy about the two of us."

She smiled, regarding Charlie, grey with dust, thickly muscled, short and squat. His hands were huge appendages not to scale with the rest of his compact body. An artist, is he? In that case, she was glad to have an artist on board. After all, the hearth is the heart of the home.

She had an urge to sit down with Charlie, tell him all about her husband and how hard he was working to pay for this dream house. Maybe ask him a bit about his own life. If he had a wife, a family. Where, exactly, did he live?

But instead, she took out her measuring tape and began to measure the windows flanking the fireplace. Stonemasons knew how to charge, and she'd found out last payday that they charged the same amount for talking as they did for laying their stones. If it was chatting she wanted, she could go to the shops downtown. She'd never been partial to shopping before, but the salesgirls were always willing to spend extra time with her. And she truly revelled in choosing sturdy yet lovely fabrics for her new furniture and warm and welcoming colours to paint her new home.

19.

Fort St. John
September 1897

Samuel eyed the pile of skins, hefted the made beaver in his left hand. He was to weigh the new skins against his perfect specimen and pay accordingly. The concept had seemed simple back at the office in Edmonton, but he hadn't been looking into two pair of hopeful eyes, hadn't imagined a scrawny girl peeking out from behind her father's leg to look longingly at peppermint sticks in a jar. Her eyes were dark, almost black. When he offered her a stick, she hesitated, questioning eyes on her father. When he nodded yes, she grabbed the stick, sucking it noisily as she darted back behind her father. He was troubled by her thinness, the dark circles beneath her eyes.

Now he understood the source of Watson's reputation as a so-called easy touch and he felt the first stirrings of real doubt. Maybe he was neither tough enough nor heartless enough to straighten out the mess the man had wrought in the outpost.

He drew a deep breath, opened his notebook and began.

That night, wrapped in his worn Hudson's Bay blanket, he tossed and turned. Things were not quite as straightforward here as he'd imagined. Exhausted from endless days on the trail, he closed his eyes and saw again the trusting gaze of the trader and his hungry child, and sleep did not come.

Samuel watched Watson pour the amber whiskey, eyeing up the levels. He accepted the smudged glass and lifted it to inhale the sweet scent.

"Now tell me," Watson said.

The lamp flickered and smoked, throwing dark shadows onto the mud-chinked walls. Samuel rose to adjust the wick, putting off the moment.

Watson's teeth gleamed pearl in the redness of his bushy beard, amusement flickering in his ocean-blue eyes. "Word was you were supposed to come up here and teach me how to be tough. Clean up the trading post," he said, raising his glass. "And now you've pulled off the God-damnedest trade I ever heard of. Worse than any I ever done."

"It wasn't a trade actually," Samuel began, but when the baby in the bunk behind him began to whimper, he turned to lift her into his arms and wrapped the blanket more snugly around her. He clumsily patted her small back, and she quieted, soft against his shoulder. He could smell her milky breath, and he was surprised to feel a flood of warmth in his chest. "I paid cash. But not much. T'was the whiskey that carried the day."

So he told Watson how he'd come across another trader, back-end of August, fellow called Nelson, along the Lesser Slave route, who'd recently bought a child from an Indian band leaving to follow the caribou. In the clearing, the man had started a small fire and unpacked his bedroll. Unbelievably, there had been a cradleboard swinging gently from a nearby aspen branch.

"Just look at her." The trader loosened the bindings of the cradleboard. "Don't know where she come from. Course the Dene won't give up any information, other than some river rat left the kid with them and they had to break camp before he returned. I figure they were feeding her for a price and didn't really want her along on their trek. Leastwise, Tall Man Sitting didn't. Can't say the same for his woman."

Samuel turned back the edge of the blanket, and the baby stared at him. She looked fine, her eyes bright, but he wondered about her chances.

"She's got a mark," the trader told him.

He showed Samuel the tiny silver arrowhead on her right middle toe. "Crazy old medicine woman mumbling about this child being marked long before she was born, in another world or some Goddamn hocus-pocus. Can't ever figure out what those Reds really believe. Chewing on something strange. Anyway, it looks like a plain old chop scar to me, although that makes not one lick of sense. Things happen up here that city folks wouldn't ever understand. Sometimes, you got to jettison whatever it is that's holding you back. Survival of the fittest, you know."

The man thrust out his hand. "Clyde Nelson. Seems I'm one of the fittest so far. Been working this territory for years."

Samuel took the man's rough hand. "Samuel," he said.

"Come and set a spell," Nelson said. "I know I'm about to. My feet are killing me. Shoulda' got an extra pair of moccasins from the Dene but they're getting too damn smart. Prices seem to go up like crazy this time of year."

Over the campfire, the trader said he had planned to leave the baby with the missionary sisters of St. Augustine over the hard winter months, and come back for her in the spring.

"How can you travel even one day with . . . ?" Samuel couldn't imagine travelling with a motherless baby in the bush.

"I been feeding her oatmeal mush mixed with water. Seems to work so far. But I think the Augustines are only one day away. I'll be rid of her soon. I mean for this one to end up with my sister in Ontario," he said. "She's barren as a rock and she's always wanted a kid. Figure she'll offer to pay, even if I don't ask. I did say once if I ever found a stray, I'd give it to her for free."

"Find a stray?" Samuel scratched his head, thoroughly perplexed. He'd never thought of finding a baby in the north. Gold maybe, certainly beaver pelts. But not a baby.

"Unless you know someone who wants a child?" said Nelson. "Might be easier to get rid of her right now than to bother with her again come spring. Meeting up as planned don't come so easy up here. All kinds of things can go wrong." The man's eyes grew smaller, and he wiped a dribble of whiskey from the deep cleft that divided his chin.

Samuel knew that Nelson had just opened negotiations. The trader's fire was hot. The birch logs were banked to burn long and slow and he made himself comfortable. When it came to trading, there were rituals to be observed.

It was an otherworldly night, the northern lights dancing across the sky, a green and blue curtain opening, closing, rising, falling. Changing colours, opening again.

Their music hummed in his head, or was it the whiskey? No use to worry, he could watch the northern lights for as long as they danced. Which wasn't usually long enough, gypsies that they are.

He started at a coyote's call from the rim of the valley. Another answered from closer to the clearing and he shivered, suddenly longing for Ellie, and home.

He rose and stretched, walked stiffly to his saddlebags hung in the crotch of a poplar tree and felt for his two remaining bottles of Seagram's with their unbroken seals.

"It's been a long night," he said, setting the bottles away from the dying fire. "And the old bones are stiffening up. Maybe another little nip would be in order just about now. And then I'd best be on my way." He poured with a generous hand for his host, and just a drop for himself.

"About the child," the trapper began, his voice hoarse and slightly slurred. "Of course, I'd like to keep her for my sister, but she's going to be a hindrance if I don't meet up with the Augustine sisters damned well soon."

"They're almost as nomadic as the Indians," Samuel said, his nerve ends suddenly tingling and oxygen flooding his tired brain. "Tracking them down this late in the year might be harder than finding the Mother Lode."

When he left an hour later, he was two hundred dollars and two bottles of whiskey lighter, but in his arms lay the child.

Watson grinned, waved expansively toward the baby sleeping in the bunk. "You're one hell of a trader, all right. Like to be a mouse in the corner when you explain this one to the brass."

Samuel leaned closer to Watson, laid his hand on the man's thick forearm. "No one can know the truth, no one but you and me. If you hear any talk, I'm counting on you to damp it down." He took a drink of warm whiskey, felt it burn the thickness of his throat. "If you can keep a secret about my doings up here, I'll do my damnedest to cover your sorry ass in head office when I get back home."

Watson tugged on his beard, his wide grin even whiter in the failing light. "I reckon it would be pretty hard to enter a trade for a baby on the Hudson's Bay ledger, or even the outright purchase of one. So you got yourself a deal. Let's drink to that. To the most amazing secrets," he said. "The secrets of the North."

The musical clink of their glasses caused the baby to stir and she began to cry, her voice high and amazingly loud.

Samuel shivered as he lifted her from the bunk, for the fire had burned low. I wonder, he thought, if she's feeling the cold. He opened his parka and tucked her inside, against the warmth of his body.

The baby opened her eyes and gazed at him, as if taking his measure. Violet eyes, rimmed with a colour that was very close to black.

"There, there," he murmured, patting her back.

She curled her delicate fingers into his collarbone. He wondered, then, if he'd really bought the baby for Ellie, for as she lay snug against him, he could hear the measured beat of his own heart and the answering heartbeat of the child.

He held her into the soft pink ribbon of the approaching dawn and felt the baby somehow become his own.

When he finally lay the baby down and crawled into the bunk beside her, he whispered a quick prayer of gratitude that the head office of the Hudson's Bay was miles and miles away.

## 20.

Edmonton
October 1897

Ellie stood at the top of the wide curving stair, admiring the wash of scarlets and blues the stained glass windows reflected onto the floor and the walls. Sometimes, she felt so happy she considered pinching herself to make sure she wasn't locked in a dream, but she didn't have that lovely, floaty feeling, not this morning.

She was tired from a restless night, full of dreams.

At first, when they moved to the new house, she would lie wakeful in her bed, hearing every creak, every snap of green lumber losing its moisture and settling into the bones of her home. But she'd grown to love the night sounds, and having the Hansons next door was comforting too. Belle Hanson was always home, and if she got lonely, she could run next door any time of the day. Belle was overburdened with the care of her six children, born in an eleven-year span, and helping hands were always welcome.

A tinkle of laughter wafted in the open window, followed by Old Mother Hubbard, recited at full volume, without a single mistake. At this early hour?

She went to the window. Little Marie Hanson was crouched on the veranda painstakingly drawing hopscotch squares. When she stopped, Ellie knew the knock would be coming soon. She'd gotten very quick at hopscotch, sandwiching a game between her household chores. It was hard to turn down the soft-spoken invitations, the hopeful look in the little girl's eye.

Not today, Marie, she whispered. I cannot bear it, not today.

The nursery, across the hall from the master bedroom in the Eaton's plan, had been changed to a room for guests, and she had decorated it in calming shades of green. But sometimes, she still imagined pink frilly curtains, and a white spindle-sided crib, painted teddy bears dancing in an uneven line across the walls and around the windows.

Smarten up, missy, she would tell herself. You are one lucky woman. You've a fine husband and more than most in this world.

And on those down days, she'd slip next door into the chaos at the Hanson's. After she'd spent an hour or two with Belle, folding the endless piles of laundry or sipping tea as they tried to talk around the noise of the children, she was glad to return to her quiet house, and the empty room upstairs seemed not quite so bad.

But last night she'd dreamed of a daughter, dark-haired, dark-eyed, like herself, and she'd woken with her pillow damp and her hair tangled and wild. For one lovely moment she'd felt the curl of five little fingers inside her own. In the light of the moon, she'd opened her empty palm.

She quickly lowered the open window, closing out Marie's laughter as the little girl hopped.

She pulled Samuel's letter from the pocket of her soft chenille housecoat and checked again the date of the postmark from Fort St. John. Her heart beat a little faster. He would be getting close to home. I'd better go to market today, she thought, and if Samuel arrives tonight, his favourite stew will be ready, and if not, I'll take out a bit for myself and deliver the rest next door. Belle would be so pleased.

"Ellie, Ellie, I'm home."

No excited cry from the backyard, no flinging open of the door.

"Damn the luck," Samuel muttered, for he couldn't wait to see the amazement on her face when he told her the child was theirs. He had been hoping to find Ellie sitting in the shade of the wide veranda, sipping her afternoon tea. "I guess it's just you and me," he told the baby. "For the moment, at least."

So with the baby cradled in his arm, he opened the wide oak door and stood for a moment in awe at the miracle Ellie had wrought in the two months he'd been gone. Longer, he knew, than he'd ever been gone before.

"We're home," he told the baby, angling his arm higher so she too could look around. "You can rest now, little one. You're really, finally, home."

Soft sunlight gleamed on the oaken floor and he rested his hand on the carved newel post at the bottom of the stair, waiting for his eyes to adjust. The baby began to howl and he looked into her wide eyes.

"Nothing for you to be complaining about," he said. "By the looks of it, this is about as fine a home as anyone could want."

She quieted then, and looked around, as if she knew exactly what he'd meant, and later he would swear that she nodded, as if she couldn't agree more.

Lily's homecoming became a story that Samuel loved to tell. The look on Ellie's face when she'd opened the door to find him holding the baby and his hurried explanation, his words tumbling like a swollen mountain stream.

How Ellie, with the true instinct of a first-time mother, had undressed the child and checked every part of her and marvelled, had run her finger over the little scar on the baby's middle right toe. "Look," holding the chubby little foot and stroking the toe, "look. Isn't that precious? She's ours," she kept repeating. "She's really ours?"

In the beginning Ellie often slipped from their bed in the night and he would find her sitting in the rocker beside the spindled crib, watching Lily sleep. He would stand behind her, his hand on her shoulder, keeping watch too.

They would watch the little chest rising, falling, rising again, listen to the soft snuffle of her breathing, until finally he would feel the cold seeping into the soles of his feet.

"Come to bed," he'd say, "she'll be here in the morning. I promise she will."

## 21.

### Samuel

I was once a good man. I know that I was. But one freezing northern night, when the sky above me was black, the stars bright pinpricks of light, I gave up the right to think of myself as good.

There were no shimmering northern lights that night, just the immense sky and the sweet smell of wood smoke in the air. The mind plays tricks and sometimes I almost believe that nothing important happened. I have only a vague recall, like when you can barely see the white of the aspens through a skin-soaking rain. Everything is fuzzy at the edges, nothing defined. In truth, I do not know what, if anything, I have done.

It was one of my longest trips, when I was bone-weary and lonesome for home. Watson was too tired for a rubber in our usual round of crib, too tired to stay for more than one small glass of whiskey. He drained his glass, set it beside the abandoned crib board and said good night. If only I had followed him. If only. But down the hill, where the Natives gathered after a day of hard trading, I heard revelry and people laughing and music wafting, fiddles and the muffled beating of drums. And I was wide-awake. I knew I would not sleep for hours and hours.

Trading stirs me up, my mind running in a maze, who to worry about most? the Bay or the trappers? Are there any real winners or losers in the beaver trade? Where, in my heart, did my loyalties truly lie?

We are forbidden to fraternize with the Natives, those of us who work for the Bay. I understand this rule for those who live in this place. But I am an itinerant traveller and these people have been nothing but friendly and welcoming to me.

The drums drummed again, the sound rising and falling and then reaching a crescendo. I could see bare-chested men dancing near the fading fire. The flames burned low, the coals a steady enticing glow. So I decided to join them and to hell with the Bay and their rules. I walked slowly down the hill, for it was dark and the path steep and studded with stones.

And I live with the persistent memory of that night, of the fine welcome the Natives gave me, of dancing, and chanting and singing, squatty brown bottles passed unceasingly from hand to hand.

How a young woman in beads and buckskin shyly asked me to dance when the fiddle finally slowed and crooned a sorrowful tune. How I held her body lightly against my own. The smell of her hair like newly fallen rain, and wood-smoke and something earthy too. How she finally took both of my hands, led me outside the circle of yellow light. I stumbled on the path, uneven in the endless night. But then the moon showed itself from behind a clump of willows, huge and red, bright, like a lantern.

"Wolf Moon," she said. "Magic moon. Only for tonight."

She stepped into a stand of sturdy poplars, and I followed her through their substantial shadows. We came to a small tipi in a clearing; she motioned me to follow, and disappeared inside.

I remember how I held her, and how she wrapped herself around me so tightly, like a fragrant twining vine.

I do not know when I fell asleep, holding that delicate nut-brown woman close to my chest, but I slept the sleep of the dead. In the morning, when the tent began to lighten, I woke and wondered where I was. I looked down at the face tucked beneath my chin, and it wasn't the face of my wife. I rose like a ghost, ran my thumb across her amazing cheekbones lightly, and I slipped away.

Confession helps the sinner, but not the one sinned against and there is nothing I can think of to tell Ellie about that night. My fears of what I have actually done or not done, my regret either way? So I hold my peace. And I have become so careful, alone in my study at the end of the day, that I pour only one glass of whiskey. I take a sip, set it away, almost out of my reach, so I must make a definite decision to take another drink. My whiskey bottle lasts so much longer these days. Sometimes, the urge to pour a good stiff drink and throw it back in one long draught is strong. I remember. Or do I? I will never be entirely sure.

When I am idle at the office, the memory of that magical night comes to me. I feel again the frost on the grass as we walked close together, smell the sweet smoke of the birch fire, our shoulders touching.

The smooth sheen of her skin in the bright Wolf Moon, the deep shadows of her eyes. Eyes that never left my face. Not once.

22.

Blessing

Ellie noticed immediately that she and the baby had the same toffee-coloured skin, the same dark hair. She thanked her Slavik ancestry for the gold of her own skin, but the source of her nearly black hair was a mystery. In the line of ancestors in their ornate oval frames, she was the lone dark-haired child. Some wild black Scotsman whose boat had gone astray was her guess, but who would ever know?

"We look more alike than lots of blood kin do. No one knows the truth. Except for Belle, of course."

"I'm not sure we know the truth either," Samuel said.

"Is there any way you could find out?"

Samuel snapped the lid of his silver cigarette case, chose a fat roll-your-own. He rasped a match across the sole of his shoe and lit up. He rarely smoked, and when he did, she usually protested. But she wouldn't tonight.

"There's one old trapper up there who's said to know every story there is to be told. But he's only found when he wants to be."

She picked up the daily paper, creased it across her thigh. "If you could just find out where she came from, who her people might be . . . "

"Didn't know you'd be so intent on details," Samuel said. "I figured Lily would be enough."

Smoke curled and drifted in the yellow lamplight. "Damn. Now you're wanting information even I don't have."

"Samuel, you know it's not for me."

"I know, I know. And I guess as long as Watson's up there, I can ask him to keep his ears open. But sometimes no news is good news, you know."

"We don't necessarily have to tell Lily anything. But it would be nice if we knew."

She rose to close the curtains, shutting out the dark, and the scent of the almond soap she'd used to wash Lily's hair rose sweet from the palms of her hands. She leaned against the window frame, moving her lips silently.

Samuel looked up from his paper. "What are you doing now? Talking to yourself?"

"Counting my blessings," she said as she came back into the light and took up her cross-stitch. "Maybe you're right. Let sleeping dogs lie."

The day started out still and hot, and then got hotter still. Ellie sat with Belle in the shade, shelling peas that had been wilting on the vine. Picking them, even in the early morning, had been a trial, but with two pair of willing hands, the three rows in Belle's garden were soon bare.

The babies were stripped down to their diapers, gurgling on a blanket at their mothers' feet.

"Iced tea?" Belle asked. "I have a jug inside, although by now it might not be really iced. But at least it'll be wet."

Ellie popped a handful of peas into her mouth. When Lily began to fuss she got up to check the diaper, but all was well. She moved a rattle to her daughter's hand, watched as she tried to grab it with a chubby fist.

She took her glass of not-quite-iced tea, took a long sip and sighed. Belle sat beside her, the children seemingly engrossed with catching the shadows of the fluttering poplars.

Ellie drew a deep breath, and twisted her napkin in her hand. "Did you ever feel a distance between George and yourself when the first baby came? Like something had changed?"

Belle turned, her brow furrowed. "Honestly, I really can't remember. We've had babies almost all of our married life. And I am so busy, I really don't have time to think about the two us."

Ellie put her two fingertips to her lips. "Of course," she said. "How silly of me."

She and Belle often cooked together, and did chores together, like mending and canning and shelling peas. They had tea together, in companionable chit-chat, but they seldom shared secrets of the heart. Their friendship was close, but not deep.

She knew better than to share her feelings with Belle, but worry had loosened her tongue. She was plagued by questions, like how often did Samuel really have to leave? Did he volunteer for trips even when he didn't need to? Sometimes she felt a piece of him had gone missing, like he'd left it behind, somewhere up there. In the north, a place she knew full well he truly loved. Her doubts slid into bed beside her in the night, when he was gone, the worse time of all to think bad thoughts. In the darkness, she would count off on her fingers. Blessings. One, she had a lovely home, thanks to Samuel; two, a beautiful

211

little girl; three, Samuel had always, always, been such a good man.

The screen door banged. It was George, home early for lunch.

"What are you two doing working out here in the heat of the day?" He stepped past Belle and scooped little Ian from the blanket, held him close to his bony chest. "You all best come inside now. We don't want these babies getting too much sun."

Ellie lifted Lily onto her hip, folded the crazy quilt blanket.

"Thanks, " she said. "But it's way past time for me to go home."

23.

Other than the Hansons next door, most of the people living in the big houses at the edge of town didn't have children, so Lily's companions were Marie and Alda Hanson and Ellie and Samuel until the year she turned six.

But once she started school, their house was almost always filled with groups of giggling girls. Ellie revelled in the hubbub, the sweaters thrown on the highboy in the front hall, the boots kicked off near the door. She loved baking cookies and cupcakes and making hot chocolate for the girls and was not in the least bothered by the endless trail of cookie crumbs that led from the kitchen to Lily's room.

She stood in her sunny kitchen, a blue-checked dish towel limp in her hand. The notes of a perfect piano solo drifted down the wainscoted hall from the front parlour. How did she do it? Even with sporadic bouts of practising, Lily's delicate fingers danced across the ivories as if she'd been playing forever. Amazing.

"How lucky," she whispered. "How lucky are we?"

She turned to her counter, rolled flaky pastry paper-thin and cut it with the rim of a crystal wine glass. She moulded the pastry to blackened tart tins, and filled the delicate shells with brown sugar and butter, creamed, to which she'd added two beaten eggs. A dollop of white corn syrup and a half cup of chopped walnuts stirred until the mixture felt right and clung to her wooden spoon in a satisfactory way. She scooped a finger full, its sweetness sending a quick shiver down her spine. Butter tarts were one of her specialties. Lily and Samuel's favourite.

On sunny Sundays, when they took Lily to the river, Samuel often packed a tin pail full of these flaky tarts. He would sit on their striped Hudson Bay blanket, watching Lily from the slope of the river bank as he nibbled pastry and absent-mindedly drank coffee from a sealer she had carefully filled and wrapped in an old wool sock.

But Ellie stood on guard at the shore, her bare feet tucked into the cooling mud, her eyes on Lily swimming just out of reach.

Lily loved to swim, and Ellie wondered if perhaps she had been born on a boat or beside a body of water. Had the insistent sound of waves lulled her to sleep? Or perhaps she remembered the months she'd floated in her mother's womb.

Lily dived and disappeared cleanly into the wide silver of the river.

Ellie held her own breath, watching, waiting, and when Lily finally reappeared, waving wildly and grinning, Ellie waved back.

"Lily. Come ashore. It's time to go."

Samuel folded his paper. "So soon? It's a beautiful day."

"Not really," she said, breathing slowly, drawing oxygen into her bursting lungs. "I believe I've taken a chill."

Samuel began to fold the picnic blanket and Ellie joined him; side to side, then end to end. When their fingers touched, she felt her freezing fingers warm in his.

Ellie took the paper and tacked it to the wall above the table. "It's lovely," she told her daughter.

After sliding a pan of cookies into the waiting oven, she stopped to study Lily's picture. Each petal was a different colour, but at least all of the stems were coloured the same shade of green. At the bottom of the paper, peeking out from behind the green stems, Lily had drawn a tiny stick-girl, with big blue tears flowing from her eyes. A small tent hid near the bottom corner of the page.

"Who's this?" she asked.

Lily stood close to her hip, touched the crayon girl with her forefinger. She ran her tongue across her lower lip. "It's me," she said. "In the forest. I've been there before but this time I got kind of lost."

Ellie sat down, pulled Lily onto her lap. "In the forest? Alone? I don't think so, my darling."

Lily raised her hand, caressed the side of Ellie's face. "Someone found me, don't worry. And I have been in the forest alone, Mama," she said. "Before. And tipis are very nice places to sleep. Cozy as could be."

Ellie looked again at the stick-girl and saw that beneath her brown legs, on the right foot, Lily had added a tiny slash of white.

"Really," she murmured. "Sometimes your stories amaze me. But I do think you have a special talent. It's a lovely picture you've made." She kissed Lily's scented forehead. "Mmm, you smell extra good tonight."

"I know," Lily said, and Ellie smiled.

"Night, Mom."

The moon shone through the bay window, bathing the room in light. Lily was afraid of the dark and Ellie was glad for the brightness of the moon. Sometimes, she had to spend an entire night lying beside her daughter to settle her.

"She's already asleep," Ellie said, and took up her cross-stitch from the chair beside Samuel. "I thought it might take longer."

"Trouble?"

She sat in her petit-point rocker and closed her eyes for a moment. Then she leaned over to turn on the new radio just in case Lily was awake and listening through the ceiling grate from her room above.

Sometimes, she would find her wrapped in a blanket, asleep beside the grate, and she wondered at her daughter's compulsion to eavesdrop, as if she didn't quite trust that Ellie and Samuel had told her all that they knew.

Lily's origins were not a secret exactly but no one's business but their own. They had made it perfectly clear from the beginning.

"Today she told me she has been in the forest alone. Lots of times, and that she likes to sleep in tipis. When she talks about before, I don't know what to say. If I even had an idea or . . . I don't know, just something I could . . . maybe she was cared for by nuns or neighbours or . . . ?"

Samuel smiled. "Well, she's got a great imagination, that's for sure," he said. "And I know she's got more sense than to go spouting off about such things when she's in school. Could bring herself a bit of trouble I would think."

Ellie didn't want to think of trouble, for any of them. She closed her book. "I think I'll turn in early tonight," she said. "Today was kind of taxing for me."

Samuel nodded.

He seemed so tired lately, and it occurred to her that they hadn't spent much time together of late. For when he came home from his trips, his friends and co-workers were always around, anxious to hear his tales. And when they finally left, Lily clung to him, like a burr.

She was glad for that.

Samuel continued to read, engrossed in the *Edmonton Journal.* He didn't get up, kiss her cheek or give her one of his famous bear hugs. Once more she felt the curtain drop between the two of them, something she had often felt lately.

She folded her clothes neatly on the deacon's bench at the end of their bed, and donned her white-dotted Swiss nightgown, so soft and so fine.

When she sometimes caught sight of herself and Lily in the mirror as she braided her daughter's hair, she was glad for the darkness of her own.


Sometimes he wished for quiet at the end of day. He never complained, but he did sometimes get up and close the door of his study to shut out the noise of his daughter and his wife.

A man should be able to read his paper in peace.

Engrossed in his paper, he would look up to see Lily standing just inside the door, fingering the spine of a book or holding a paper she'd brought home from school.

She was attuned to his moods, connected to him somehow. She would be absolutely silent until he put the paper down and raised his eyes. Then she would come to perch on the edge of his desk, or in earlier days, on his knee, as they'd talk about all the things that mattered to her.

Like how the Hanson girls were so much fun and how she wished for a sister of her own, how difficult her math assignment was and how she needed his help for just a while, how she longed to learn to skate someday soon, how Dianna Collins had left her out of a game of hopscotch at noon for two days running and wasn't that a poor thing for a best friend to do and maybe she should find a new best friend. How she loved to play the piano and could she get some new sheet music on Saturday and how she was thinking now of trying the fiddle.

## 24.

### Lily and Samuel and Ellie

Lily was at the kitchen table, piles of buttons in front of her, six buttons per pile. "What's this?" he asked. "Taking up sewing? Making a button necklace? Or . . . ?

"Papa, I am doing math. My six-times table. I'm trying to see."

"To see what? Math is memorization. I'll make some flash cards and we'll work on the tables. Then it will come easy."

Lily reached out, moved two piles of six buttons. She studied the arrangement, which looked willy-nilly.

She moved one more pile. "Six times nine is fifty-four."

"Yes," he said, "it is. But how did you . . . ?"

"The pattern," she said, pointing to the piles of buttons.

"Really?" He couldn't see the pattern but Lily could, and she was only eight years old.

One night, she'd taken his hand, opened the screen door and pulled him outside. Northern lights flickered across the sky, gorgeous greens and pale yellows, scarlet and pink and purple blues reflecting in her wide eyes.

"Just look, Papa. They are so, so beautiful. I remember sleeping beneath them before, lots of times, so close that

219

I could reach out and touch them with my hand. Well maybe not touch them, really, but I've heard them sing."

He reached for her hand. "Really? Are you sure? I've heard of that, but in all of my travels, I can honestly say I've never heard them sing. Not even way up north."

"It was a long time ago. You know, before."

"Before what?"

"Before here."

The lights shifted and changed. He stayed still, waiting for Lily's reply. When does memory begin? And when does it end?

"You come up with the strangest of notions, Lily. And as far as sleeping outside, you know how Mama is about the very idea."

"Please, Papa, can you convince her? I think the northern lights are lonesome."

He sighed. "I don't suppose the northern lights get lonesome. You'd best not mention this notion to Mama."

She pulled her hand from his.

"But why?" Her eyes were dark, full now of shifting shadows.

"You never know. She might get upset. And I would like to keep our Sunday peaceful. What do you say we get inside, see if we can find a butter tart or two?"

Lily was easily distracted by the very idea of sweets. Butter tarts were her and her papa's favourite. Just one more way he felt they were the same.

"Okay." She blew a kiss to the lights. "Bye. See you again. One of these nights I'll be out here long enough to hear you sing."

She was a determined little thing, you could say that. Only one week later, she was out there again, flat on her back in the backyard.

He remembered flopping down on the grass years and years ago, when he was a child. And watching the stars. So he let the screen door bang and went to Lily, eased himself down.

"Aren't they pretty?"

He didn't answer, so awed was he by the vast sky. Why did adults forget to lie in the grass and really see?

"The lights are keeping watch."

"You think so?"

Lily's teeth flashed white in the darkness as her lips curved into a smile. "I know they are."

Wouldn't that be a comfort? To her and to me. To some poor trapper out in the bush. To Ellie. "I'll bet your mama wonders where we've disappeared to."

Her hand was on his arm. "Papa, can I sleep outside tonight? Please?"

"It's cool these nights. More like cold I'd say. Seems to me your bedroom is the sensible place to be."

"But it's all set up. Tonight they promised to sing."

"It's late, Lily. So I guess that's one concert you're just going to have to miss."

"But Papa, they said that tonight . . . "

The lights flickered.

"The northern lights don't talk to little girls," he said. "But fathers do. And what this father says is its time to go inside."

He took her small hand and pulled her up. He led her toward the square of yellow glow that gilded the wooden steps and the railing and lighted a little patch of the yard.

She and Papa were both pulling hard on the toboggan. The tree seemed perfect while it was standing at the edge of the ravine, but felled, it was too long for the toboggan and very heavy and so its narrow end hung off the back and dragging it through the snow was hard and they still had a ways to go. All uphill!

She hoped they wouldn't break the tip of the beautiful tree, for that was why she chose it. She could see an angel with sparkling wings perched on top, plain as could be.

They'd have a time getting that big tree in the front door, that was for sure.

They did it! The tree was in the stand and Mama had secured the holders for the little candles they would light on Christmas Eve. She put the candles on herself and chose the red ones because she really loved red.

The tree was now sparkly with silver balls. And wrapped with a white garland made from popcorn. It took forever to make. Two perfectly popped kernels for the garland and then two each for the stringers. She and Mama were groaning with bellies full of popcorn before they were done.

"Mama, please hurry."

Ellie was in the kitchen, already starting Christmas dinner. But when she came into the living room she was carrying hot chocolate in two steaming blue mugs. Marshmallows floated on top. Lily reached for her cup, took a careful sip. Papa laughed at her chocolate moustache and then made one of his own.

She got everything. A soft red scarf with mittens to match, a silver locket with curling cursive on the front.

Lily it said. Inside, a place to tuck a picture. She would have to find one to cut out, to make it fit inside that delicate heart.

New winter boots and some soft flannel pyjamas with white snowmen dancing around on a red background. Art pencils and a new sketch pad. Oranges and candy canes.

"Your turn," Mama said and she handed a large package to Papa. It had snowflakes on the darkest blue background and was tied with a silver ribbon.

"This is too pretty to open," Papa said. And he waited some, just holding the gift.

"Come on Papa, open it, please."

Slowly he peeled back the paper, careful not to rip it. He folded the paper and set it aside. Finally, he opened the box.

"Please hurry, Papa!"

When Papa went to the office he always wore dress shirts, mostly white but sometimes a pale blue. She loved the smell in the kitchen when Mama was ironing his shirts. It was like summer sunshine and flowers in bloom, and maybe a little of Papa's essence too.

He lifted a soft flannel shirt, black and red plaid. He took off his morning robe and put the shirt on. "It's beautiful, Ellie," he said. "Although my pyjama bottoms don't do it any justice at all."

A window opens before me. I can look through it, through the very walls of our living room and into another room somewhere. There is a tall slim man there, and a woman too. He is hanging his red and black plaid shirt on a hook by the door, and he walks past two chairs, one red and one yellow. He walks to the rumpled bed in the corner, kisses the woman and touches her hair. He looks into the cradle close by her side and he smiles.

Then a black dizziness washes over me and the window is closed.

"What do you think Papa?" Lily burst through the door, pirouetted for his inspection.

Her mother had bought her another new dress that she didn't really need. They spoilt her, really, they did.

"Mmm, very nice."

"Nice? That's it? I only look nice after all the time we spent primping?"

"Primping for what?"

"It's the Autumn Equinox dance tonight and I'm running for Harvest Queen."

"Right. I sort of forgot. And actually, you do look better than nice."

He took her hand, pulled her closer to the light. "But I think if you wash some of that rouge off, your real beauty could shine through."

"Oh Dad, you're so old fashioned." She kissed the top of his head. "It makes you kind of cute sometimes."

"Hummph."

Lily's frequent forays into his study had slowed imperceptibly over the years; at first, he barely noticed. So quickly she'd gone on to the upper grades and found good friends to turn to. Who needed a chat with dear old dad when you had Katie and Elizabeth or whoever else might be inner circle just now.

He felt hollow sitting here alone. Perfect peace at last.

It felt nothing like the way he'd thought it would.

Of course he knew that children had to grow up and away, at least they should, if you'd done your parenting well. But he was surprised at how much he missed her. He thought mothers had a corner on that. It seemed that the gift of Lily had only just come into their lives, but when he counted the years since the day he'd brought her home, he knew he was dead wrong.

The lampshade was working its way loose again. He adjusted it again. For the second time this night. He was not sure why Ellie had bought him a banker's light, as he was not nor had he ever been a banker.

But he did love the soft green light pooling on the oak, the puddle of brightness holding the darkness at bay. He pulled the paper closer.

Why, suddenly, does the writing seem so small? It seems his arms are not quite long enough.

A little too much time on fussing and primping and of course, the prime seats were gone.

Still, it wasn't hard to find Lily in the crowd of graduates.

Lily was the tallest girl in her class and the most beautiful, although he would never say it aloud. He checked the program again, anxious for the speeches by the principal and the chairman of the board to be over and for Lily's toast to the parents to begin.

Good God, was that Sheila in the front row and Miriam too? Had they not been in his house just last week, learning to bake chocolate chip cookies in Ellie's Eaton's catalogue kitchen? Sliding down the bannister and landing with a thud? Screaming with laughter?

225

And now they were wearing make-up and high heels too.

How has it happened? Where have I been?

Early on, he'd protested Lily's easy life, the fact that Ellie did everything for her. But she'd dug in her heels, uncharacteristically stubborn.

"Maybe she started out hard, for all that we know," is what Ellie had said, "and now that she's ours, I am going to make sure the rest is easy."

"Easy isn't always best."

"I am the mother here," Ellie told him. "And mothers know."

Loud clapping. Surely he hadn't nodded off? On such an important night. He leaned forward, and admired Lily's easy grace as she walked to centre stage.

Ellie was leaning forward too, so he took her hand, gave it a little squeeze.

"She'll do fine. Lord knows, she's taken over my study almost completely for this entire week. Gone over her words with a fine-toothed comb."

*Dearest Parents, as graduates, and as incredibly lucky people with our futures before us, we cannot begin to thank you for always being here to support us, for answering our questions and for all that you have done.*

Oh Lily, what questions did I answer? How do you pick the perfect stone? How do you make it skip? Can you find Orion for me? Can we go to the beach today, please? Can I sleep outside? Have you ever heard the northern lights sing? Wasn't it only yesterday I brought you home, and stood at the bottom of the stairs, listening to the howl you'd begun almost the moment I stepped inside the door?

∾∾∾

Ellie was sniffing beside him and she pulled her hand from his, dabbed daintily at her glistening eyes. He fumbled for the silk hankie Lily had tucked into his vest pocket as they were leaving the house. Really, it was too fine to use.

But come washday, Ellie would put it right. She had a real knack for that.

He handed her his new hankie and patted her shaking shoulders as the music of Lily's voice rose and fell.

## 25.

### Lily

What is memory and what is a dream? Do I remember a cozy cabin, flour-sack curtains lifting in the breeze?

Do I remember the feel of fresh moss against my skin? The sparkling yellow eyes of a silver-tipped wolf?

A nut-brown woman holding me?

Always, I am rushing, rushing, rushing along with my heart beating hard.

Even if Mama leaves a lamp lit in the hall, even when she tucks me in and tells me all is well, the dream is waiting. Fear is waiting.

It makes no sense, for I love swimming, being in the river, being caressed by the cool and deep water.

But I am afraid of being on top of the water. So afraid that I have never even been inside a canoe, although Papa has tried to convince me many a Sunday. It's fun. We'll rent a red one. Or any colour you pick. You'll love it. I know you will.

No.

Please. It will be lots of fun.

No. I cannot bear the rushing sound.


"Mama!"

She comes then and sits on the bed. "There, there. Don't be frightened. It's only a dream."

"Mama, it is real. I remember. Really, I do.

I remember.

I can see the reflection of my face in the glossy patent of my brand new shoes. Mama got them at the Bay. For turning six. I knew she would get me these shoes when she noticed me admiring them in the window. So I have to be careful with Mama. She would get me everything!

The piece I will play tonight is already inside my head, but the notes are on this sheaf of papers. A complicated piece. I want to play it perfectly, and I know that I can.

Mama and Papa are in the front row. They have clapped politely for Delores and for Miriam, but they really are here only for me. Papa is leaning back, his arm along the back of Mama's chair and his eyes wander around the room. But Mama is leaning forward, her hands clasped.

My eyes glaze for a moment and I see her lick her lips twice and then take out a silver tube and apply a layer of pink perfectly inside the line of her lips. She does this without a mirror, which seems an amazing feat.

And then, of course, I know that what I've seen isn't real at all. For my mama uses only a home-made concoction on her face at night and that is the only beauty thing I have ever seen her do. My mama says if you want red lips you can eat some cherries. I think my mama is beautiful just the way she is, even in the morning. She always looks good to me.

As I watch, she lifts her right hand and carefully pats down her curls before straightening the errant pleats of her cornflower dress. Her cheeks are a little more rosy than usual and if I were sitting beside her, I know I'd hear the shortness of her breathing and maybe a whispered prayer. She is nervous for me. I know this because my mother does not ordinarily fidget and fuss.

Mrs. Klemke introduces me and I glide across the polished floor, lower the seat of the piano stool three turns so my feet can reach the pedals, set my sheet music on the rest, and position my fingers. One deep breath, and I am sure my mother takes one too. When I strike the first notes, everything falls away and it is just the music.

The swell of applause comes from miles away. I twirl the piano stool toward the audience and am bathed by my mother's luminous smile. Papa looks happy too, although there is no tinge of relief in his smile for I know he never had a single doubt. He believes I can do anything I set my mind to doing. He's told me so.

My classmates are whispering, but as I draw near, they fall suddenly silent. Tears prickle my eyelids as I keep on walking, past my so-called friends. Everything was fine when I left school on Friday. What has happened? What?

The last bell has rung and I catch Miriam in the porch as she is pulling on her red rubber boots. The newest thing and a springtime special at the Bay.

Out the small portal window, little boys are stomping through muddy puddles on their way to the gate, the water splashing up onto their pants and the hems of their jackets. I would like to stomp too, but I am too grown up now.

"Miriam. Everyone is talking about me."

"Don't be silly."

"They are, I know it."

"If they really are talking, it might be something good."

She smiles as she pulls a scarf over her carrot-red hair and tucks the ends into the collar of her coat. She opens the door and steps outside and a curtain of rain quickly obliterates her. I wipe at the clouded glass and peer harder but my friend has disappeared.

Another day of whispers and sudden silences. What have I done? This morning I couldn't eat and last night, although Mama sat on the edge of my bed and patted my back, like she used to when I was little and the terrors came, I could not sleep.

Go to bed, Mama. I'll be just fine.

I am not fine. I keep my eyes down, do not approach those whispering girls. I avoid Miriam. But when she slides onto the bench beside me at lunchtime, I am so grateful.

"I can't stand it anymore," she says. "You're going to make yourself sick. But we promised to keep it a secret."

"Keep what a secret?"

"Your birthday party. On Friday right after school. It's supposed to be a surprise. That's what everyone is talking about. Promise not to tell your mom?"

"That's all?"

It was fall when Papa brought me home. Do I really remember that? A slow climb up polished stairs. How carefully he held me. The light through windows, rose and violet and green across the walls in the upstairs hall.

"Ellie, are you home? Come here. I have a surprise."

❧❧❧

The birthday they chose for me is April 22nd. A nice enough date. It's my favourite time of year, the grass new and green, the buds of the maple trees unfurled, the leaves opening like a small hands, waving to the sun. The Canada geese returning, black vees high in the sky and the call of their joyful cries.

It is the strangest thing. Mama is planning my party but I know she's got it wrong. But who would dare to tell her such a thing?

"It's too chilly for swimming today."

"Look, Mama. The clouds are breaking. It'll be perfect by the time we get there. Please!"

I can't get enough of swimming but I know my mother and she's not about to change her mind. But then I hear the study door open, my father's soft footsteps.

"I've had enough of ledgers for a Sunday. Got any of your famous butter tarts lying around? Wouldn't mind a little picnic on the riverbank today. I think the sun's about to shine."

One deep breath, bigger I think, than a whale can take, and then dive. I love the silken feel of the water as it parts to receive my body, its cool blue fingers closing over my sun-warmed back. I even love the murkiness as I wiggle along the bottom, greens and browns almost obscuring a fish hovering in a patch of reeds. I swim closer to look that fish in the eye, but he wavers like the reflection in a blackened mirror and then he is gone. Arctic Char or maybe a Grayling?

When I get back home, I will find my father's fishing guide on the shelves in his study and look it up. So I have to remember. The size, the colour. The details of this not-quite-hidden fish. I would like to stay down here forever. But my land lungs are screaming now and so I rise quickly, because even I, who love the water so, do not love sucking in a mouthful of river and coughing it out again. I break the surface.

Sunlight off the water almost blinds my underwater eyes and I wish to be down there still, in that softer light.

My papa is tall and muscled, his thick hair brighter than newly polished silver. He lounges on the striped Hudson's Bay blanket we always bring, reading the paper, folded and refolded so the wind doesn't whisk any part of it away.

I love Sundays when he is in his study and I know that he's there. Sometimes I slip inside the double doors and stand by the bookcase and pretend I am reading something. I love the feeling, him in deep concentration, me so close. The quiet from him seeps into me.

But he's aware of me, I know that he is, and when he's ready, he will raise his head and smile. "Okay, something's up I'm sure. Might as well spit it out. See what I can do."

I am not always there asking for something. Sometimes I just like to watch my Papa. Papa is so quiet, so good.

But today, on the grassy knoll, my papa is engrossed in the news of the day and he doesn't feel my concentration, doesn't see me wave or blow him a kiss, so I fill myself with air again and sink beneath the blue.

This time I stay down longer, a record I think. Maybe my lungs really are getting bigger. I have been practising deep breathing in the mirror at home, holding huge breaths until my face is scarlet, and my eyes bulge like a frog's.

233

I punch my way to the surface. Yahoo! A new underwater record! Me!

But Miriam isn't watching, Papa isn't watching, and if no one sees your accomplishment, it doesn't get to count.

Then I see my mother. She is standing on the strip of sand we call the beach, her dark eyes raking the water like a searchlight. Back and forth. Back and forth again. Her shoulders are slightly rounded, like the rest of her, but the softness of her body is taut right now, wound tightly by her worry.

I am bobbing like a cork, up and down, scissoring my legs just like the frogs in the brackish pools near the rocks.

Mama! But the wind whips the word away so I raise my arm and wave. I can even swim with only one arm working. That's how good I am!

She sees me instantly. The tension leaves her body in a rush, like a wave leaving a shore.

Come, she beckons wildly. Come here.

She hates it when I am beneath the water. Can't you just float, she asks me? Grab a piece of driftwood and ride it along the surface? The river is so deep, so cold, and there are currents that can reach out and whisk you clean away. People have disappeared out there, stronger swimmers than you.

"You don't have to worry about me. The river knows me. The river is my friend."

When I say that, she looks at me with puzzled eyes.

I am puzzled too. The river knows me? The river is my friend? What the heck?

"You gave me a start this time," my little mama says as she enfolds me in a beach towel and holds me close.

234

I have been in the water for a long time, but it is she who is shivering, she who needs to be held and warmed.

The afternoon of my birthday party starts off very slow. After school, I hope to find a new red bike in the front hall. I really mooned over that bike, dog-eared the page in the catalogue so I could find it in an instant. So my papa and mama could find it too.

But the hallway is bare, the wood gleaming gold in the afternoon sun. And there's no sound anywhere. Not even the sound of Mama puttering in the kitchen, no clink of silverware, no ping of water hitting the tin basin.

There is a wicker settee along a sidewall near the front door where I sink down and slowly unlace my shoes. Did Miriam lie? Is there really to be no party?

"In here, Lily."

Strange to come home from school and find my mother in the parlour and not in the kitchen, but I know exactly what to do. I make my face expressionless, like a blank page, and then open the door.

My friends all jump up and yell, "Surprise, surprise!"

"Oh my goodness, I can't believe it. Really I can't."

Mama smiles and claps her hands. "Good for you girls. I wondered if we could pull it off. Secrets can be so hard to keep."

The girls are here not just for the party, but to spend the night too. Even Sheila, who most often isn't even asked, although I'm not sure why.

When Papa comes home, he is wheeling the red bike. Balloon tires and shiny chrome and nice high handlebars.

I want to ride it right away and so I do, just down to the corner and back to the gate. Then Papa says I have company to attend to right now and that tomorrow, when my friends go home, he'll adjust my bike so it fits me perfectly and I will fly down our street, a blur of red.

My new bike is leaning against the half wall of the front veranda. I can see it from my bedroom window and I keep looking out to make sure it's still there. I am full and happy, and with my friends sitting cross-legged around me on the braided rug, I feel like the luckiest girl in the world.

"Wanna play a game?" Sheila asks.

"Sure," Miriam says.

"Truth or Lies. You go first," Sheila says. "Tell us something you've never told before and we'll decide if it's true."

Miriam closes her eyes, pushes her fingertips against her temples. "Timothy O'Leary kissed me behind the outhouse at recess." A faint rosy blush slides up her neck and onto her cheeks.

"That's a lie," the others holler.

Timothy is shy and scared to death of girls, but I wonder because of the blush and so I vote for Truth.

I write down the question and the yeahs and nays inside one of my birthday gifts, a black and white checked notebook that has a little metal lock and a fancy key.

Miriam doesn't have to say one way or the other until the game is over.

The ending will be another surprise.

We are practising to be good liars, but then I think, what the heck, it's only a party.

"We are going to ride to Boston in a bed-sitting car," Caroline says. "At night, the sofa folds down and the two of us will sleep there as snug as could be. And the porter will bring us hot chocolate if we ask."

"False!"

We know Caroline's mother is afraid to go across town by herself, let alone take the train to Boston. There is a wistful look in Caroline's eyes and I wish, for her sake, that the story is true.

Then I stand up, folding my hands below my breastbone as Mrs. Jackson has taught us in elocution. I wait until all the girls have given me their undivided attention. I have no idea what I will say until my mouth opens and the words tumble out.

"I have rafted alone in the Peace River."

Miriam is grinning and shaking her head as if I've said something really funny.

"There's more." I say. "My real parents got lost in a forest and when they knew they were truly in trouble, they put me on the raft and it floated down that river."

"Liar," Sheila hollers. "That story is straight out of the Bible. If you studied it, you'd know."

I know now why Sheila's party invitations are few and far between.

I truly am a real bad liar. Where would I come up with a story like that? I am so relieved that my friends don't believe.

"This is a stupid game. Let's go downstairs and see if we can finish off the rest of my cake."

My sleep is full of dreams. The swiftly flowing river, the rocking craft, pinhole stars in the inky sky, the crescent moon, loons calling and coyotes answering, the silver river, rushing, rushing, caught in an eddy and swirling and swirling, spray across my face and the touch of icy water.

Here in my pink room beneath the sloping eaves, I am safe. Not dizzy and certainly not cold, but still I shiver and pull the blankets tight around my shoulders.

In the morning, my mother says there are bluish circles beneath my eyes.

"Did you silly girls stay up all night? Or did you eat a little too much cake?" Her cool hand touches my forehead. "I think you've got a bit of a fever. Maybe you should rest while I see everyone home."

My friends kiss me and hug me and thank me for the lovely party and tell me it was the most fun ever. When they leave the kitchen, I scoop pink frosting onto my finger and suck at its sweetness. It has been the absolute best birthday I have ever had. And the absolute worst.

Every day, I have been whizzing around the neighbourhood on my red bike. I love the speed, my hair blowing in the breeze. At first Mama worried, so we went for a walk and she laid out the borders within which I am allowed to ride. I have promised to stay inside her imaginary lines. I don't play hopscotch or even double-dutch skipping anymore. After the freedom of my bike, those games seem too slow. If the boys are playing a pick-up game, I stop to watch. They never ask me to join them, and even if they asked, I wouldn't. I don't like playing games I'm not good at. So I stand behind the backstop and watch the ball humming over the plate, hear the solid smack as the bat connects and I wish, I really wish, that I was a boy.

When I tell Papa I would rather be a boy, he asks me why.

Now every night, we are in the backyard, playing catch. At first, my papa threw the ball nice and easy. And he showed me how to throw my whole arm into the ball. He showed me where power and speed come from. I am getting better and better and now Papa burns those balls at me and, most of them, I catch. And I throw them back hard. Next week we are going to start batting practice.

I am thinking about the home run I will hit in front of Stewart and Garry when the ball hits the edge of my glove and glances up into my face. I drop my glove. My lip really hurts and I wail.

And then Papa is holding me, pressing with a cold cloth. "I'm sorry," he says. "I'm so, so sorry. I threw it too damned hard."

My Papa rarely swears so I know he's upset. I smile at him even though it hurts.

"Don't worry Papa. Next time I'll keep my eye on the ball."

I spend the rest of the summer practising, throwing the ball up onto the slope of the roof, catching it when it rolls down. Sometimes I misfire and I am concentrating on the ball so hard that I trample Mama's flower beds. I feel real bad for that but it doesn't stop me. Over and over, till I can catch it almost every time. Then to teach myself how to hit, I toss the ball in the air and swing my bat when the ball comes down. At first there are a lot of wild pitches and fruitless swings but after a while, I get pretty good at that too. Then I ask the boys if I can play. And we play until it gets too cold outside.

Marie and Laura Hanson got new skates for Christmas and so did I, but it's a long way to the big rink and Mama won't let me go all that way without her. What if you get cold? What if you want to come home and Marie and Laura aren't ready yet? And I don't think those Hanson girls are really old enough to be keeping track of you. Really, they are only children themselves.

So when the Hansons leave with their skates slung over their shoulders, I can only watch from the window in the parlour.

The only good thing on those not-skating days is seeing my papa walking up the sidewalk and opening the front door.

"Anybody home?"

Of course I am, because Mama wouldn't let me go.

Then Papa asks me to help him stomp down a big square of snow in our front yard. It takes us a very long time, especially when we have to make a nice even ridge around the outside to hold the water in when he floods the square.

"That's what we're doing? Making our very own rink?"

"You bet."

We stomp that square every evening after supper for three days straight and now Papa is outside in the dark, pouring water onto the hard-packed snow. He says it's too cold out there for me to help, which I don't think is true, but there's no use arguing.

The ridges hold and the water is contained. Tonight it will freeze quickly. Papa says he has to add water at least three more times to make it smooth. "I want it to be just like glass."

Soon I will have my very own skating rink. Then Marie and Laura and I can skate all we want. I am so excited I could almost die. My papa is really something. When Mr. Gullickson told him the ice would cut off the oxygen and come spring the grass wouldn't grow, my papa just smiled. "We don't worry too much about growing grass around here. We're busy growing children just now."

Mama is roasting a chicken for supper, with stuffing too. I ask for mashed potatoes and offer to help her peel them, but she shooshes me away.

"Play while you can," she says. "You'll have all kinds of duties soon enough."

Outside, I skate and skate, sweating in the crisp air, full speed around the outside curve.

My mother's voice trills across the stillness of the twilight. "Lily. Lily, darling. It's suppertime."

The shovel I use to clear the ice is still lying on top of the banked snow and I know it must be put away. Papa is very fussy about his tools. So I pick it up and walk kind of carefully on my skates to the backyard shed.

The light from the kitchen window is yellow, my mother walking into view and then quickly out again. I hope she will let me un-stuff the chicken. I love the stuffing, so moist and fragrant with onion and sage. I love to pop the little browned pieces that have fallen into the juices of the roasting pan into my mouth. Of an entire roasted chicken, those little golden pieces are the very best.

But I pause on the back step to gaze at the sliver of bluish moon, at the milky light shining on crusted snow. Delicate frills of frost edge the barren branches of the apple tree and the twisted iron railing of the step. It is so white, so still, so very, very beautiful. I want to take it all inside of me. So I bend and quickly lick the frost on the railing. And I am stuck there, howling for my mother, the copper taste of blood on my tongue.

She comes in a flash, frees me with warm water poured quickly onto my pulsing tongue.

Oh, it hurts, it hurts so bad.

How can anything so beautiful be so dangerous?

Mama is shaking her head, hugging me as she leads me inside. "Really, Lily. You know better. You have to learn to stop and think."

Maybe I stayed out in the cold too long, numbing my toes and numbing my brain too. For my tongue and my toes are now throbbing together, in unison with the beating of my heart. And I know what my mama said is true.

I love to slip into Papa's study and inhale the smell of old books, admire the red and tan tartan wallpaper that Mama chose. I love to watch him as he slowly sorts through his papers, the complete concentration he brings to his tasks tracing furrows on his face. I am not sure I will ever be able to concentrate like that, for I have tried to, especially in history class, and I cannot make it work.

But today, when Papa asks me to go into his study, I wish I could be anywhere else. For an official visit to Papa's study always means trouble for me.

"Sit down, Lily."

And so I do, perching on the edge of the green corduroy chair.

"Is it true you punched Ian McAlister at school?"

I fidget, trying to think what I should say and then I look into my papa's eyes.

"Yes, Papa. I did."

"Do you mind telling me why?" His quiet voice makes me more nervous than anything and my throat is full of dust and I don't know where to start.

"I'm waiting."

"He said something really rude to Miriam. I can't tell you the words."

"Then Ian has shown extremely poor judgment. But a punch in the eye? Especially from a young lady. You've made him a laughing stock. And that's worse for a young fella than a shiner any day."

He leans forward and opens his hands. His face looks very grave, as if I have done something really wrong this time.

"Papa," I say. "Ian was rude and Miriam just ignored him and kept on walking. But he tripped her, right at the top of the stairs. And she dropped her books and her lunch bag and her dress flipped up and she was all tangled up and no one stopped to help her and when I tried to go to her, Ian put out his arm so I couldn't get by."

"This is nothing to do with you," he says. "So just keep on walking if you have any sense at all. Which, probably, you don't."

"He was laughing and so were his friends. So I punched him right in the eye."

"Hmm," my papa says. He toys with the pen from the silver holder on his desk. "Your teacher has asked for an apology."

"Oh, Papa . . . . "

"But I don't think you're the one who needs to apologize." He comes from behind his big desk and pulls me to my feet. Suddenly, I am wrapped in his thick arms and he is patting my back.

"You are one good friend," he tells me. "And all anyone needs in life is one good friend. I'll speak to the principal tomorrow. As will Mr. McAlister, I am sure."

I am almost out the door, so relieved.

"By the way," he says, "I hear you gave him quite the shiner. Left hook or right?"

"Left," I say, and Papa is grinning wide.


"Mama, he's not going to let me go. I just know it."

"He's thinking it over, Lily. Your going on a date is a something I am sure your father has never really thought about. He still thinks of you as his little girl. Men are slow to notice what's right in front of them sometimes. And your father is one of the species, even if an unusually good specimen."

"But it's not a real date, it's only Garry. I've known him all my life. And I am just dying to go to graduation. Not many Grade Ten girls even get asked."

Mama takes my new Easter dress from the closet and shakes it. "Here, let's do a final fitting."

She folds her arms, and I slip into the satiny fabric. The fabric falls over my shoulders, swishes over my chest, my hips, the back of my legs. It feels like falling into water, water stirred by a gentle gust of wind.

I run my hands down my thighs.

Mama turns me around as she carefully pins the back, taking it in here and there, so it will fit perfectly. It's pretty enough to wear to graduation, a soft peach colour with pin-tucks down the front and a very trendy dropped waist. And it's only a little bit too big.

Mama says it will be easier to alter than to send back to Eaton's and wait for a replacement to arrive. Easter Sunday might be over and summer too, before we'd get another. "I'll work on your papa," she tells me through a mouthful of pins. "He'll come around. He's a reasonable man."

I have known Garry Hanson as long as I can remember. A date with him will be like spending an evening with my own brother, although I have never had a brother, so how do I really know?

Pale pink streamers and silver balloons almost camouflage the brick of the gymnasium walls and candlelight makes the basketball hoops and lines disappear.

Me, attending graduation! Even though it is only Garry; Miriam is very impressed.

An orchestra is playing dreamy songs.

And oh, Garry Hanson can really dance. That's one thing that I didn't know.

The tentative touch of his lips on mine as we stand on my veranda is nothing earthshaking, that's for sure. There's no quick rush of blood to my face, no swoony feeling, like Miriam told me happens to her when she kisses Allan. But still, there is a flicker of something and when I open my eyes, I see Garry Hanson in a different way. He has always been handsome and fun and when you play One-a-Cat or Kick-the-Can, you want to have Garry on your side.

But with this one kiss, something changes.

The kitchen is warm, so warm that sweat is beading on my upper lip. I wonder why I begged Mama so hard to let me help make perogies. It is a lot more work than I ever dreamed. This much work might just take the fun right out of eating them. They have always been one of my favourites, so I guess I will see.

Mama sprinkles a little more flour on the maple cutting board and I notice that her dark hair is shot with a few strands of silver. My mama? Going grey?

There is beef stew bubbling on the stove. I stir it and watch the liquid swirl. It swirls and swirls, sucking me down.

"Mama. Do you ever cook the heart?"

"Never."

"The hunters long for it. It makes them wise and brave. But it's the eyeballs the children want."

"Lily. Stop it. If you're trying to make me lose my urge to cook, it's working for sure."

I quit stirring, move back to the cutting board.

"They eat them raw," I say.

Times in this kitchen are so dear to me. First of all, because I have to convince Mama that I really do want to learn some things from her and it is her job to show me, and second, because I know that there are only six more months until I graduate.

And what then?

When he graduated, Garry Hanson left home and never came back. He sent me two letters from Calgary in the first month and then nothing at all. There is no good

246

excuse for his continued absence, especially now that the train runs from Calgary to Edmonton on a regular basis. But Mama says she always wondered how a quiet, contemplative boy like Garry came out of a house so full of chaos and that maybe he has grown used to the quiet, living by himself like he does.

I think of how gracefully Garry could dance, the velvet of his soft lips, and I know that he is probably doing more than just sitting around enjoying the quiet and thinking all the time. He comes home once a year at Christmas, but I don't see him.

Mama says Mrs. Hanson lives for that day.

26.

Samuel
August 1914

Samuel watched his daughter and his wife from the kitchen doorway, leaning quietly there. Lily bending to heed her mother, her apron stark white against her golden arms and her gleaming dark hair. The muted sound of Ellie's voice.

"See? Like this. Roll it across twice, once this way, and then across in the other direction. Try to keep the pressure the same. Don't pull the edges or you'll end up with holes."

They were immersed in flour and fillings, rolling, crimping, things he had no idea how to do.

Lily had developed a real flair for cooking, despite Ellie's insistence that she didn't need to learn, at least not right now.

He wanted to memorize the two of them, to freeze this ordinary scene.

For two weeks hence, Lily would board the train, on her way to Ottawa and Mrs. Brighton's boarding house and The Ottawa Ladies College. A world he could only imagine, but one he was sure would be perfect for Lily, eventually. Although she might not think so at first, not at all, and neither would Ellie. For himself, when he thought of Lily gone, there was an actual sore spot in his chest.

He sometimes wondered if they'd done something wrong bringing Lily up or if she'd been born with a stubborn streak as wide as the Peace. She'd darn near worn him down with her dogged insistence that she get a job at the Bay.

For Lily, he had always had bigger dreams.

But with the unforeseen fact of the war in Europe, he wondered if he was doing the right thing. Sending her off to broaden her horizons in such an uncertain time. Still, the war was an ocean way and Lily would not be in any immanent danger. Surely, the experience of attending school with young women so different from her would be worth it for her in the end.

He'd kept his reservations to himself. He was used to keeping his counsel with Ellie, he'd done it for years, since his betrayal, but for him and Lily this was a first. It kept him awake at night.

Finally, she'd promised him one year at the college in Ottawa and he'd allowed that if, by the end of that year, she was still set on her original plan to stay in Edmonton and work at the Bay, she could come back home and give it a try. Although he would have nothing to do with securing a job for her. If she chose that path, she'd have to make it on her own. A woman working in the Bay wasn't something he'd seen. But times were changing. Who could say?

As he hauled her trunk onto the platform, he wondered if his idea to send Lily so far away was a huge mistake.

Ellie was bundled up, as if against a great cold. She held her arms close to her sides, didn't really look at him. "It's so far," she whispered, "so very far away."

And Lily, he thought, looking at his daughter as she lugged her satchel up the sturdy stairs to the platform. Lily, alone?

It would be just him and Ellie again. He couldn't remember how that had been, can't imagine, now, how it will be.

## 27.

### Lily

If the train had arrived two minutes late, I would never have gotten on. Mama, looking so small and so sad. Papa being dignified and brave. Me, wanting to beg them. Please, please, let me stay.

I couldn't imagine living so far away. Attending classes with girls I'd never met. Staying in a boarding house, even a highly recommended one. Tears welled in my eyes, threatened to spill down the front of my smart blue jacket.

But as the train came to a screeching stop, I blinked them quickly away and turned to Mama and Papa with my widest smile. I knew how bad they both were feeling and I didn't want to make it worse.

The porter heaved my bags aboard and Papa tipped him large. The clock on the station wall kept ticking, its hands moving, faster, faster, faster.

"All aboard," the conductor hollered through billows of steam creeping around him like a thick fog. "All aboard."

It felt like another one of my dreams, only in this one, there was no water, only the gaping grated steps of the waiting train and Mama hugging me hard, telling me to write as soon as I arrived.

"No," my papa said. "Send a telegram. Bugger the cost."

That almost made me smile, for my papa was not one to curse. Not often anyway.

"Really, Mama." I hugged her one last time. "I promise to write all the time."

I ran up the steps at the last possible moment and flopped into a maroon corduroy seat embossed with roses. I pressed my nose against the pane as Mama and Papa grew smaller and smaller until I could no longer see them waving.

It was then I began to cry.

The clickety-clack of the wheels on the steel lulled me to sleep. I awoke to a different landscape, to twisted trees and stunted bushes and thinly layered rocks. I had no idea how long I'd been sleeping, but I was hungry for sure.

A rotund porter led me to the dining room and seated me at a tiny table before fluffing a large white napkin onto my lap. I studied the menu he offered, but in the end, I ordered toast with a side of crisped bacon and a pot of English tea. My stomach was rolling, whether from all the crying or from the motion of the train, I couldn't really tell.

"Excuse me, miss." A man stood beside me, short, slightly balding and the skin on his elongated forehead shone. "Do you mind if I join you?"

Of course I minded, but what could I say?

"Lovely evening," he said, and I had to agree that is was. The sky was full of towering clouds, backlit by the sun so their edges glowed luminescent white. "Donald is my name." He placed a brown leather valise beside him on the adjacent chair, squared it and patted it like it was a sleeping babe before he turned to me.

"Lily," I said.

"I couldn't help but notice. A young girl like you, travelling alone."

So I had to tell him all about the school in Ottawa and about how hard it had been for me to get on the train and leave my mama and papa behind.

"I'm sure it was," he said. "But it sounds like you're off on a great adventure. Somewhat like myself."

I didn't feel as if I was off on a great adventure, and I knew it was rude of me not to ask about his. But he told me anyway. "Oh yes," he said, "I am about to become a salesman with a territory of my own. Watkins products. I have been told they almost sell themselves but I don't believe that for a minute. I can see the spices maybe, but cleaning supplies? My sales base is in the middle of Manitoba, where I have never been before. Would you mind," he said, gesturing toward the bulging case. "If you could maybe listen while I run through my spiel? I've tried it on my wife, but I don't believe her comments are exactly objective. Considering I've been out of work for thirteen months."

"I'm sorry to hear that," I said.

"Well, that's life. But now, with this Watkins thing, I feel as if I've gotten another chance. So you can see why I want to practise a bit? Before I begin my new venture?"

"I'm not a very experienced audience," I said. "My mother could no doubt help. But I've never bought household cleaners or spices in my entire life."

"If you could just . . . "

"I'm truly sorry but I'm just grabbing a quick bite. And turning in. It's been a tough day."

"Oh, of course. Maybe later, if you have a moment?" His eyes were blinking quickly and his small hands twisting at his napkin. "It's just that I've never been a salesman before and day after tomorrow is my first day and I thought if I just ran through things one more time with an audience it might . . . and those Manitoba farmers are not so well off and I don't want to pressure the women and have them buy things that will cause strife when hubby comes home, but still I want to be a good salesman and . . . "

"I'm sorry," I said.

Tucked into my tiny bunk, rocking with the rhythm of the train as it swung through curves and hills, I could not sleep. I kept seeing his earnest face, the nervous flush on his cheeks and the unconscious busyness of his hands.

And I knew that all of my life I would remember. Perhaps this was the first lesson. That it is better to regret things you have done rather than things that you have not.

And the train was still swaying across that moonscape and I was sad and tired and alone. And I knew that I had been unkind.

It was not an auspicious start, but after the endless train-ride and my unforgiveable rudeness and a mix-up finding my luggage, I arrived at Mrs. Brighton's boarding house in the late afternoon. Mrs. Brighton was a short, squat woman, her thin silver hair combed straight back, like a man's. She showed me to a cramped little room painted a nauseating purple, not a rich dark plum like my favourite velvet Christmas dress. There is purple and then there is purple.

In that tiny room, on the very first night, my old dream returned. The sound of rushing water and me so dizzy and the sound of rapids somewhere up ahead and knowing full well I have only moments to veer towards shore, and no way to navigate, just the pell-mell rush down and down.

When I finally pulled myself from the dream, sweat was running down my neck and my pillow was bunched in my hands.

The yellow light from the streetlight outside was unfamiliar and all of the shadows in that room were strange.

I sat on the side of the bed, and my shoulders shook.

The squeak of footsteps on the stairs. Moments later, I heard the rushing water again but this time it was only one of my roomies using the wash room, situated on the other side of my headboard, with only a thin wall between. I clearly heard the bodily function we never talk about. And I longed for my big room at home, and for my mama and papa.

Mrs. Brighton's boarding house had been in operation for ten years, ever since her late husband fell from a ladder while trimming the apple tree. This she told me the first morning, as she poured me a cup of very strong tea. She spoke of her husband as if he'd just left the room. In her eyes, he was obviously very close to being a saint because it was Stanley this and Stanley that every single day. But I wondered, had he been such a fine husband, how had she been left in such dire straights, for the upholstery was faded and the carpets worn and the whole house had an air of neglect.

And surely, she was taking in boarders only because she had no choice.

We ate mostly stews and soups, full of root vegetables and very little meat, but Mrs. Brighton had a wonderful way with biscuits, filled with grated cheddar cheese, which made up for the lack of meat. She ran her house with a determined air of cheerfulness and optimism, as if sure that Mr. Brighton himself would one day walk back in the door and put things right.

If he had happened to materialize, I might have just told him what I knew.

That he'd gambled all his money away on the horses and hadn't sent it to the African missions, as he'd claimed. That he'd never been honest with his wife; he'd been short of money only because he liked to buy a drink or two for the ladies the days he went to the track.

But if I'd said such a thing aloud, Mrs. Brighton wouldn't have believed it, not for a minute. She'd have been very angry too, that much I knew.

How could I explain to anyone that this insight into Stanley came the first time I rested my hand on the arm of his favourite chair? A chair Mrs. Brighton reserved for herself only, as if it were some kind of shrine. It was the strangest feeling, like the chair was full of secrets and had just been waiting.

Sometimes I was so close to knowing things, so close I could almost see. But before I could capture my big revelation, the knowledge always faded away.

This knowing about Stanley's character came so fast and so clear, it frightened me a bit.

*September 27, 1914*

*Dear Mama,*

*Although I miss you and Papa all the time, I am most lonesome in the hours before dinner, when I used to be in the kitchen with you. Mrs. Brighton's cooking is okay but a varied menu is something she hasn't heard of. The entire house smells of boiled cabbage so sitting in her kitchen is something I avoid. Besides missing you, I miss the kitchen! Strange isn't it?*

*I fill my time by taking long walks up and down the streets of Ottawa. The buildings are so magnificent, brick and stone, carved cornices, and ornate doors. I have discovered some delightful places. One of my favourites is N. Mark's Jewellery Store, right in the middle of town. The walls are the deepest navy I have ever seen and the display cases are gleaming dark wood and polished glass. Lights sparkle everywhere, making the gems flash and the gold gleam.*

*There was a write-up about Mr. Mark in the Ottawa Citizen, Sunday edition, and this is what it said: "The elegant and costly character of Mr. Mark's stock, and the taste displayed by Mr. Mark in serving the wants of his customers are the result of 15 years in London, England in the jewellery trade. For the elegance of his stock and the perfect accomplishment of its display, Mr. Mark's estab-lishment is one which admirers of that variety of goods will be delighted to inspect."*

*I should say! For I have lingered in his store more times than I can count.*

*A thick gun-metal grey carpet runs up the middle of the store and Mr. Mark has three small tables situated along one side and each table has two oak chairs pulled up close, one with arms and one without. It is there fine gentlemen dressed in suits and satin-clad ladies sit, daintily sipping tea from delicate china cups. They wait as Mr. Mark disappears into the bowels of his store. They are always smiling, sometimes holding hands for just a moment or two.*

*When Mr. Mark finally returns, he cups a small square of purple velvet in his hands and when he opens his palms under the light, diamonds spill out like pieces of the sun after a rain, brilliant rainbows of colour flashing everywhere.*

*Someday, maybe, I too will sit at one of those little tables, and a handsome gentleman will buy a sparkling gem just for me.*

*Oh Mama, whatever am I thinking? I am not in Ottawa to find a handsome young man, but to get myself, as Papa says, a first-rate, well-rounded education so that I can go places! Although right now, the only place I want to go is home.*

*Please don't show Papa this letter — he might get worried about my dedication to my schooling and I can assure you, I really am doing well although I have to admit I don't love it here.*

*Much love — Lily*

*November 10, 1914*

*Dear Mama and Papa,*

*Things are looking up for me, though not for our poor boys sailing to Europe! I have met a girl at school who has* lived in Ottawa her whole life but she is not stuck up at all. She finds the fact that I have been raised 'out in the wild, wild West', a plus, and she's always pumping me for details. I think I finally have her convinced that bears don't lurk behind the bushes in my backyard and that cowboys and Indians aren't fighting in the streets. Still, she doesn't quite believe that Edmonton is a city just like Ottawa, only newer, and that I don't have any experience in the wilds! Now, if Papa had taken me, just once, to Fort St. John, I could say that I do and then I think she might be satisfied.

I may have to bring her home with me in the summer so she can see for herself what Edmonton is like. That seems like so long away when I write it! I wish wish wish I could come home for Christmas.

My new friend's name is Yvonne Harris and she has invited me to her house, which I am really looking forward to. She says her parents will be delighted. I hope she's right.

Her father owns a sawmill on the Ottawa River and Mrs. Brighton tells me he is quite a well-known businessman. Yvonne told me that she and her parents were actually invited to the Winter Solstice festival at Rideau Hall!

I had thought that winter in Ottawa would be negligible compared to our indescribable cold, but it is definitely winter here too. Maybe I feel the cold so because it's a humid, hoarfrost cold, not like the freeze-dried temperatures we have at home.

All around me is frosty and white, and overhead, the bluest of skies, which at night, becomes the most glorious diamond-studded canopy. (back to Mr. Mark!)

*Yvonne says the toboggan slide at the Hall is really something to see, long and straight and banked on either side by huge snowdrifts topped with flaming torches and long strings of coloured Chinese lanterns. The slide, in that light, she said, seems almost perpendicular, so it took every bit of her courage to let loose when standing at the brink. I think it sounds even better than skating as fast as you can. I can only hope I get to try it sometime, on a Sunday when the Hall is open to the public, as it is occasionally.*

*Yvonne loves ice-skating there, the rink lit all around by twinkling white lights. Sounds a little grander than the one Papa and I made every winter, don't you think? Although I suppose, not this year, when I'm not there to help (or skate).*

*If I ever did really help, that is!*

*The next time the Hall is open, Yvonne and I are going to go. She says it might be a long time until her family gets invited again for a private event. Apparently, it is a real honour to get invited there and the Governor General's wife tries to spread the glory around.*

*Once I have seen the place with my own two eyes, I shall send you a full report!*

*Love Lily*

28.

Edmonton

Ellie kept Lily's letters in the second drawer of the
hutch in the kitchen, in a small cardboard box. She put
them in chronological order, and often, while cooking
or cleaning, she'd sit for a moment feeling close to her
daughter.

She re-read the first letter and the second and then
flipped through the growing pile.

*April 23, 1915*

*Dear Mama and Papa,*

    *I wish you had been with me yesterday. Although I was
at Yvonne's house at Christmas I am just now taking it
all in. And I didn't really tell you much about it. Yvonne's
house is bigger than anything I could have imagined.
There is a long curved drive leading to the front doors
and a wide veranda across the front. Even though spring
is new, the ivy is already thick on the brick and on the
columns and hangs like a curtain so that you don't notice
the size of the place until you walk up the front steps.*

    *Mr. and Mrs. Harris are lovely people and they made
me feel right at home, even in that mansion of a house.
That is, until we went into the dining room. Mama, they
have a butler! Can you imagine? There were so many forks*

*and knives that I had no idea where to start. So I watched Yvonne and did as she did.*

*But I was nervous, no doubt.*

*Yvonne's father talked politics and the war all through dinner. It seems people here are obsessed with government just like people at home are obsessed with the weather.*

*The closest I've gotten to politics is touring the Parliament Buildings, very impressive to say the least. Still, I know nothing about what the Tories are up to and about the new direction the Grits seem to be taking. That was the dinner table talk and it sounded like a foreign language to me!*

*I was so glad that no one thought to ask my opinion for I am not informed enough to have an opinion. Although it seems everyone here does, informed or not.*

*The incessant talk of war upsets me and somehow it all seems much closer living here. The very idea of it often keeps me awake at night.*

*My first sad Christmas away from you and Papa seems so far away. I tried to get into the spirit of the day but Yvonne's mother knew, as mothers do, where I really wanted to be. And now, I have been at her house so often I feel quite at home here. Yvonne and I come and go as we please. Like real grown-ups I guess!*

*I was glad when Yvonne and I spent last Sunday touring the town, mostly to escape a croquet tournament her parents were hosting. I cannot for the life of me see the point of the game. I think people might play it just to be a little snobby, because it really is so British and it's not something most people grow up playing. Although Yvonne's parents are far from snobby, so maybe croquet is for everyone now.*

*I wasn't keen on trying and making a fool of myself in front of people I don't know at all, so Yvonne, who knows everything about me, decided we should go to Russell House Hotel for high tea.*

*It is very grand, with soaring ceilings and gold leaf mirrors and old masters in ornate frames everywhere. It has been rebuilt and refurbished and has two elevators (we didn't ride them, although Yvonne thought we should), and with bathrooms in every room — imagine — and outside fire escapes, which is apparently a big drawing card.*

*I had never even heard of High Tea, although I didn't let on so to Yvonne when she suggested that we go. Do you know about High Tea, Mama? You probably do!*

*If our urge to escape croquet was to avoid being too proper, High Tea was not the place for me. Except for the music.*

*At four o'clock, women began to arrive dressed in all their finery. Sandwiches and dainties were served on gigantic silver trays, and of course, endless cups of tea poured by a waiter dressed in a charcoal tuxedo with satin-lined tails. The talk was subdued, the clink of bone china and silver supposed to be soothing to the ear made me want to jump up and run outside.*

*Yvonne and I sat in two large upholstered chairs tucked into an alcove, and we ordered only one pot of tea to share. And we tried most of the dainties, of course. But mostly we watched the ladies, and listened to the piano player, who played Beethoven and Brahms and all kind of music I've never even heard before.*

*After High Tea, eating dinner would be out of the question. But maybe, for those old ladies, that is the whole*

263

*idea — no need to have dinner alone. (I feel kind of silly calling it dinner, as it was always supper at home).*

*There was something sad in those birdlike old women perched on velvet chairs, their hats and gloves adjusted just so.*

*I felt like such an interloper, more strongly than I usually do.*

*Yes, Mama, I am still missing you and Papa and I can hardly wait until this year is over and I can come home, for despite getting to know Yvonne and spending time at her home, I strongly feel I do not belong here, not at all.*

*Much love — Lily*

∿∿∿

*May 26, 1915*

*Dear Mama and Papa,*

*I have gotten through my first set of exams and as you can see from the enclosed transcript, things are going quite well. Except of course, for French. A lot of the girls in school can already speak the language and those who can't have at least heard it before. I studied, I really did, and Yvonne tried to help me, but I cannot make sense of French verb tenses no matter how many times I try.*

*I am starting to wonder about the value of learning it, as I'm sure once I am back home, I will never use the language at all.*

*I know the Ladies College is a top-notch school but I believe more than ever that it's not really for me. Being ladylike in all of your dealings and worrying about deportment and the pitch of your voice is something totally foreign and to be truthful, I can't see the point.*

*Remember when I used to listen for the slam of the front door at the end of the day, and no matter where I was in the house, I would holler "Papa, Papa, is that you?" and then throw myself into his arms, sometimes even before he had a chance to set his briefcase down?*

*Well, a lady never hollers, so I've been told, nor does she run into anyone's arms. I am not sure that being a lady is such a good idea! Seems what real ladies do is take the fun out of everything.*

*Have you heard anything of Miriam? I got one letter and I wrote back right away but it has been months. Maybe she is too busy with her job at the bank and with organizing all of the details for her wedding. I can hardly believe that is true — Miriam about to be married.*

*It would be nice to be so sure of what I want.*

*Not much else is new here, so I will sign off for now.*

*Hugs and kisses.*

*Lily*

The clang of the mailbox lid dropping made Ellie jump. She'd been rolling out sugar cookies, Lily's favourite kind. And really, what was the point of that, except to find a little comfort for herself? Of course, Samuel was always up for a cookie of any kind and grateful for them too, so cookies never went to waste.

Lily, sprinkling pink sugar carefully onto the bell-shaped cookies, her tongue caught at the corner of her mouth, eyes dark with concentration. "Is this good, Mama? Or should I add a little more? Can we make another batch so I can take some to school? Miss Johnson says your sugar cookies are to die for."

Ellie quickly dusted flour from her hands and ran to the door. Lily's letters arrived faithfully, written every Sunday, but it had been almost three weeks and they hadn't heard a word. And mail delivery had become pretty dependable the last few years.

After the first week without a letter, a knot had formed in her belly, and no matter how she tried to ignore it, every morning when she woke, it was there, like a lump of oatmeal porridge congealed in a bowl.

She flipped open the mailbox and when she saw the light blue envelope with Lily's neat handwriting, she sank into the wicker rocker on the porch, and quickly opened the letter. No date? Unlike Lily somehow.

*Dear Mama and Papa,*

*First of all, forgive me and don't be too mad. I know a good education has been Papa's dream for me.*

*But it's Papa's dream, not mine. And even after all these months, I feel like a fish out of water here, like I will never really belong.*

*Last Friday, when Yvonne and I were leaving the National Gallery, we ran into — not quite literally — a friend of hers. Surprising because I thought that I knew all of her friends. She introduced us right away, as a well-brought up young women should according to the Ottawa Ladies College! But it's also something you and Papa taught me years ago. His name is Ward Spencer and he's come all the way from England. He's fallen in love with what he's seen of Canada so far. He's dying to come west, and I have decided that he needs a guide! So*

*I've quit school and by the time you get this letter, I'll be halfway home.*

*Your loving daughter — Lily Charlene*

*PS: He's very good looking and knows how to dance!*
*PPS: Papa — My quitting school really has nothing to do with meeting Ward. After we talk, I'm sure you'll understand.*

Ellie tucked the letter into her apron pocket, a grin tugging at her lips. Lily rarely signed her full name and she and Samuel only used it when the girl was in trouble. No doubt she realized she'd be in a bit of trouble now.

She supposed she should be upset that Lily had quit school but with her daughter gone, the big house had seemed too quiet and the days too long. Try as she might, she could not return to hours with just her and Samuel and she spent much of her time alone. Her new aloneness had a forlorn quality, like faded curtains hanging in abandoned houses, and she missed Lily more each day.

She decided to roast a nice rack of lamb for supper, something special for Samuel before she gave him the news.

The rack of lamb hadn't helped a bit.

"What do you mean, she's coming home? As we speak? When did she leave?"

"She doesn't say." Ellie handed the letter to Samuel. "Here, read it for yourself. I wonder if she was afraid to tell us?"

"When has Lily ever had reason to be afraid of us?"

Samuel began to read, then fumbled for his glasses and held the letter further away. "Light in here isn't too good, is it?"

The creases on his cheeks seemed deeper, his hair a little more grey. "Why don't you try the study? You've a better reading lamp in there."

She quietly washed and dried the dishes, hearing the crisp re-folding of the *Journal* from the drawing room and Samuel's muttered cursing.

When her chores were done and she really couldn't delay any longer, she went to him, perched on the footstool near his feet.

He ignored her, did not even raise his eyes.

"Now Samuel," she said, "nothing's ever been so bad that we haven't been able to at least talk. And Lily hasn't done anything truly awful. All she's doing is coming home. Who knows, she might go back to finish her schooling some day."

"Sounds like she's already made up her mind about that. And it seems to me you're mighty pleased about something. So I assume you're with Lily on this."

"Samuel, it's not as if we have to take sides. Sometimes things just are, you know?"

He didn't reply. He rose like an old man, and went slowly up the stairs. Soon she heard the scrape of a suitcase across the floor above.

"Samuel?"

He was tossing clothing into a battered valise, a flurry of shirts and sweaters and socks.

"What are you doing? Packing? For what?"

"For a trip."

"Why Samuel, I do believe you're running away."

"I am not running away. It's been months since I've checked in with Watson. I can't just assume things up there are going along tickety-boo."

"But Lily will be disappointed if she arrives and you're not home."

He snapped the valise closed, let it thud to the floor. "Well, I guess she'll just have to be disappointed. Maybe it's about time that girl found out that the world doesn't revolve solely around her."

That night, when she fitted her body to his, felt his barrel chest rise and fall, she knew that Lily would most certainly get over being disappointed, but she wasn't so sure about Samuel.

She fit her hand to the curve of his cheek, stroked his lovely bones.

The smell of boiled coffee teased her awake. When she arose, she pulled her plaid housecoat close, for there was a chill in the air.

In the kitchen, she found Samuel's cup rinsed and turned upside down on the draining board. Polished pewter clouds lowered the sky.

As she stood staring out the kitchen window, she heard the splatter of oncoming rain.

29.

Home

I am so glad to be home. To wake in my own room, a place the smell of boiled cabbage has never touched. Mama doesn't boil cabbage, she first fries onions golden and then quick-fries the cabbage, so it's crisp and delicious.

My first week is spent only with Mama, mostly in the kitchen, where we both like to be.

Papa is still in Fort St. John. I think he must be more than a little bit mad, or surely he would have found some reason to come home as quickly as he possibly could. But when he does come home and he meets Ward, I know my papa will understand.

At least one person is happy, and that's my mama. She's making Ward feel right at home, cooking and fussing, and I can tell she likes him a lot.

My first night home, Mama and I stayed up late, sipping cocoa, and for me, a few butter tarts. Oh, I'd forgotten how good. Much better than anything at High Tea. I don't think Ward was tired at all, but I think he knew we needed some time alone so he turned in early. He's very thoughtful, Ward is.

Mama had a lot to say. He's quite good looking, she told me. And charming too. Have you met his family? Will he be staying here long?

I opened my mouth to answer her cascade of questions, but she wasn't quite done.

"Is there something between you and Ward? Something a mother should know?"

When I didn't answer right away, she reached across me and added another teaspoon of clotted cream to her cocoa mix.

"Silly me," she said. "That's not a question I meant to ask. I know you'll tell me everything in your own sweet time."

News spreads quickly in a town the size of Edmonton and I was really pleased when Miriam called and asked me to come for tea. It has been so long since I've talked to any of my friends. Friday, she told me, at three-thirty, which seemed rather strange. I would have grabbed my coat and run over there right away if she hadn't said that.

∾∾∾

It was evident to me from the moment she opened her front door. As she pulled me into a hug, I felt the swell of her belly, the fullness of her breasts where before she had been all angles and bone.

"I am so glad you're back," she said. "It's been ages since I've had anyone to talk to."

And I wondered how that could be true, for Miriam, here, in the town where we both grew up. With a husband who must surely know her heart.

Miriam talked and I listened. She is most definitely expecting. Expecting a perfect child, expecting Allan to get a raise and perhaps a promotion very soon, expecting to build a new home on the north side of town. Expecting, I think, a perfect life.

And oh, how I envied her certainty, the settled-in feeling of her life. I was glad she was so involved in her own plans and didn't think to question mine, for what could I possibly say?

That I had dropped out of school and although Mama has said nothing, I know that I have sorely disappointed my papa? That I have no idea what I intend to do? That there is something between Ward and me, something I felt the first time I met him, like a part of me I hadn't even realized was missing had just clicked into place? How I thought that perhaps Ward felt it too but so far has not said anything to me?

That right now, he is so taken with exploring Edmonton that I barely see him from morning until night? That he is looking for a job, and a place to move into as soon as he can?

The only thing I am really sure of is how pleased my little mama is to have me home again, how the kitchen brims with the smells of roasting and baking.

How she bustles about, a hen with her only chick.


"Samuel," Ellie called from the kitchen. "Is that you? Finally? Come, there's someone here I'd like you to meet."

He set his suitcase on the polished oak floor, hung his hat on the hat rack. He remembered the days when Lily used to run to greet him every afternoon.

They were all three back there in the kitchen. He could hear them and he felt like a stranger, walking by a lighted window at night and peeking into someone else's life.

But then Lily flung the kitchen door open and ran down the hall, and she hugged him hard and took his hand.

"I'm so glad you're finally back. Don't be mad at me, Papa. Please?"

She led him to the kitchen, full of scents and warmth.

"My father, Samuel Vining," she said, her face lit from within. "Ward Spencer, my friend."

He was tall, the young man, with a flop of blond hair above ice blue eyes. The hand offered was smooth and firm.

"Pleased to finally meet you, sir," he said. "It's easy to see you have Lily's full admiration and that's something, I think. Your daughter has been such a good friend to me."

He wanted to ask why are you here, in my home? Are you just Lily's friend? But Ward was a guest, so he only shook his hand.

"Pleased to meet you." That was a lie. He would rather not have met him, would rather that Lily were still in school.

The comforting smell of slow-roasted beef was in the air and Ellie's face was flushed from the heat. A smudge of flour on her cheek made him think that tonight there might be dessert served too — maybe even a bread pudding with butterscotch sauce, Lily's favourite, and his too. Ellie hadn't made bread pudding since Lily left home.

"Looks like you've pulled out all the stops. We'll probably need a leaf in the table tonight. Ward, want to give me a hand?"

As he soon found out, Ward had secured a good-paying job. The government's promise to finish the bridges required to complete the half-built road through the big Muskeg was perfect timing for a young man with training in Engineering.

And thanks to men like him, he could now drive a buckboard and a wagon from the muskeg crossing to within twenty-five miles of Fort St. John in five days time. This was miraculous, considering how long it used to take to make that trek.

Although he'd secured his own lodgings, Ward was very at home in their house, something Samuel was not quite sure about. Perhaps this time, he had stayed away too long. Who was this young man, who seemed to hold both Lily and Ellie in his thrall?

❧❧❧

In the last four months, Miriam has become very fat. But it is I who have become lazy. I do the minimum at work, and I rush out the door the earliest moment I can, sometimes even before closing if no one is around to take note. I never thought I'd turn out to be an employee like that. It's a good thing Papa doesn't know!

I have taken over Mama's garden, mostly because the feel of the black soil on my fingers is soothing to me. I have to fight the urge to lick my fingertips, they look so like they've been dipped in dark chocolate.

I love to watch the drooping tomato plants perk up when I give them a satisfying sun-warmed drink from the rain barrel Papa has set up at the corner of the garage.

The sight of yellow beans hanging heavy on their scrawny hosts is enough to make me laugh aloud. You can almost hear those overburdened plants sigh when I pick a pan of ripened beans. And I love the snap, when I break them. The sight of butter melting onto their already golden skins.

There is poetry in a garden, and somehow, poetry is very appealing to me just now. A really good poem is a springboard to dreaming.

So as I find and pull the odd determined weed, or nip faded flowers from the riotous pink petunias, I dream of Ward, how his face softens when he looks at me, the absolute sense of belonging I have when he hugs me.

How I wish he would soon finish building his bridges and spend more time with me.

I know that I too, should be making plans but I am stuck in this dream, as if I am waiting for my life to unfold. Ordinarily, I would hate such a feeling, but right now, I like the floaty sensation. It is like being carried by a strong current, one that you know you must ride out and not struggle against, one that will lift you up and deposit you where you are meant to be. Like being in the river again.

Mama and I spend endless hours together. Today we are making red current jelly, picking the berries together in the early morning light, listening to the musical ping of berries hitting the bottom of our empty pails and then the pouf of berries on layers of berries, some bursting with their ripeness. Washing and cleaning, the slow boil until the skins split and give up their rosy juice. The gauze bag crimson above the drip pan, the absolute patience we need to wait until the precious juice has all dripped down. No squeezing the bag to speed things up a bit. We don't want cloudy syrup, which is what happens if you try to hurry things along.

Mounds of white sugar dissolving slowly into red, the edge of pink foam clinging to the side of the pot as we boil and stir. The slow drip of syrup from the spoon as we test for thickness. Is it ready? Is it not?

How I love the sight of the full jars lined up on the windowsill, their jewel colour lit by the setting sun. It is a sight prettier than the sparkling diamonds in Mr. N. Mark's jewellery store.

He can hear them in the kitchen, the familiar clink of cutlery, the swish of water as they finish up the supper dishes, the soft murmur of their voices. Sometimes he envies them. Standing side by side in front of the sink, both facing the window and the world outside, yet tethered together by their ordinary tasks. His den is down the hall, but it is a world away from his wife and daughter.

He is already halfway through the old *Edmonton Bulletin*, savouring the quiet and the burn of a bit of Irish whiskey poured from the crystal decanter.

The territory is of great area and vast and varied resources. It differs most radically in its different parts, from the high rolling bluff studded prairie of Peace River — the most beautiful prairie land in the world — to the bare rocky shores of Lake Athabasca at Fond du Lac, also on the edge of the Great Grounds of the Arctic. There are hundreds of miles of fine agricultural and grazing land soon to open for homesteading along the Peace River. (*Edmonton Bulletin*, Aug 31, 1899:3)

There is nothing written of the hardships of the north and how a simple miscalculation could easily have cost a man his life. People would have read this glowing report and thought they could homestead for a while and come back home rich.

It had been like the gold rush all over again, only with land this time. And he remembers how many fools rushed in, dreaming of wealth and ending up defeated by an early frost, just when the wheat was turning to gold. So many died, so far from medical help. He'd seen many an unhinged mind from all that solitude.

Ah, but the north is mile upon mile of endless beauty.

God knows he loves the sight of it, but put him in a cabin again in the middle of all that beauty in the middle of an endless winter and he's not sure just how long the appreciation would last.

He refolds the yellowed paper, and looks up to see Ward, lounging against the doorjamb, flipping through the thick spine of *The Book of Home Remedies* in exactly the manner Lily used to do. He doesn't exactly live in the house, but for the last six months, he's been spending every spare moment here.

"I didn't want to disturb you."

"Sit down," Samuel says.

The kitchen music has damped down now. The settling sounds of night-time have already begun.

But still, Ward lingers. Samuel places his *Edmonton Journal* into the right-hand drawer with the rest of the yellowed pile. "Kind of a history buff, he says. Maybe

277

because I've lived some of it." He picks up a more recent *Journal* open on his desk. "Look at this. June 2, 1913 — 'Opening of the High Level Bridge.' Made a big difference to unite the north and south halves of this town. City, I guess I should say."

Ward shifts and his chair creaks. "Don't get me going on bridges."

"Maybe we'll take a tour out there some day. It's quite the accomplishment. Some said it couldn't be done. Sorry I'm rambling on tonight." He glances at his watch. "Didn't realize it was getting so late."

And still Ward sits in his study, looking at his hands. "There are a few things about me I feel you should know."

That he is from England, twenty-two, blonde, blue-eyed, that he likes to play soccer and that he's good with math and geography. Samuel knows all that. Why he is here and not fighting for his country is puzzling, though.

How he met Lily is a tale she has told more times than enough. It is amazing how one small action can impact so many lives. Yvonne, who introduced Lily to Ward, who altered his daughter's path, is still in Ottawa, living her unchanged life.

"Of course," he says. "Go ahead."

"Besides Lily, I have another pressing reason for coming west." Ward is now sitting, apparently mesmerized by something he sees in the palms of his hands.

"And that would be?"

"My father. He disappeared out here when I was a boy."

"In Edmonton?"

"I don't know for sure."

Samuel's gut tightens. He's not sure why.

"I had an easy time growing up. Good parents, brothers to tumble with, mostly fun with a bit of work thrown in. I apprenticed in a factory, worked my way up through drafting, engineering. We truly didn't know how good we had it. But the war . . . My brothers signed up. They were young and strong, invincible too. And the war was supposed to be over in mere months. Mum cried until her eyes were slits . . . "

Samuel reached for his decanter, poured himself a scant inch.

Ward took a deep breath. "But she was also set on the fact that I must not ever enlist. 'I need to have one of my boys close,' she said. 'One at least.' I really did try to enlist. The medical officer advised me that I was not fit for service. The rejection really hurt. I expected sympathy from my brothers when they were home after training, but they'd been into the drink that night. Like real soldiers.

"'Strange that me and James are just fine but you're not. Ever think to wonder why?'

"On that rum-soaked night Collin told me my mother was really my aunt, as if it were common knowledge."

"Say again?"

"One moment I am Ward Spencer, with two brothers and a mother and father who love me. Then I find I am not Ward Spencer at all. It took me quite a while to get the truth, for my mother didn't want to talk about it."

Samuel is silent, still trying to make sense of his words.

"My mum, or Auntie Joan. I am not comfortable right now calling her either one. She told me everything, eventually. That my 'brothers' actually were my cousins. That I was born Ward Armson, with a mother who died giving me life and a father who immigrated to Canada. It was a to be a temporary arrangement, she said, me living with them. 'Your mother was my darling sister,' she said. "And when we lost her, I was only trying to lend a hand. Until your father got squared away. Which apparently, he never did. But you're ours now. You have been since you were a baby. Surely, nothing you've learned can change that."

Ward finally stops talking, drags in a huge gulp of air. "I have to admit, that and being deemed unfit for service, it nearly knocked me off my pins. And the work I was doing though deemed essential was a joke for the fellows doing the real work of war. It was rough." His hands are shaking. "I was ready to escape the whole mess. Joan had received two letters from Canada, which, thank God, she'd saved. Intending to show them to me when the time was right, she said. My father's last letter was posted from Edmonton. I hoped to find out something, but so far I've had no luck at all. Not even in the archives of the *Edmonton Journal*, a twenty-year span, which I've studied very thoroughly at the library. They're very helpful there."

Samuel takes another sip of whiskey. "People don't just disappear without a trace. You still go by Spencer? Even now?"

A flush pinks Ward's cheeks. "I didn't see any sense in taking the name of a man I'd never met. A father who chose to leave me behind."

Samuel reaches for his banker's light, pulls it a little closer. Tilts the whiskey and checks the level in his glass.

"I intend to tell Lily all of this very soon. For as I'm sure you already know, I am in love with your daughter. And with your blessing, I intend to ask for her hand."

Samuel reaches for his pipe, holds it for a moment and then puts it back. He doesn't smoke anymore, but the feel of the pipe in his fingers is soothing.

Even the sight of it, leaning on its rack.

"I wanted to tell you. To, you know, see if you have a problem having a son-in-law who's not sure, really, who he is."

Dots of light refract from the crystal glass onto the soft green desk pad.

"Of course, I hope to be your son-in-law someday soon, but Lily will be the one to have the final say in that. But before I speak to her, I am asking your permission."

Samuel lifts his glass, finishes the last whiskey and realizes that he hasn't offered Ward a drop. He is pale and looks like he could use a good stiff shot.

He is about to offer him one when the clock in the hall begins to strike and keeps striking. Eleven.

You need not ask for my permission, he wants to say. For as I'm sure you've already figured out, Lily has always been the one in charge. But you need to tell her everything. For secrets are never good.

Lily. Even Ellie has no idea that he bought their darling for two hundred dollars and two bottles of whiskey.

The wolf moon and a woman, a secret still. An overwhelming sense of fatigue washes over him.

He leans across his desk as Ward offers his hand, this tall and handsome young man that Lily has grown to love. The uncharacteristic slouch of his broad shoulders tugs at his heart.

Samuel ignores the hand, comes around from behind the desk, and hugs him hard.

30.

Lily

Papa was proud of me when I got my job, I know he was, although all he said was "Hmmph, I've spent my whole life working for the Bay. Never thought my daughter would be so intent on doing the same. Never thought they'd hire a woman actually. Not even now."

I've started in the accounting department and I like it just fine, although sometimes the work is a little bit boring. All of those ledgers and easy sums and no one my age anywhere around. Miriam thought working at the Bay would be so exciting, that I would soon meet all kinds of men. Which I have, if you are interested in men forty and over, and I am definitely not. The dashing young men she was sure I'd meet must be overseas fighting or out in the field, travelling, trading for furs, doing all those exciting jobs that people in head office only dream of.

When we took inventory last month, I got to go out on the floor and I talked my way into another kind of job. As we painstakingly counted overstuffed racks of merchandise, I thought of Mr. N. Mark and how he so cleverly arranged his stock, and how when you looked at his jewellery displayed so beautifully, it made you long to buy.

"I think," I told Mr. Anderson, "that I have some good ideas to get this inventory moving. It's so disorganized it's hard to even see what we have."

He was counting a pile of Hudson Bay blankets, and just as he was nearing the bottom of the pile, the tower toppled and half of them landed on the floor at his feet.

"I can certainly see the logic," he said, his hands already busy re-piling the blankets onto the crowded table.

"Give me one day a week," I told him, "working the floor. If sales don't pick up within a month, it will be back to full time accounting for me."

He put his clipboard aside, looked at me as if I were a species he'd never encountered before. He looked off into space for a bit, and finally tilted his head. "Well, as my father used to say, nothing ventured, nothing gained. Let's give it a try."

I felt like whooping and throwing my papers into the air, but instead I just smiled. "Thank you," I told him. "You won't be sorry." I set my own clipboard down on the floor, and began folding and stacking the blankets. "We can't shake on it, because as you can see, I'm pretty busy."

"Well anyway, it's a positive start. A girl not averse to pitching in when the merchandise hits the floor. Literally," he said.

So in the end, my schooling in Ottawa was beneficial, although the skills I was using had nothing to do with any of my classes at the Ottawa Institute for Young Ladies.

I started with window displays, of course, because first you must draw potential customers inside. And there are more people are coming into the store and Mr. Anderson is pleased.

I dropped by Miriam's place on my way home the day I finished my first window display to tell her of my little vignettes that would entice customers to buy.

"I so envy you," she told me and I wondered why, looking around her perfect house. Her son, chubby and blond, tugged at her dress as he tried to climb onto her knee. She lifted him up, shushed him with a cookie. "Look at this mess," she said, with a sweep of her hand. "I do the same job ten times a day and no one would ever know. At least you can see, at the end of a day, what you have accomplished."

"True," I told her. "But your job is far more important than mine."

She grabbed her coffee cup two seconds before her son did and set it out of harm's way. "Says who?"

She looked worn out, deep blue shadows under her eyes, and the front of her blouse was stained.

"Says me. Why don't you come downtown tomorrow and we can slip out for lunch? At least you'll be getting out of the house."

She sighed. "I'd love to. But that's easier said than done."

A little girl's bedroom, all pink and white gingham, complete with two teddy bears leaning against each other at the side of the gleaming spindle crib. A small quilt thrown casually over the arm of a nearby rocking chair.

I see Miriam standing outside the window, a look of longing on her face. I recognize that look because I've seen it on my own face when I am looking at wedding dresses, when I'm locked in a dream. When she finally comes inside, Miriam buys the entire display. This is how

I know she is expecting again. I was going to ask her to be my bridesmaid, but a pregnant bridesmaid won't do.

She snaps her purse open, tucks the sales receipt into a pocket. "Let's get to that lunch. We'll talk about the newest style of dresses. And dancing, and dinners. And how you will soon be running your own department." She smiles. "At least when I see you, there's hope for women in general. Although maybe not for me."

"Oh, Miriam," I say. "You've a lovely life. I envy you. You've always known what's important. You really have.

One quick look around the store. I smooth a pile of our signature woollen blankets. They are soft, so, so soft.

"Come on!" Miriam says. "I've got some news."

I, of course, already know.

While I have been dreaming of my wedding day, Mama has been handling all of the real-life details. A late morning brunch of muffins and pastries, which she, of course, will prepare. The baking she plans to produce in her kitchen the week of my wedding would put a bakery to shame. I just hope she doesn't wear herself out.

My wedding will be small, because Ward, of course, has no family here. But still, it will be as beautiful as I have always dreamed.

St. John's is a lovely old cathedral, only ten blocks away, and Mama and Papa and I are going to arrive there in a horse drawn buggy.

Ward will be waiting alone at the front of the church.

We have decided it will be just him and me. No Matron of Honour or Best Man, partly because I don't want Ward to feel sad for even one moment on our wedding day and partly because Miriam is far too pregnant to be in a wedding party.

Two pregnancies so close together. Her ankles are terribly swollen I'm sure she could never squeeze her poor feet into a pair of fancy shoes even if she wanted to.

Both Mama and Papa will walk me down the aisle, something the Reverend has never heard of before. He was hesitant to change any part of the ceremony, but I persuaded him. After all, I told him, the world is changing fast right now and the church should change a little bit too. I know he thinks that Papa's sending me going off to Ottawa to be educated was definitely a mistake. But Mama and Papa and I have attended this church for years and years, and Papa is generous with his donations, so what can he do? When the service is over, and we are finally man and wife, Ward will take the reins and drive the carriage back to Mama and Papa's.

The Hanson twins are going to move the living room furniture out to the walls and roll up the rug while we're away getting married, so once we're back, we'll have lots of room to mingle and we can start the dancing at any time.

I wonder if anyone will feel like dancing after they've eaten all the food that Mama plans to prepare.

For just a moment, I think about Garry Hanson. I wonder if he is married. I wonder if he still likes to dance. Is thinking of another man something a woman should do? Only weeks before her wedding?

I love my cozy room, its double dormer windows facing south and pulling in the light and warmth, even on the coldest of days. The walls are a pale pink wash, like the earliest hint of dawn. The colour was chosen by Mama when I first came and it's never been changed. I don't ever want it to change, and neither, I think, does she.

Now that I will be soon leaving this house for good, every nook and cranny has grown more dear.

Two dresses are lying across my canopied bed. One is long, oyster-white satin, a simple A-line cut with a high neck and long flowing sleeves. The other is bouffant, all frills and fluff, tight at the waist with a sweetheart neckline and small cap sleeves of beaded lace. The hemline falls just below mid-calf and I can just see myself in the highest of heels, dancing the night away.

"Mama," I call. "I've brought something home I think you should see."

I picked them out today, on my coffee break, although I have been looking in the ladies department every time something new comes in. And checking the Eaton's catalogue too. Mama came down for lunch at least three times, and we looked at every single wedding dress in the whole downtown, but I never found that perfect one I would know the moment I saw it. But our new inventory arrived last week. And now my luck has doubled.

But how will I choose?

I open the closet door, run my finger through the fabric of the dresses. One so smooth, the other frothy. So different, but both so beautiful too.

The floor creaks. I hear Mama's indrawn breath.

"Oh Lily," she says, running her fingers over the satin and the lace. "Let's have a look. Which one first?"

I choose the A-line. Mama does up the buttons that trace a line down the dress all the way to the small of my back, perfect tiny buttons, shiny with ivory satin, twenty-six in all. The softness of satin caresses my skin.

"Walk in it," she tells me. "See how it feels. You want beautiful, but you want comfortable too." My little mama, practical even when it comes to my wedding dress.

Next I try on the lace, its weight a dandelion about to go to seed. It seems to float around me but with Mama's help, I slip inside and turn so she can button the buttons, and the lace snugs around my waist, which I am proud to say is a trim twenty-four inches.

"Is it scratchy at all?"

"No Mama, it's perfect. Both of them are."

I must be looking woebegone, for she starts to laugh.

"Oh Lily," she says, hugging me hard. "I wish for all of your problems to be so small."

But in the end, we really can't decide.

When Papa comes home, we go through the entire performance again.

"Which one?" I ask.

Papa doesn't say a word, but I see the look in his eyes when I walk into his study wearing the ivory satin.

He opens his ledger, parallels his pen. "They're beautiful. As any dress you wear would be. Pick your favourite. Or if you love them both, just draw straws."

I kiss the top of his head and he reaches for my hand. Whatever was he thinking? Drawing straws? "Never mind," I say. "I just wanted you to see. Actually, I've already made my choice."

But of course I hadn't. Papa had.

## 31.

### Samuel and Ellie

He finds Ellie perched on a stool in the kitchen. The moon is full and it's easy to see clearly the fine web of lines that will some day soon define her face. She's got a tattered book in her hand but she's not reading, just staring out into the yard, brightly lit by the full moon.

"I hope you're not searching out more recipes. I think, my dear, you've worked hard enough. It's time to enjoy these last few days."

"Oh Samuel," she says, turning. "I don't know that I can. For when Lily marries Ward and goes north, she will really and truly be gone. For good this time. "

"We can see Lily often," he assures her. "I'll stop at their place every time I go to see Watson. Keep an eye on things. And I'll take you along, leave you to visit with Lily while I do my business. It won't be so bad."

She turns to the window again. "It doesn't seem possible does it? Wasn't it only yesterday you brought her home?"

"Ellie! Ellie, I'm home."

No answering call from the yard, no clatter of dishes from the kitchen.

The baby cradled in his left arm, he steps into the miracle Ellie has wrought.

"We're home. You can rest now, little one."

Soft sunlight on the oaken floor and the baby begins to howl.

"Nothing for you to complain about. By the looks of this, it's about as fine a home as anyone could want."

My eyes found hers. And hers mine.


Ellie's cool hand on his arm.

"Samuel," she is saying, "let's have a hot toddy tonight. Maybe it will help us sleep. You get the whiskey and I'll boil the kettle."

She continues to amaze him, for hot toddies in the dead of night are something they have never done. But big changes are coming. He can feel it. Maybe Ellie can too.

"A little more sugar for me." He pushes his mug across the table. Kitchen music, the tick of the clock, the clink of silver against mug.

"I was hoping they'd stay in Edmonton," she says. "I don't know why they're so set on homesteading. What do either of them know about farming? Especially in the Peace. Oh, I know they've studied up on it and they might have enough knowledge, but that's not nearly enough. Book learning's not the same as living it, not one little bit. And they could have done well enough with the jobs they already have."

"I still think of Lily as a little girl," he says. "Remember how she begged to come north with me when I travelled, and wanted to get a job with the Bay so she could travel there herself, if I would not take her along? Be damned if she's not going anyway. But if they stick it out and end up owning some of that rich black soil it'll for sure give them a head start in life.."

"Do they really need that?" Ellie says. "When we're gone, all we have will be theirs. And I do think we have quite a lot."

"We do," he says. "Maybe it's the legend?"

"What legend?"

"Watson says that anyone who has even so much as dipped a toe into the Peace River will forever long to return, and that longing will be passed down to their children and to their children's children. And our girl was born somewhere in the north, as far as we know."

"But we have no idea where, do we?"

"Lily might have been baptized in the Peace."

"I think it's very late and you're being fanciful," Ellie says. "Just a tired old papa." She reaches across the faded oilcloth and takes his hand. "She's probably never been anywhere near the Peace. And anyway, I don't think it's possible for a river to cast a spell."

He finishes his last sip, takes their cups to the sink. "I'm not so sure," he says.

He does not tell his wife that when he lays eyes on that wide ribbon of silver after a long stretch in the city, his heart lifts. The business with Watson and the ledger at the store was cleared up long ago, but he has always manufactured reasons to return.

As he's sure Ellie has known for years and years.

The old dream slipped through again last night. The rush of water, the pell-mell ride. Me, cold and hungry and wanting to howl.

291

I am far too mature to have Mama come running in the night, and if she heard me that's exactly what she would do, so I sat on the edge of my bed, watched the moon on the trees in the yard. Sipped cold water until my heart finally slowed.

I am tired this morning, up far earlier than Mama and Papa, which is another change. I pour a cup of steaming black coffee and go to sit on the back step. The tiny scar on my middle right toe is throbbing, as it sometimes does when the weather is about to change. Or when I am about to suddenly see, like I did with Stanley when I touched the arm of his chair and knew he hadn't been such a wonderful husband, like poor, hardworking Mrs. Brighton pretended.

Like I did with Miriam and her exciting news.

Little things, like knowing before the doorbell rings exactly who will be standing on the step. Like knowing exactly what day Mama's letters would arrive, so that I always asked Mrs. Brighton where my letter was.

"Uncanny," she'd say. "You must be very tied to your mother still. An invisible cord."

Of course, it's not infallible, because I didn't know about my birthday party all those years ago. Had no inkling of that surprise.

I hope the throbbing doesn't signify anything today. I want the entire week of my wedding to be glorious with sun.

I rub the scar with the sole of my left foot, something I often do to soothe myself.

The barking of a dog, the long mournful whistle of a train, the slamming of a screen door. Ordinary sounds of a waking neighbourhood.

The daughter I have imagined flits from shadow to shadow, bluebells bending as she goes — will she be born with the same mark as mine, a perfect arrowhead on her middle right toe?

A calico cat meows. I watch as she climbs the maple tree and lies languid on the lowest limb, neatly camouflaged by a riot of red and orange and yellow. The sparrows have spotted the danger, though, their incessant twittering silenced as they watch. Slowly and thoroughly, she licks the pads of her feet, first the right foot, then the left. Her cleaning job complete, the cat drops silently to the grass and slinks away.

When cats clean their paws, there is pure concentration, a dedication to their task. And pleasure too, I think.

I too stretch, long and slow, like the cat.

Soon the maple will be bare, touched by a blanket of pristine snow. Snow the colour of my dress. I feel like pinching myself, hardly able to believe that my wedding is now only three days away.


Ward has laid his worn map open on the desk. Red circles dot the south shore of the Peace near Spirit River. Good God, it is so far. So very far.

Samuel runs his finger along the course of the river, remembering the first time he stood on the shores and watched it rushing quickly by. A sight he will never forget.

"I'd like to get a homestead right about here," Ward says, "or maybe here. Lots of good land the Dominion has surveyed is ready to go. Ten dollars for a hundred and sixty acres sounds insane but the fellow at the local Land Branch confirms that it's so. I've no experience in farming, other than feeding the chickens when I was a boy, but I'm a quick study and Lily seems game for anything I decide."

"It's a long way up there," I say.

"If I can throw up some kind of temporary shelter, I figure I can get started breaking this fall. Stay up there working as long as I possibly can. Come spring, I should be ready to put in a few acres of crop. If the weather will just hold for a month or two."

It is already August and the chances of the weather holding for a month or two are non-existent. But Ward, of course, has no idea. "And Lily . . . ?"

He re-folds the map carefully in half, and then in half again. "You needn't worry," he says, "these first few months I will be on my own. But once she joins me come spring, I promise I will take good care of Lily until the day I draw my final breath."

Samuel thinks of the toll that the north can take on the toughest of men, and Ward's earnest oath does nothing to ease his worry about Lily.

The climb up the stairs from the main floor to his office seems steeper today and he feels every one of his sixty-six years. The desk is piled high with paper but he ignores it all and instead stands staring out the window, watching the pigeons on the adjoining roof squabble over a piece of bread that one of them has dropped.

He has only one day of work left, for he intends to take two days off before the wedding. To help Ellie and to savour these last few days.

"Good morning, Samuel." Jane plunks a steaming cup of coffee onto the desk. "Looks like you could use this today."

"You're right." The coffee is brewed strong and black. Perfect.

"Oh," she says, "I almost forgot."

She runs from the office and almost instantly returns. "This came yesterday about four. I decided not to bother you at home."

"You should have," he says.

"I know, but you hardly ever take a day, and I thought you were looking awfully tired lately and with the wedding coming up so quickly . . . "

"It's fine. Don't worry about it."

But that's not what he's feeling. Not one little bit. As soon as she leaves his office, he tears the telegraph open and adjusts his new glasses. He walks to the window, holds the paper to the light.

Finally found something. Check late train. Stop. Package addressed to you personally. Stop. Very Important. Stop. Watson.

*Yesterday? At four?* Very Important?

He almost runs from the building, heart beating hard. The station is busy, even at this early hour and he has to wait in line at the freight window. Four people. Three people. Two. "Samuel Vining," he says when his turn finally comes. The man behind the wicket moves maddeningly slowly. "Vining?" he says. "Can't say as I recall. What was it you were expecting?"

"I'm not sure. A package of some kind."

He slowly sorts through a stack of boxes and letters on a cart behind his counter. "Sorry," he says, his palms open.

"There has to be something. I have a telegraph. It says so right here."

He scratches his head, straightens his cap.

"Please, can you check again? You have no idea how important . . . "

"Maybe someone else picked it up?"

"No. For sure, no one did. Can you just check?"

"Everybody thinks their package is the most important one. But hold your horses for a minute. I'll take another look."

He starts the slow sort again, his movements like treacle. Finally, he comes up with a small package, wrapped in brown paper and tied with twine. "Don't know how I missed it first time," he says. "But here you go."

Samuel carries the parcel carefully, as if it is made of spun glass. What seems like forever later, he opens the door to his office, settles into his chair, counting the measured ticking of the clock to calm the erratic beating of his heart.

He centres the package on his desk, slowly unties the twine.

An old Bible and an aged paper.

He unfolds the lined paper.

*Samuel — remember how we sometimes talked of the baby and where she'd come from? How could we be so set on maintaining total silence when we wondered so often ourselves? But over the years, for whatever reasons, we've let that conversation die.*

*I know how she used to drive you crazy with questions. Does she still?*

*The enclosed might provide answers, if anyone still wants to know. Of course, it's truly your call. My lips will always be sealed.*

*James Williamson, a surveyor for the Crown, stumbled upon this. Pounding in stakes for the new homesteads is what he was up to. Very strange, that he'd find things undisturbed, after all of these years. Luckily enough, his first stop after his discovery was here for more supplies.*

*He'd found a Bible in a small dugout dwelling, well hidden, and protected by a huge fallen pine. The dugout had sturdy half-walls and roof supports that still held, allowing only the dimmest of light inside. So probably not much rain or snow.*

*The poor bugger also found the skeleton of a man with a baby bottle by his hand but no sign of a baby. He was spooked and not sure he should have even picked up the Bible. But once he had, he felt compelled to take it somewhere. And of course, that somewhere was here.*

*When I mentioned I'd been here long enough to be a historian of sorts, he gave me the Bible and I gave him a bottle of rum.*

*Sounds a bit like history repeating itself, wouldn't you say? Of course, I have no idea if this has anything to do with Lily. But the baby bottle? Thought it might be worth a shot.*

*God bless you. Hope this missive finds you well. Let me know if it sheds any light.*

*Always, Watson.*


The smell of damp rises in the room. The Bible is leather clad, its gilt edges curled. He picks it up, opens it, holds it to the light.

"Oh, sweet Jesus," he says, following the wavering words with his forefinger as he reads and re-reads.

The first entry is written in a firm hand, steady and sure. The final entry is spidery and faint, trailing almost completely away.

He sets the Bible down, begins to fold the paper that enclosed it and feels something else, so opens the paper again.

A small soft pouch, and inside, one crystal marble, with a purple heart, twinkling in the sun.

He would never forget the tenderness in Ellie's hands, that first day, when she unwrapped the baby. How she noticed right away, and held the little foot, marvelling at the minute perfection of the arrowhead scar on her middle right toe.

## 32.

His house stands square and solid, like it did this morning when he left. The wind tousles the tops of the yellow chrysanthemums that grow in pots placed by the front steps. The house gleams white in the September sun, and he feels the warmth of the metal rail beneath his hand. He leans on the railing, uses it to pull himself up. The door is gleaming with varnish and Ellie's care. No dust here, even on the outside.

The scents of Ellie's incessant baking, of which there is now no need, waft around him as he steps inside. Cinnamon and ginger, molasses and allspice. Sweet and sharp, the comforting scents of home.

"Papa, is that you?"

A sudden whirlwind in the yard picks up a handful of gravel, splats it on the window.

"Yes. It's me."

She drifts from his study to the hall, as delicate and beautiful as a butterfly.

"Oh Papa," she says, and she throws her arms around him. Just like old times. But she is shaking, shaking like aspen leaves in a breeze.

Sunlight gleams on the oaken floor. He rests his hand on the carved newel post at the bottom of the stair, waiting for his eyes to adjust. Crystal tones of rose and purple and green wash through the stained glass window at the top of the stairs, the soaring walls. When he can truly see, he tilts his head and looks into the dark of her eyes, the rim of purple around the iris. "What is it?"

Lily's shaking is quieting now. "I've already told Mama. She's upstairs crying."

Her body fits to his, the top of her head tucked neatly beneath his chin. He remembers how easily he held her the day they first stepped through this door.

"Told her what?"

"I've cancelled the wedding." She straightens her shoulders and steps from his embrace. "Papa, I'm so sorry. I love Ward, I really do. But not the right way."

"Not the right way?"

She is twining her hair around her bare ring finger. "I told Mama, but I didn't tell you. How I felt I already knew Ward the first time we met? Like he was a part of me that was missing, a part that just clicked into place? But the more I got to know him, well, the more I felt like he could be my brother or my cousin or maybe just a really good friend, and not so much the love of my life. As I'd first thought." Her face is flushed, her eyes glazed.

"Whoa. Just breathe."

Her fingers are plucking at his shirt-sleeve, and then she closes her hands around his wrists. "Our plans for a life together and filing on our homestead, working our land together, maybe even trying our hand at cattle. Ridiculous as that sounds for Ward and me . . . "

He couldn't help but smile, because no way could he see Lily mucking out a barn or holding her ground against a cranky black Angus cow.

"All the preparations Mama and I have done and that beautiful wedding dress and . . . I so wanted it to work.

When I first began to have doubts, I thought it was too late to change anything but I . . . . I, well, lately, I dreamt of a child, a little girl. So beautiful, flitting across the yard. This yard, so dear to me. Even more so, now that I have been away."

He looks down the long polished hall to see the backyard through the kitchen window. A little patch of green, edged by a caragana hedge, black soil beds, dotted by almost spent daisies. Fall flowers too, warm bright colours like bonfires in bloom. The garden, mostly harvested and put to bed now, waiting for the blanket of winter snow. And further on, stands of poplar and birch, their thin white skins edging their world.

"But last night, in my dream, when I turned to Ward to share that special look that parents always share . . . when I turned to my husband, it wasn't Ward, with his blond hair and his blue, blue eyes. My husband was someone else entirely. His eyes were liquid chocolate, and his hair bluish-black. He was watching the little girl too, and he was smiling and smiling, his wide smile deepening the dimples in his cheeks."

Samuel remembers then those welcoming people he'd sat with around the campfire that night so long ago. Their liquid chocolate eyes.

"And when he saw me, he put two fingers to his forehead, kind of like a salute. To say I see you. And I know you see me. And I am waiting. Waiting for you."

"Oh Lily."

She takes a great gulp of air and continues. "That's how I knew for sure that Ward and I could never be. And now I have to find a way to tell him so." She pulls her hands from mine, rubs her red-rimmed eyes. "Oh Papa! What will I say?"

He leads her into his study. Perhaps Ellie has cried herself to sleep. He opens his battered briefcase, soft and scarred. Mucous clogs his throat as he hands her the Bible.

"This came yesterday. It's from my old friend Watson in Fort St. John. He was the first person I know to lay his eyes on you. Even before your mother."

Lily takes it into shaking hands, hands so small and fine, nails perfect ovals, burnished the palest of pink. "And he you sent this?" She opens the Bible, the scent of must rising in the hall. "Why?"

He feels for his shirt pocket, the small deerskin pouch tucked inside. "Because I asked him to."

He stands closer, flips the fragile pages, puts his hand on Lily's arm, steadies her as she begins to read the first entry, the strong and precise writing.

*Born this day, April 30th, 1897, a baby girl with vocal cords in fine working order. Parents: Edward and Isabelle Armson Baby: Sarah Louise*

The next entry is spidery, the writing wavering painfully across the page.

*Godspeed to my precious daughter, Sarah Louise Armson. May God watch over her and keep her from harm on her perilous journey down the Mighty Peace.*

*Sarah's special mark — an arrowhead scar on her middle right toe.*

*And to my son, Ward Armson — now mothered by Joan Spencer — sister-in-law in England, I leave my fatherly love and — a sea of regrets.*

*My dying wish is that my children will come to know each other, somewhere, sometime.*

*If this missile is ever found, contact my sister-in-law Joan Spencer, care of Barton and Beverly, Solicitors, Brighton, England.*

*Edward Armson — on the shores of the Mighty Peace — a place so very close to God.*

Lily traces the words with her index finger, her eyes so dark and deep, scanning once, twice, then one final time.

"I've already sent a cable to Barton and Beverly. But really, there's not much doubt. Ward is your half-brother, God help us all."

She sets the book on the corner of the desk. He wants to reach for her but she is stiff, her arms now wrapped around her midriff, as if holding herself together.

Eventually, she straightens, leans on his scarred oak desk, slowly rubs the sole of her left foot across the top of her right. Rub, pause, rub, pause again, a soft sound like silk sliding on silk.

"The night Ward came to my study to ask for your hand, he told me a bit about his life in England and his family there and what happened to send him here . . . and, well, I already know quite a bit about Ward and why he felt compelled to come to Canada, but this, only . . . "

She closes the Bible, strokes the worn cover with her dainty fingertips. "What do you know?"

He takes the Bible, marks the page with a paper before closing it with a thud. "He didn't tell you? Why he left?"

"Very little. Just that he grew up in a nice, normal family and that he has two brothers, back home. And that he'd had some kind of unmanageable difficulty crop up in the family after his brothers signed up to go to war." She twists her hair around her index finger, a sign of angst that she's had her entire life. Her life that he knows, that is. "I was hoping to meet them all some day. Not at the wedding, of course, because it's so very far and expensive. But maybe in the future, when we could afford to go there. I was curious to see the place he grew up. To meet his mom." She fumbles in her pocket for a tissue, and wipes her scarlet nose. Then she squares her shoulders. "I had the idea I could help him mend his fences, especially with his mother because whatever the original tiff was about, mothers and sons should never be estranged. It doesn't bode well for future relationships if you've turned your back on you own mother." She hiccups, wipes her eyes one more time. "Last week, when it came to me so clearly, the certainty that Ward and I could never be, I didn't listen. Pre-wedding jitters, I told myself." She leans on the desk, re-opens the Bible to the dedication page, runs her dainty fingers over the words.

"And so I was right. And Ward and I can never . . . "

"Yes," he says.

And he knows that when Ward has heard this devastating news, he will bring him into this study and pour him a stiff whiskey and put the soft pouch enclosing the lone marble into his hand. Perhaps it will help.

33.

Lily
Condie Meadows Nursing Home
Manning, Alberta
June 22, 1994

When I woke today I saw the morning star.

The walls in my room are painted cream — real cream that has risen to the top of the crock. Not exactly yellow, but nowhere near white. The white trim, installed before I moved into this room, is at least four inches wide, the better to protect the walls from wheelchair damage, I think. I have always tried to steer my craft with care, but lately, the chair has taken on a life of its own. I am only one more tired passenger, waiting for my final stop.

The lacy curtains that my daughters have hung across the bay window on a silver rod filter the morning sun. My girls are trying so hard to make this place feel like home to me, which of course, it never will.

My tough little money-tree plant, also a gift, is not growing, but not dying either.

Dinner is cooling on the tray. The kitchen has sent my tea in a clumsy ceramic mug. The mug is green and the tea is too.

Red Rose is my drink of choice. Obviously someone new has started and not read the prep notes, what we like and what we don't.

I absolutely cannot stomach green tea, which to me has always smelled of hay.

I decide what I really, really need is water.

Clear, cool water.

That's one need I still have some control over. I have a low sink and a lever-handled tap and I can still walk just fine without that cursed walker, although most of the nurses give me a darn good scolding when I do.

Right now, the walker is folded and tucked away behind my closet door. Not exactly helpful to me and definitely out of my reach, but still, I can find a way if need be.

Bed to bedside table, table to back of my flowered chintz chair, chair to narrow table by the bathroom door. Hands on familiar landmarks, then on the bathroom doorway. Small spaces are good for those us of requiring boundaries, something to remind us of where we now are, something to steady the hand.

Eventually, because nothing happens quickly anymore, I stand in front of the sink. I stopper it and turn on the water full blast. Very soon, cool water cascades over the counter's edge and falls to the floor like a miniature waterfall.

Nothing like the rushing water. I remember it from the one trip I made up a shallow river with my father, one week before I left for school.

A trip of a lifetime, is what he said.

The waterfall was an amazing sight, if you were standing at the base looking up and not thinking of being tossed above it by that roiling water in a fragile craft, losing the battle with the current and about to plunge down the abyss.

I have to admit, even with the comforting presence of my father, the sight of it gave me nightmares for months.

For all of my life, I have heard rushing water in my dreams.

In the mirror, I see a faintly familiar woman. Who is she? A neighbour? An old friend? "Do you hear it? Do you hear the rapids?"

The old woman doesn't reply, but she frowns, a deep crease between her eyebrows. Obviously, frowning isn't new to her.

I take some soft soap in my right hand, smear it thickly on the mirror. She disappears and I am glad. Now I won't be bothered by her obvious disapproval. I flip the handle, turn on the water full bore.

Then I relent, grab a stiff blue towel and scrub at the smear of soap until I can again see her lined face.

"You seem so alone. So I will tell you a story," I say. "If you could please quit your scowling, just for a moment or two."

She seems a little more pleasant now. Maybe she just needed a little human contact. Poor thing, maybe she's no family at all.

"When I was a baby, I was set adrift on a raft in a great shining river. They say babies have no recall, but I, for one, know that's not true. Sometimes I still feel the rise and fall of the water beneath my craft, the brightest of stars lighting my way. The great yellow moon hanging so low I wanted to touch it. But I could not, for I was bundled tightly and all I could really move was my eyes. I could hear the rapids. Coming closer. Rapids I could feel but not yet see."

I try to turn off the gushing tap but my gnarled old hands have seized, and maybe the tap has too. I fold a threadbare towel and place it to stem the spreading tide.

I could be in serious trouble for this. But I so love the sound of water splashing and a feeling of such utter peace floods my bones.

I turn again to the wasted woman in the mirror. Even blurred by the murky mist of soap, she looks so old, so very, very frail.

"Have I told you this before? Not everyone believes me," I tell her, "but when I was young, I rode down the mighty Peace River in a very small raft. My trip lasted for days and days, or so it seemed."

The water squishes between my freezing toes.

"So a little water on a bathroom floor will never do me in."

I throw down one more towel. Not very thick, unfortunately, and definitely not white and soft, but that is how things are in this place.

A place I can afford. And not become a burden to my girls.

"Waves smacked against the side of my snug little craft and it was a small miracle that it remained upright."

The water, molten metal in the moonlight, rushes under me and around. One by one, the stars wink out. But the northern lights remain. Scintillating scarlet and the palest of pinks, vibrant greens and the deepest ocean blue, turquoise too. Like sheer silken curtains, they curl and flutter, ghosting in the unearthly light.

Their soft whooshes whisper an ancient secret in my ear.

The Peace is not called the Mighty Peace for nothing.

I trail my hand in the cool quickening water and I am not afraid.

My cousin Robert, who grew up in the Peace River country, sent me a clipping of this story, found in his father's effects, and suggested it was a tale I should tell. I tucked the raft baby story away in a pile of writing ideas for 'sometime later.' I was a short story writer, and writing a novel was beyond my skill-set. How to attempt such a task? I finally decided that all I could do was try.

I have always loved the Peace River country, partly for it's beauty, and partly because the branch of my family that moved there in the "dirty thirties" has remained close to all of our prairie hearts. I clearly remember my very first view of the Peace, as most who've seen it do.

I have taken liberal license with the facts of the raft baby story, first explored when I read a review of the book *Hatchet Mark in Duplicate* by Rev. Garrioch, (Ryerson Press, Toronto, Canada, 1929). Originally, I tried to stay true to historical fact, but I was not able to do that and fully imagine the characters. As I began to write, the people I'd imagined took their own routes through the facts as I knew them and eventually I realized that I must follow their lead. And so in the re-telling, fiction took over fact, as it often does.

For instance, in *Hatchet Mark in Duplicate*, the mother does not die in childbirth but is present on the trip down the Peace. She dies in the dugout along with her husband. But somehow, during the writing of this story, the birth mother wished to leave the story. So I did as directed.

The one true thing, that Edward Armson's Bible was found in time to cancel the wedding planned between

Lily Vining and her half-bother Ward Spencer, is a miracle in itself.

In this story, it is Lily who "knows things, things that cannot be known", and it is Lily who calls a halt to the wedding. In history, it isn't so.

Some of the names and dates have been changed, some left as they were. I have renamed Lily several times on her life journey. But whatever her name, I know that Lily, as I have imagined her, is real to me.

The timing of the short-lived gold rush in the Peace River country has also been altered, as has some of the history of the development of the Hudson's Bay Company.

I have used racialized terms that were common usage at the time but were not right and are not right in the world we live in. If I offend anyone, I deeply apologize.

Some true things. Edward Armson's children both recovered from the heartbreak of finding out they were never meant to be husband and wife, but in reality were half-sister and half-brother, born worlds apart. Life is stranger than fiction.

Lily was married not much more than one year after she found out who she truly was. Perhaps to the dark-haired man she'd seen in her dreams. Ward also eventually married, a woman from England, newly immigrated to North America.

## ACKNOWLEDGEMENTS

I would like to thank the following people for reading drafts and for their valuable feedback: Dianne Warren, Elizabeth Philips, Steven Ross Smith and Susan Majeran.

A special thank you to my editor Michael Kenyon for his insight and skill in helping to shape this novel. His questions and suggestions have helped to make *Raft Baby* a better book.

To the SK Arts for their support during the writing of this book, the Banff School of Fine Arts for time to set apart from the world in a magical place and to the Saskatchewan Writer's Guild for their support of artists in this province.

And to Jackie Forrie and Al Forrie at Thistledown Press for keeping the faith.